AF260478

FAMILY

F-BOMB: SEALS LOVE CURVES, BOOK 6

MARY E THOMPSON

Family

F-BOMB: SEALs Love Curves, book 6

Copyright © 2020 Mary E Thompson

Cover Copyright © 2021 Mary E Thompson

Cover Photo from depositphotos, Copyright © puhhha

Background from depositphotos, Copyright © yupiramos

Flag from Pixabay, CC0

Published by BluEyed Press, All Rights Reserved

No part of this book may be reproduced in any form or by any electronic or mechanical means, including information storage and retrieval systems, without written permission from the author, except for the use of brief quotations in a book review.

This is a work of fiction. All characters, businesses, locations, and events are either products of the author's creative imagination or are used in a fictitious sense. Any resemblance to real persons, living or dead, is purely coincidental.

Ebook ISBN: 978-1-944090-79-1

Print ISBN: 978-1-944090-80-7

Audiobook ISBN: 978-1-944090-81-4

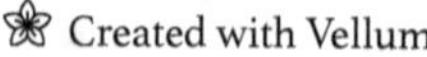 Created with Vellum

F-BOMB: SEALS LOVE CURVES

Welcome to the world of F-BOMB where a group of former SEALs have come together to protect the curvy women they love and the country they call home from the dangers of the world. They have the training and the knowledge, and they have the ability to kick some ass when needed. And it'll be needed.

F-BOMB: SEALs LOVE CURVES

Freedom

Fiancée (subscriber exclusive)

Forgotten

First

Failure

Friends

Family

Forbidden

Future

Finally

SUBSCRIBE NOW AT MARYETHOMPSON.COM

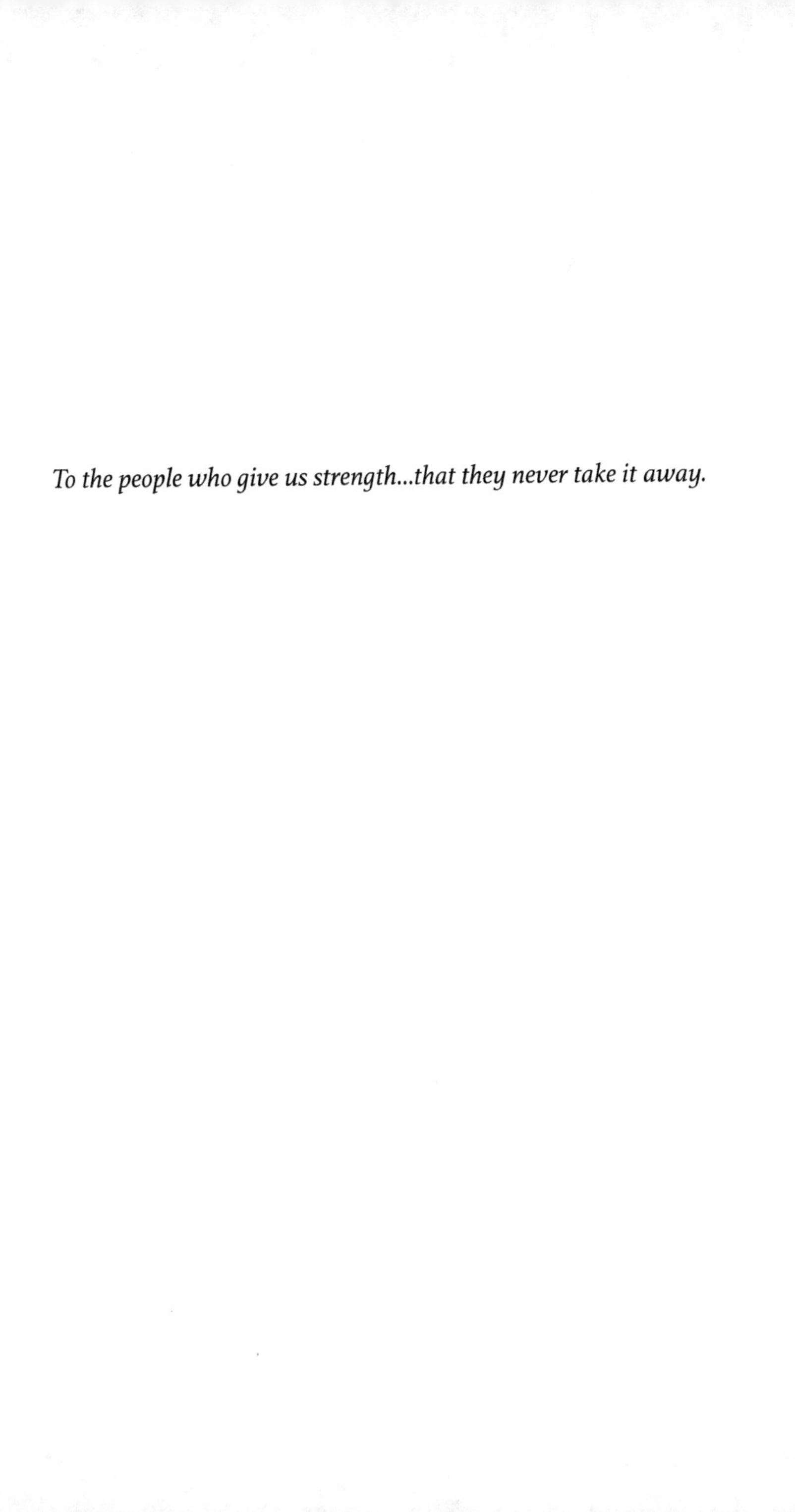

To the people who give us strength...that they never take it away.

1

Adrian Malone rolled his neck to the side to work out the kink in it. He was sore and stiff and in desperate need of a shower and a few hours in a bed. After spending the last thirty-six hours on surveillance in the back of one of the team's SUVs, he was dead on his feet.

Even worse, they didn't catch the guy they were after.

Adrian, known as Rocky to his closest friends and teammates, was a member of an elite group of former SEALs who spent their days and night protecting the borders. Stationed in Niagara Falls, New York, they did everything they could to make sure no one came in or out of the country without permission.

Unfortunately, people always slipped by. Which was why Rocky was part of a multi-day surveillance. A failed one.

Rocky sifted quickly through the mail and tossed it on the counter. He barely noticed what was in there and figured there wasn't anything that couldn't wait until he got some sleep and food. Preferably something that didn't come out of a bag and wasn't room temperature.

"Anything good?" his friend and roommate, Ryker 'Dex' Hamilton, asked. Dex was on the same surveillance as Rocky and just as tired, but he wore it better. His eyes actually stayed open on the drive home.

Rocky shook his head and walked toward the fridge.

"What about this?" Dex asked, holding up one of the envelopes.

"What is it?" Rocky asked without looking.

"From the living donor registration place. You could be a match for someone."

Rocky shrugged and continued his search for food. He'd been registered as an organ donor forever, but it was only in the last month that he'd signed up as a living donor, willing to give pieces and parts of himself while he was still breathing to help others. He wanted to give back, but at the moment, food was a higher priority.

Their fridge was sparse and the cabinets worse. He debated ordering a pizza, but after the chips and sandwiches and junk he'd eaten lately, he couldn't stomach the thought.

"You need to open this," Dex pressed.

Rocky wasn't sure about it. They were in the middle of a huge case that required all hands on deck. They'd been working around the clock for weeks. He was starving and exhausted and not looking for something else to do at the moment.

The sound of tearing paper met his ears, and he spun around. "What the hell?"

Dex shrugged and pulled the letter out of the opened envelope. "It says you're a match. Someone needs you."

"The team needs me," Rocky said, his senses of duty warring. "I can't leave right now."

"You can always leave," Dex said. "We always have a big

case, and we're always working crazy hours. You wanted to do this. You chose to do this. How can you walk away now that it's here?"

Rocky shook his head and turned his back on his closest friend. He and Dex went through BUD/S together, then were matched to the same Team. Rocky had spent most of his career with Dex by his side. They knew each other better than most people knew another person, but at the moment, that only meant Dex knew how to push Rocky's buttons.

"What if it's a kid?" Dex asked. "Can you turn your back on a kid?"

"They don't give out any information about who it is. I'll never know. And right now just isn't a great time. I'm starving. Do you want food?"

"Yeah," Dex said. He continued to stare at the letter while Rocky pretended it didn't exist.

Rocky settled on veggie pasta and a meaty sauce in the freezer. While the water boiled, he defrosted the sauce. Dex went to his room to shower, leaving Rocky alone with the letter. He shook his head at himself and tried to ignore it, but he couldn't. All his life, he'd been called to give back, to serve. His mom was a nurse, and his dad was in construction. They always helped people and taught Rocky and his two sisters to do the same. It was why Rocky trained as a medic in the Navy and became a SEAL. And why he signed up to be a donor.

He added the pasta to the boiling water and stirred the sauce. He continued to stare at the letter without actually picking it up or reading it. It scared him. No matter how much he felt the pull to help, the act of surrendering his health for another person was terrifying.

His phone buzzed in his pocket, startling him. He dropped the spoon he used to mix the sauce, cursing when red splattered all over the floor. He left it there and dug his phone out of his pocket.

"Yeah?"

"Can you come in for a meeting?" Daniel Dunn was his XO as a SEAL and his boss as a civilian. Rocky trusted Dunn with his life.

"What time?"

"Thirty minutes."

Rocky groaned and nodded. "Yeah, I'll be there."

"Thanks."

Dunn hung up, and Rocky hung his head. He was not in the mood to go into work. He knew if he did, he would spend the day there and get even less sleep. But it wasn't the first time and wouldn't be the last he had to spend the day at work without any rest.

He finished cooking and wolfed down his breakfast, adding a cup of coffee to the mix. The combination would have made him sick years ago, but he learned as a SEAL to eat what you had and not worry if it went together.

Dex got the call, too, and shoveled his food in as quickly as Rocky had. They were out the door in fifteen minutes and on their way to work. When they arrived, the rest of the team was rushing around the office. Rocky didn't know what was happening, so he followed Dex to the conference room to wait, knowing the team would fill them in. Rocky put his head on the table and closed his eyes for a minute.

The next thing he heard was a mug of coffee placed on the table in front of him. A soft hand on his back would have made him jump a few years ago, but he stifled the urge to attack whoever touched him and looked up at Kyra.

"I figured you could use this," she said with a smile.

Rocky nodded and accepted the mug gratefully. Kyra

was their office manager and friend. She was also crazy in love with one of Rocky's teammates, Slade.

"Thanks," Rocky said, smiling at her. He brought the mug to his lips and drank. The hot burn of the coffee and the jolt of caffeine helped him as the others walked in and took seats around the table.

"We have a problem," Dunn said as he set his stuff down on the table.

Rocky just closed his eyes and groaned internally. He was definitely not getting any sleep.

IT WAS dark when Rocky and Dex made it home again. Exhaustion had set in and neither of them were in the mood to talk or think or eat. They bypassed the kitchen and went straight to their rooms without a word. Rocky didn't bother stripping out of his clothes before he headed for bed, falling onto the covers and passing out almost instantly.

His internal clock woke him far too soon, but Rocky knew it was useless to fight against it. He never slept past six, and even sleeping that late was a challenge most days. He went for a run and lifted with the free weights he kept in his room, then showered and returned to the kitchen for breakfast.

He groaned when he opened his fridge and saw the same nothing he had the day before. He shook his head, grabbed his keys, and decided to stop for something on his way to work.

The letter caught his eye, and he paused to read it. It ended with a phone number to call for more information if he was still interested. He pocketed the letter and went straight to work, forgetting all about breakfast.

"I need you to check this out. Tell me if it's legit," Rocky said, handing the letter over to their resident computer expert, Liam Johnson.

English looked up at him when he saw what the letter said and simply nodded. Then he went to work and within a few minutes, he had his answer. "It's legit. Are you going to do it?"

Rocky took a breath and shook his head. "It's a shitty time to be out of the pocket. I wanted to, but I can't leave the team. Not when we're this close to closing this case."

"Want to know who it's for?" English asked.

Rocky snatched the letter away and shook his head. "No. I think it's better if I don't."

English shrugged and went back to whatever he was doing.

NICOLE BURKE SAT across the desk from Dr. Andrews and held her breath. She knew finding a donor was a long shot with her son's rare blood type and antibodies, but she had hope that somewhere out there, someone was a match.

"I wish I had better news," Dr. Andrews said. "There is a match registered in the system, but the person has declined."

"Why?" Nicole asked. Her throat seized, taking all her breath with it. She was out of options. Out of hope. Her son was only six. A six year old shouldn't have to go through what Sly had gone through. But things were only going to get worse for him. Without a donor, and soon, her son was going to die.

"We have no way of knowing that. Sometimes donors change their minds, sometimes they aren't available for some reason, and sometimes they have medical issues that prevent them from donating. We really don't know."

"What am I supposed to do?"

Dr. Andrews said the words Nicole never wanted to hear. "Enjoy the time you have and prepare yourself."

She sucked in a breath and nodded, but inside, she wasn't accepting that answer. She would find another option, a solution that didn't involve waiting and struggling and praying for someone else to do something. She was a mother, and she was not going to let her son die. She didn't care what it took, she was going to fix this. She was not going to sit back and watch him fade away. That wasn't an option. There had to be another choice.

And she was going to find it.

THE NEXT TWO weeks were a whirlwind for Rocky. He worked nights with Dex, and they were called into the office half the time for meetings. Every time they thought they were getting close to closing the case, something happened, and they ended up three steps backward. Until it all blew up in their faces and months of work led nowhere.

"Dammit!" echoed down the hall when the team returned.

Fists beat against the walls as each member of the team took out their frustrations on the inanimate objects around them. It was going to be a busy day in the gym with all that anger.

Rocky stood at his doorway and waited for Dunn to reach him. He didn't need confirmation from Dunn that everything went sideways. He already knew, but Dunn jerked his head toward his office for Rocky to follow.

"What's up?" Rocky asked, taking a seat across the desk.

Dunn took all his weapons off, setting each on the desk before pulling off his bulletproof vest. When he looked more like a normal guy, he sat down and asked, "Why didn't you tell me you were a match?"

Rocky groaned and closed his eyes. "Dex needs to stay out of my business."

"He came to me because we all know you signed up for a reason. He knows this will eat at you if you don't go. What's going on?"

"The timing sucks," Rocky said simply.

"There's never a good time. Never will be. But whoever it is you're helping needs you now, so you have to go."

"I just—"

"When I was off with Ashleigh and Junior, you guys survived. We've all been out of commission for injuries. This team doesn't function if we're not all at the top of our game. You're distracted by this because it's what you want to do. So, why aren't you?"

"If I do this, I won't be at the top of my game. I'll be down a kidney."

"And you think we'll give you desk duty?" Dunn asked. He leaned back and cross his arms over his chest.

Rocky shrugged.

"Will you be able to forgive yourself if you don't go through with this? If you know someone out there is out of options and you said no?"

Rocky blew out a breath and closed his eyes. He'd been pushing the entire thing out of his mind for that very reason. He didn't want to think about who wouldn't make it.

"You're a healer, Rocky. You're the guy who takes care of everyone else. If you decide not to do this, I'm not going to think any differently of you, but I think you will. I think you'll regret it."

"It's a month," Rocky said.

"What is?"

"I would need to be there for a month. Because of what we do, I would have to be observed for a month by whatever doctor so they know I've healed completed before they'll let me return to work."

Dunn shrugged. "And?"

Rocky shook his head and ran a hand over his face. He hated missing anything, but missing a month was not going to be easy. "I—"

"Don't," Dunn said. "Whatever it is you're feeling guilty about, don't. You are saving someone's life. That's why we do what we do every day. You're just doing it in a different way. An easier way than we usually have to do it."

Rocky stared at his boss and friend and admitted the truth. "I'm not sure I can walk away from this."

"Then don't. Do what you need to do and go save someone. We'll survive without you, but this other person might not."

Rocky took a breath and nodded. He felt like a weight had been lifted from his chest. He was going to help. To give back. To do what he knew was right.

He was going to save a life.

IT TOOK a few weeks to get more testing done to confirm Rocky was, in fact, a match. When he was finally given the go ahead, he booked his flight to Tennessee and headed south. Rocky checked in with Dunn and Dex when he arrived and ordered a car to take him straight to the hospital. His surgery was scheduled for the next morning, and they wanted him admitted overnight so they could monitor him and start surgery at the crack of dawn.

Rocky walked into the waiting room and glanced around. He didn't know who he was donating his kidney to, but he was still curious. Could it be the teenaged girl in the corner with her mom and dad? Or maybe the toddler sleeping against his dad's shoulder? Or the young boy...

Rocky tilted his head to the side. Wow. The boy looked just like Rocky's dad. Same shape of his eyes. His ears stuck out a little too far. His chin was long and thin.

His father died when Rocky was at BUD/S. He was repairing a weak spot on the roof of his house and lost his balance. He was on life support for two days, but his mom knew he would do more for the world if she agreed to donate his organs. Rocky wasn't there when the rest of his family said goodbye. His dad was proud of him, and his mom assured him his dad would have wanted him to stay at training and finish, but the guilt of not being there and not having patched the roof before he left ate at Rocky.

Rocky smiled at the boy and knew he made the right choice. If he was seeing his father's face, there was no doubt in his mind that walking away from his team and giving up his kidney to help a stranger was for the best. He'd go back to his team when he was healed, but the person he was matched with couldn't wait any longer.

His phone buzzed. Rocky pulled it out and smiled at the screen. His teammates had been sending him texts since he left, mocking him and saying he was a hero. He shook his head. They were teasing, but they meant it, too. Every single one of them was signed up to donate their organs if something happened. Rocky was the only one who signed up to be a living donor, and even though it scared him, he felt good about finally agreeing to go through with it.

Someone sat down next to him, and Rocky shifted to give her space. He glanced over and smiled, then did a double take.

"Hi, Rocky," she said, sounding less than happy but not surprised to see him.

"Nikki?" he asked.

She nodded and tucked her blonde hair behind her ear.

"What are you doing here?"

She chuckled. "I'm here for the same reason you are."

"You're a donor?" Rocky asked, surprised at the coincidence. He met her on leave seven years earlier. They spent a weekend together, more time in bed than out. Rocky told himself she was better off not knowing his real name and refused to tell her who he was, using only his nickname when they were together. She played along, only giving him her first name.

Rocky thought about trying to find her after she disappeared their last night together, but he figured it was for the best. Still, he never forgot her, or the connection he thought they had.

Nikki shook her head and looked at the boy Rocky had been staring at. "I'd almost given up hope. I never thought you'd be the person who showed up."

"What do you mean?"

She took a deep breath and blew it out slowly. "You're here to save my son's life. His name is Sly. Sylvester. I named him after Sylvester Stallone."

Rocky chuckled. "What are the odds? I got my nickname after his iconic character."

Nikki nodded. "I always assumed. That's why he has that

name." Her eyes filled with tears, and she let them fall when she met his gaze. "He's named after you. You're his father, Rocky."

2

NICOLE LOOKED AT THE MAN SHE SAW IN HER SON'S FACE EVERY day and drew a breath. He was in everything Sly did. She hadn't known Rocky long or well, but she knew him intimately. She knew him in ways she hadn't known any other man before or since. And those little pieces of domesticity she saw when they spent a weekend together years ago were in her daily life with her son.

Sly was her world. When she found out she was pregnant, she was scared, but every decision she made since then was for him. Right up to and including telling Rocky her son was his.

"How is this possible?" Rocky asked, staring at Sly from across the room. "Why didn't you tell me?"

She stared at him for a long moment, letting the reality sink in. She knew Rocky wasn't his real name, that it was a nickname given to him by the SEALs. It didn't bother her at the time because there was no reason she'd see him again, or need to. She only told him her first name, never a last name. They agreed to keep things anonymous. She had no way to find him once she found out she was pregnant.

"You didn't know my name," he said after a moment. "Shit, Nikki, I'm sorry. I... I'm sorry. How is he?" He shook his head. "Stupid question. What happened?"

Nicole shrugged. "The doctors aren't completely sure. They said it could be hereditary, especially since I didn't know your medical history. He also fell when he was little and could have damaged something that went unnoticed. It's been tough, but I haven't spent a lot of time looking for reasons why. I've been more focused on helping him feel better. I've done everything I could, but his doctor said a transplant is his only hope for a long life. Without it, he has a year at the most. Dialysis has been hard on him."

Rocky ran a hand down his face and leaned forward. He stared across the room at Sly. Nicole tried not to be jealous of how longingly Rocky looked at her son. She hadn't had a man look at her like that since she last saw him, either. He was her last lover, and the memory of their weekend together got her through some rough days and nights.

When Sly was little, she imagined life with Rocky by her side. Helping her with midnight feedings and diaper changes, kissing scraped knees and elbows, and holding and loving her all night long. But Rocky was a figment of her imagination. Just like the hope they would find a donor had been.

Hope that sent her looking at other options. Options that would cost everything she had, except her son.

"How are you? This can't have been easy on you. Are you okay?" Rocky asked, turning to her suddenly.

Nicole took a minute to soak him in, all those memories of dreams she had, of him coming home after a long day and asking exactly that, fogged her brain and made it hard for her to think straight as she sat next to the man she never thought she'd see again.

Nicole took a breath and said the same thing she said to everyone else. "I'm fine. It's not easy, but Sly's a great kid. I wouldn't change anything in our lives because we're together."

Rocky held her gaze for a long moment, as if he could see the lies buried beneath the surface. She cried herself to sleep most nights of his life. She used him as her crutch. She spent every spare moment and every spare dollar on him, and she loved him, but a part of her resented Rocky for it. Not Sly, because he couldn't help being sick, but Rocky for not being there. Even though he didn't know, Nicole resented him.

"You must hate me," Rocky said, as though reading her secret thoughts. "I wish I'd been here for you. For both of you."

Nicole pulled herself together while Rocky stared at their son. He'd gotten older in the years since she'd seen him. He was still as lean and strong as ever. She had memories of outlining his muscles with her tongue, of tasting every inch of him. He did the same for her, something she wasn't sure about at the time. He loved her curves, and he wasn't afraid to tell her and show her how much. Years later, with a son and not enough money for both of them to eat healthy, she had even more curves hidden beneath her oversized sweatshirt and jeans.

Not that it mattered. Rocky wouldn't see her naked again. Ever.

"I did the best I could," Nicole finally said.

Rocky's dark gaze snapped back to hers. "I know you did. He looks happy and you've done everything to make sure he's healthy. I'm not trying to say you didn't do everything. I just wish you weren't going through all of this alone. Well, I mean, maybe you're not. I'm sorry to assume."

The question in his gaze almost made her laugh. Nicole had been alone since she walked out of his hotel room in the middle of the night, leaving behind the only man she was ever willing to be her full, true self with. But he wasn't supposed to be hers.

Nicole shook her head. "No, I'm alone."

Was that relief or heat in his eyes? It didn't matter. Nicole was both too tired and too over men to even think about getting involved with someone. Maybe if Sly got better... No. She couldn't think about that. Her son was her priority. Her only priority.

"Mommy," Sly said, running over to her. He held up a toy he'd grabbed from the play area. It was a humvee, his favorite vehicle. "Look, Mommy!"

"I see, sweetheart. That's really cool."

"Can I get one?" Sly asked, his brown eyes hopeful. That was the thing with Sly, he was full of hope and faith. He never gave up on it. He trusted he would get better and be able to have a full life. He trusted their situation would improve and he would have all the toys he wanted. He trusted everything would work out all the time.

Nicole didn't have the same levels of hope or faith. She didn't trust anyone or anything. If something was going to happen, she had to make it happen.

"We'll see, honey," Nicole said, giving him a sad smile. She'd looked at something similar for him as a gift for getting through surgery, but she couldn't afford it. Not when the hospital bills were going to cost her thousands. She had insurance, but it wasn't great insurance. She had a tiny bit of savings, too, but she was going to use that for a new car since hers was barely holding on.

Now that she didn't need that money to buy her son a kidney.

"Okay, Mommy," Sly said, his smile only fading a little. He knew he'd never have one of his own, and instead of getting upset about it, he went back to playing with it, soaking up as much fun with the truck as he could get while it was in his hands.

He raced back across the room to the play area and zoomed the truck around the mat on the floor. Nicole watched him, smiling at the one person who'd never let her down.

"Wow," Rocky breathed, startling Nicole. She'd forgotten he was there for a minute.

"What?"

"He's... He reminds me of my dad."

Nicole smiled. She wasn't going to tell him she reminded her of him.

"Even the way he talks and how happy he is. It's like a piece of my dad is here again."

"Your dad is..."

Rocky looked at her. For a second, she could see that he was somewhere else, but then he snapped back to reality. "He died a long time ago."

"I'm sorry," Nicole said. It didn't matter that she never met the man, she could see the pain it caused Rocky.

He nodded. "He was a great man. The kind of father and husband I always hoped I would be."

Nicole glanced at his hands, panic rising up. "You're married with kids?"

He shook his head. "No. I just always wanted them."

"Ever been married?"

"Nope. How about you?"

Nicole shook her head.

"Any other kids?"

Nicole shook her head again.

"Boyfriends, girlfriends?"

"No one. It's just been Sly and me since I last saw you."

Rocky took a breath and leaned forward again. His gaze was zeroed in on Sly. "Does he know who I am? That I'm his father?"

Nicole shook her head. "I didn't know it was going to be you until I saw you today. He has a rare blood type, one I assumed he got from you. I figured there was a chance you would be the donor, but I also thought it was just as likely to be a stranger."

"So, he doesn't know anything about me?"

"He knows his father was a SEAL and that if you knew about him, you would be a part of his life."

"You told him that?"

She shrugged. "I figured you would never know so I'd never have to tell him I was wrong."

Rocky held her gaze, then drifted back to watching Sly. "You weren't wrong. I want to know him, Nikki. If it's okay with you, I'd like to get to know our son."

Rocky watched Nikki as she processed his words. He wondered if she knew how much she telegraphed her thoughts in her eyes. She didn't trust him, and she wasn't sure if she wanted him around her son.

He didn't really understand it. It wasn't like he walked away from them, or even from her. When he woke up the morning he had to leave, she was already gone. She snuck out during the night. He had always been a light sleeper, so Rocky had no idea how she'd gotten out of the room without him knowing, but she did. She didn't leave a note for him. She just vanished.

For a while, he was pissed off about it, but Dex convinced him it was for the best. Rocky didn't plan to keep in touch with her, so what difference did it make that she left without a word?

But it bothered him, and until that moment, when he was sitting next to her in the waiting room, getting ready to donate a kidney to their son, did he realize why it bothered him so much.

Because he didn't want it to be over.

"I'm sure he'd like that," Nikki finally said.

Rocky could barely remember what they were talking about. Oh, yeah, getting to know Sly. That was honest. He did want to know his kid. He just wanted to know Sly's mom, too. But he wouldn't use Sly to get to Nikki. If things worked out with them, that would be great, but if not, Rocky still wanted to know his son.

"So, Nik—"

"Adrian Malone," a nurse called from the open doorway.

Rocky stopped and looked up. He lifted his hand and stood so the nurse knew he heard her. He turned back to Nikki.

"Your name is Adrian Malone?" she asked with a laugh.

He raised an eyebrow.

"No wonder they call you Rocky."

He grinned at her laugh and remembered the first time he heard it. She was across the bar, and he had to know where it was coming from. She was like a siren, calling to him, and she still was.

"Mr. Malone," the nurse said again.

"Nikki, please come find me. Okay? Don't vanish on me again. Please."

She stopped laughing and sucked in a shaky breath. She looked up at him and nodded, her eyes locked on his.

Rocky took half a step toward her and stopped. He couldn't kiss her. She wasn't his. He couldn't even hug her. But he wanted to do both.

"I'll see you soon."

She nodded again.

He held her gaze for another second, then followed the nurse through the security door. She verified his identity and took his vitals before showing him to a room.

"Your procedure will be first thing in the morning. You won't be able to eat after nine o'clock, but we can have dinner delivered to your room if you'd like. There is a menu on the table next to the bed and instructions on how to order are on the back. Please change into the gown so we can monitor you overnight. I'll be back in a few minutes."

Rocky nodded at the nurse. When she left the room, he changed and packed his clothes into his bag. He pulled out his phone and charger and set them on the table. He had a few missed texts from the team, but nothing that couldn't wait.

The nurse hooked him up to machines and left again. Since he wasn't really a patient yet, he figured they'd mostly leave him alone.

He replied to the texts and debated filling them all in on everything that happened. Dex was the only one who really knew about Nikki, but he might not remember her. Besides that, Rocky wanted a little time to process what happened and everything he learned before telling anyone else.

He ordered dinner and spent some time looking through his emails. He turned on the TV and stared at the screen, his mind and body screaming at him to do something. He wasn't used to sitting around.

He picked up the phone to call the nurse's station.

Maybe if he found out what room Nikki and Sly were in, he could go visit them.

"Can I help you, Mr. Malone?"

"Yeah, can you tell me what room Sylvester... um, shit. I don't know his last name."

"I'm sorry, Mr. Malone, but I can't give out patient information."

"But his mom... he's... Okay. I understand. Thank you."

"Is there anything else, Mr. Malone?"

"No."

Rocky hung up and stared at the four walls surrounding him. It was going to be a long, boring month.

NICOLE FLUFFED the pillow behind Sly's head and smiled at him. "Are you feeling okay?"

He nodded. "Who was that man you were talking to, Mommy?"

Nicole took a breath and avoided looking at her son. She assumed he would notice and ask her, but she thought she could tell him Rocky was just another patient. She didn't expect him to want to be involved in their lives.

"He's donating a kidney tomorrow," Nicole said.

"I'm getting a kidney tomorrow," Sly said with a grin. "Is he giving me a kidney?"

She sat on the bed and took her son's hands. She forced a smile for him. "He is. He came here to give you one of his kidneys."

"That was really nice of him. He's a nice man. Did you tell him thank you?"

She smiled. "I... don't remember. But you can tell him. After tomorrow."

"I will? I'll be able to meet him and tell him thank you?"

She nodded and took the plunge. "You will. Because he wants to get to know you. Honey, he's—"

"Hello, everyone!" Dr. Andrews said, bursting into the room.

Nicole chose him as Sly's surgeon because of his reputation as a top pediatric specialist. She liked him because he was always bright and happy and positive. He made everything seem possible, even the impossible.

"Hi, Dr. Andrews!" Sly shouted. He loved the man, too.

"Well, now, Sylvester, what are you here for? Is it a nose transplant?"

Sly giggled. "No."

"Oh, I know, a funny bone transplant."

Sly laughed harder and shook his head.

"It has to be an armpit transplant," he said, tickling Sly.

Sly giggled and struggled to get away. "No, Dr. Andrews, it's my kidney."

"Oh, kidney!" He slapped his forehead. "Silly me. I should have known that. How is everyone feeling tonight?"

He looked at Nicole even though he was really asking how Sly was.

"I'm great. Mommy met the man who's giving me a kidney. She said I can meet him later and thank him."

Dr. Andrews gave Nicole a funny look. She wasn't supposed to know who was donating, but it wasn't an issue if she found out. She knew he was going to ask.

"Well, that sounds great," Dr. Andrews told Sly. "How about you let me check you out real quick, and we'll get all ready for the morning."

Sly nodded and stretched out on the bed. He did as Dr. Andrews told him and smiled when the report was good.

Dr. Andrews talked a few more minutes, then asked Nicole to speak to him in the hall. She knew what was coming.

"How did you figure out who the donor was?" Dr. Andrews asked.

Nicole took a breath and admitted, "He's Sly's father."

"Really?" Dr. Andrews asked with a grin. "Well, that's great news. I thought this was a registry match?" He flipped through Sly's chart.

"It is. His father hasn't been a part of our lives. I didn't know how to contact him," Nicole said.

Dr. Andrews nodded like he understood. "Well, whatever the reason, I'm happy to see things are going well and that Sly will be healthy. How are you, Nicole? Are you getting enough rest? The next month or two is going to be tough on you."

"I'll be fine, Dr. Andrews. As long as Sly's okay, I will be."

Dr. Andrews smiled at her and put his hand on her shoulder. "Tomorrow is going to be a good day." He squeezed, a grandfatherly gesture from a man who really cared about his patients. Dr. Andrews was well into his fifties and shared with Nicole that he had grandkids close to Sly's age. He said he enjoyed working with kids because they make the world a better place. She was sure he saw more than his fair share of heartache, but he still dealt with every child as though they were his favorites and they all had a great chance of recovery.

"Thank you, Dr. Andrews."

"Do you want me to check up on the father? Make sure he's good?"

Nicole smiled and shook her head. "He's a good man. He didn't run out on us. He never knew about Sly. I didn't know how to reach him once I found out I was pregnant. But he said he wants to get to know Sly."

Dr. Andrews nodded. "Well, if you change your mind, let me know. Try to get some sleep tonight, Nicole. I'll see you both early in the morning."

"Thanks, Dr. Andrews. See you tomorrow."

Nicole went back into the room where a nurse was talking to Sly. She was showing him the options for dinner and flipping through the channels on the TV. Cable TV was a luxury they didn't have at home, so Sly was in heaven.

"Hi, Mom," the nurse said. "We're talking about dinner. He's hungry. He wants pizza and a cheeseburger and fries and a cookie and ice cream."

Nicole crossed her arms and gave Sly a look that said not a chance. "Maybe about half of all that."

The nurse grinned and winked at her. "That's probably for the best." She handed Nicole the menu. "I'm Shelly. I'll be here until he goes into surgery tomorrow, but I'll be back for nights through the weekend. Dinner for you is included, too, Mom, so order whatever you want. I'll pull the chair out for you whenever you're ready. And let me know if there is anything else you need."

Nicole nodded. Shelly started to walk out when Nicole remembered Rocky. "Is it possible to tell me what room another patient is in?"

"It depends. Is the patient family?"

Nicole smiled and lowered her voice. She glanced back at Sly, but he was focused on the TV. "He's my son's donor, but he's also his biological father."

Shelly nodded and smiled. "What's his name?"

"Adrian Malone."

Shelly tapped the screen of her tablet a few times, then said, "Room 412."

"Thank you."

Shelly nodded. "Good luck."

Nicole smiled. She was going to need more than just luck.

3

———

ROCKY'S DINNER ARRIVED WHILE HE WAS TALKING TO DEX. He decided not to tell him about Nikki and Sly yet, even though Dex could tell something was off. He kept asking what was going on, but Rocky insisted he was just anxious about the surgery and being gone for a month.

"We're fine. There's nothing going on here that we can't handle," Dex said.

"Yeah, I know. I just wish I could be in two places at once."

Dex told him to enjoy his dinner and to call once he was up the next day and said goodnight. Rocky dug into his dinner and was about to enjoy dessert when the phone in the room rang.

"Uh, hello?" he answered it.

"Hey, Rocky. It's Nicole."

"Oh, hey. How are you? Is Sly okay?"

He could hear the smile in her quiet voice when she answered. "He's fine. He just fell asleep. He gets tired easily."

"Is that because of his kidneys?"

"Yeah. His body has to work harder, and it wears him out. But that's not why I called."

"Okay, why did you call?"

"I wanted you to know what room we're in. I mean, if you want to know. I don't know if you really meant it when you said you want to get to know Sly, but if you do—"

"I do, Nikki. I meant it. I want to know him. But you're his mother, and if it's not okay with you, that's your call. I haven't been here. You don't know me, so I get that you need to be careful."

"No, I..." She sighed heavily. "You're his father. I'm not going to keep you from him. If I knew how to find you, I would have told you when I found out I was pregnant."

"I know," Rocky said. "I was the one who didn't want to use full names. It's on me, not you."

Nikki was silent.

"So, are you going to tell me what room you're in?" Rocky asked with a laugh.

"Yeah, um, sorry. Sly's in room 768."

"Okay, good. Thanks. Does he have to stay in the hospital for a long time, too?"

"A week or two, yeah."

Rocky scoffed. "Seriously?"

"Yeah, why?"

"They want me to stay a month."

"We live close to here. Dr. Andrews said I can monitor him at home. Sly's going to be recovering for a few months, but he can recover at home."

"Is Dr. Andrews a good doctor?"

"The best. He's amazing."

The irrational jealousy Rocky felt at Nikki's praise of the doctor made him want to punch something.

"So, um, I'm going to get ready for bed. It's going to be a

long day tomorrow. I just wanted to make sure you could call us."

"Thanks, Nikki."

"Yep. So, um, good night."

"Good night. Oh, wait."

"Yeah?"

"What's your last name?"

"Burke."

"Nikki Burke. It's nice to meet you."

"You, too, Adrian Malone."

"Good night, Nikki."

"Good night, Adrian."

He smiled as he hung up the phone. Nikki Burke. And Sylvester Burke. His son. Who would be getting his kidney the next day.

His mind bounced to Dr. Andrews, and curiosity got the better of him. Rocky searched for more info on the man Nikki was so fond of. He needed to make sure the doctor was as good as Nikki made him sound.

The glowing reviews online made it seem like he was even better. Rocky liked him more when he saw a picture of the man with his wife of over thirty years and their children and grandchildren.

He wasn't going to admit that, though.

He started to put his phone down but paused and searched for Nicole Burke. Her name was common enough that he had to sift through people who weren't her to find Nikki's unused social media profiles. Her accounts clearly hadn't been updated in years, and the other information he found about her wasn't much more recent. Rocky knew he could find out just about anything he wanted to know, but he wasn't going to violate her privacy anymore than he already had.

His nurse came in around eleven to ask if he needed anything, but Rocky told her he was going to try to sleep and was okay. She turned off his lights and pulled the curtain to block the light from the window in his closed door.

Rocky didn't take long to fall asleep, with dreams of Nikki and Sly to keep him company.

Morning came far too early, but Rocky was happy for it because it meant Sly was going to feel better. He was prepped and taken up to the surgical floor before the sun was up. People buzzed around him, connecting him to machines to monitor everything while he was under. Rocky let them work and tried to relax and think about Nikki.

He wondered how she slept, and if she slept. He had no idea what it was like to be a single parent, but even if he did, he figured it was that much more difficult to be a single parent to a sick kid. The look on Sly's face when he asked about the humvee told Rocky things weren't easy for them financially, and he felt even more guilty for not knowing about Sly.

"Good morning," a cheerful voice said. "Can I get a moment with our patient?"

The rest of the staff filtered out, and one person said, "Good morning, Dr. Andrews."

Rocky looked up at the covered face of the man who was going to save his son's life and smiled. "Nice to meet you, Dr. Andrews."

"You know who I am?"

"I asked Nikki about you. She said you're great."

"Nicole and Sly are wonderful people. Thank you for what you're doing for them."

"I would have been here sooner if I'd known, sir."

Dr. Andrews nodded slowly, cataloguing Rocky. "I

believe that. Nicole said you want to get to know Sly after this?"

Rocky nodded.

"He's a special kid. And Nicole is an amazing mother. I know it isn't my place, but without her parents in the picture, I think of her as another daughter. I hope you don't intend to hurt them."

Rocky shook his head and held the man's gaze. "I wish I'd known about Sly years ago. If I had, I would be a part of their lives already."

"And Nicole?"

Rocky sucked in a breath. "I hope she'll let me get to know her. But beyond that, sir, quite honestly, it's not going to be your business or anyone else's."

Dr. Andrews was silent for a moment, then nodded. "Take care of them, Mr. Malone."

Rocky nodded. "I will."

Dr. Andrews left the room, and the hustle resumed. It wasn't long before someone was telling Rocky to count backward from ten and he was drifting off to sleep.

NICOLE PACED SLY'S room while she waited for news on the surgery. Dr. Andrews said it would take a few hours, but every minute that ticked by had Nicole more and more anxious. She just wanted to see her son again, and know he was going to be okay.

The door opened, and she jumped. Dr. Andrews strolled in and smiled. Nicole nearly collapsed with relief. Dr. Andrews gestured to the chair behind her and took the other one himself. He patted her hand on her knee.

"Everything went well," Dr. Andrews said. "It was textbook, to be honest. Having a kidney that came from a living relative was perfect, and so far, everything looks great. Sly is still groggy, but that's to be expected. They'll have him back in here within the hour."

"Thank you so much, Dr. Andrews. Thank you."

"Stay strong, Nicole. I did the easy part. As always, you have the tough part. Go get something to eat and relax for a minute."

Nicole nodded. "I will. Thank you."

Dr. Andrews squeezed her hand and stood. He was almost to the door when he stopped. "Do you want to know about the donor?"

Nicole looked up at him. "Can you tell me?"

Dr. Andrews nodded. "Since there is a relationship, yes."

"There's not a relationship. We're not... I mean..."

"I just meant he's Sly's father. Is that not the case?"

"He is. Sorry. I thought you meant... How is he?"

"He did well, too. I would expect a full recovery from him as well. And for what it's worth, he seems like a good man, Nicole."

Nicole nodded. "He is. He'll be good for Sly."

Dr. Andrews smiled. "Maybe for you, too."

Nicole shook her head. "He doesn't live here, I don't think. And we don't really know each other. He wants to know his son, but that's it."

Dr. Andrews grinned. "I'm not so sure about that. Get something to eat. I'll be in before long to check on Sly."

Nicole nodded, ignoring what Dr. Andrews said about Rocky. Besides, it didn't matter because Sly was Nicole's one and only priority.

She went downstairs to the cafeteria and got coffee and a breakfast sandwich. She didn't want to risk not being there when Sly got back to the room so she carried her food upstairs. She'd just finished eating when Sly was wheeled back into the room.

"Good morning, Mom," the nurse said. "I'm Dana. I'll be the nurse for today. Dr. Andrews said this guy did awesome. We'll be watching him closely for today and for the next forty-eight hours, but then we'll get him up and moving. He's still pretty tired."

"I'm hungry," Sly mumbled from the bed.

"Can he eat?"

Dana nodded. "Absolutely. Soft stuff to start because he was intubated and his throat is likely to be sore. The menu has breakfast options and the soft foods are marked. Not a lot of kids like things like oatmeal, but pancakes are probably soft enough. Maybe some fruit."

Nicole looked over the menu and thanked Dana. Once she ordered breakfast for Sly, he asked if he could watch TV.

He zoned out while the cartoons played on the screen. Nicole closed her eyes and said a quick prayer of thanks to whoever was listening.

ROCKY GROANED when he tried to move. Pain shot through his abdomen, like someone shot him.

"Stop moving, dude," Dex said.

"What the hell happened?" Rocky asked. His brain was foggy from the anesthesia.

"You had surgery to give a kidney to a kid," Dex said.

Kidney. Kid. Sly. Nicole. It all came back to Rocky in a flash. The only thing he couldn't figure out was why he was hearing Dex's voice.

He pried his eyes open and saw his friend and roommate sitting next to his bed. "What are you doing here?"

Dex snorted. "Did you really think we were going to let you go through all this alone? I took the first shift."

"Shift? The rest are here?"

Dex shook his head. "Not yet. I'm here for a week, then Mason's going to come. Slade and Kyra talked about coming, and you know Lily isn't going to miss a chance to baby you."

Rocky snorted, then winced when the pain sliced through him. "Don't make me laugh."

Dex chuckled. "Sorry, man. You need me to call your nurse? She said you can have something when you wake up again."

Rocky shook his head. "I'll be fine."

"No need to be a tough guy. If you're hurting, take the meds. You know that."

Rocky nodded. "I know, but I need to judge how bad it is before I start taking stuff."

"Suit yourself. Hey, do they tell you how the kid is? The one you gave your kidney to? Or they can't because you don't know who he is?"

Rocky met his best friend's gaze and drew in a breath. "I know who he is."

"What do you mean?"

"Do you remember Nikki?"

"Nikki? The chick you lost your mind over that one weekend and never got over? Uh, yeah. But what does she have to do with this?"

"It's her son. The one I gave my kidney to."

"No shit? What are the odds she would have a kid you were a match for?"

Rocky waited for Dex to put two and two together. When he figured it out, his jaw dropped.

"No. No fucking way. Are you kidding me?"

Rocky shook his head.

"How long have you known?"

"Since yesterday when I saw him in the waiting room and she sat down next to me and told me."

"Fucking hell. Why didn't she ever call you?"

"She didn't know my name."

"Shit. Are you okay?"

Rocky shrugged. "I haven't really had time to process it all."

"Why the hell didn't you tell me last night when we talked? I knew something was off."

Rocky shrugged. "It threw me. A lot. I always wanted a family, but... not like this. I wanted to be there to see my kids grow up. I wanted to have a wife and be a part of everything."

"You blame her for this?"

"No. Fuck, no. Nikki is an amazing mom. She's done everything for Sly. And she said if she knew how to reach me, she would have."

"Do you believe her?" Dex asked, not in a malicious way.

Rocky nodded. "I do. I don't think this was easy on her. She said she's alone. No one was here with her. She's done the best she could, but she said she's open to me getting to know Sly."

"Sly? His name is Sly?"

Rocky chuckled. "Like father, like son. She knew me as Rocky and named him basically for me."

"I like her already."

Rocky smiled. So did he.

"Am I going to get to meet her?"

Rocky nodded. "I'm sure. I wanted to call once I was up to see how Sly's doing. Can you hand me the phone?"

Dex got up and picked up the phone. He dialed the room number while Rocky held the handset to his ear.

"Hello?" Nikki answered on the first ring.

"Hey, Nikki. It's Rocky. How's Sly doing?"

"He's good," Nikki said, a smile in her voice. "He's eating and watching TV, so pretty much living the dream."

"Good. That's great news. Did you see Dr. Andrews yet?"

"Yeah, he was in here right after surgery. Said everything went well and we should be good. Obviously, it's a long road to recovery, but we will recover."

"Great news. I'm happy to hear it."

"Yeah, me, too. Thank you. We..." She choked up. "We wouldn't have gotten here without you."

"I'm glad I could help."

"Dinner?" Dex whispered.

Rocky waved his hand at him. "Shut it."

"What was that?" Nikki asked.

"Nothing. Sorry. Just a pest in my room."

"Seriously?"

"No. A friend of mine. He came down to make sure I'm following the rules. He wants to meet you and Sly."

"Oh, well, that's fine, but um, maybe not today. Let's give him a day or two. We can talk tomorrow. If that's okay."

Rocky nodded. "Of course. I think I need the same."

Nikki gasped. "I'm so sorry. I should have asked. How are you?"

"I'm good. And you shouldn't have asked. You have someone a lot more important to worry about."

"Yeah, but—"

"Nikki, don't worry about it. Sly is your number one priority. This ugly jackass in front of me can worry about me."

"You looking in a mirror?" Dex asked.

Rocky snorted.

"What did he say?" Nikki asked.

"He asked if I was looking in a mirror. He thinks he's funny," Rocky told her, then flipped Dex off while she laughed softly.

"Do you live close to here? I never asked you."

"Nope. We live in New York. Niagara Falls."

"Wow," Nikki breathed. "I've always wanted to go there."

"You should come visit," Rocky said without thinking.

"Maybe," Nikki answered. All of a sudden, she was reserved and pulled back. "Um, I need to go. I'll talk to you soon."

She hung up before Rocky could say goodbye. He looked at the phone in his hand.

"Scared her off?" Dex asked, taking the receiver and setting it down.

"Screw you."

Dex snorted. "You saw her for the first time yesterday in what? Seven years?"

"So?"

"And you're inviting her to visit you? She's a single mom with a sick kid. You need to take this one slow, or you're not going to get anywhere with her," Dex said.

"I'm not trying to get anywhere with her. I just want to know my kid."

"You aren't still hung up on her? Because if my memory serves, you were pretty broken up about her running off on you. And I don't think it was just your ego. I think you liked her. A lot."

Rocky shrugged. "It doesn't matter. She's not interested, and that was a long time ago."

"If you say so," Dex said.

Rocky rolled his eyes. "Hey, do you think you can do me a favor? Since you're here?"

Dex raised an eyebrow in question.

"Find a local toy store and go pick something up."

"Something in particular?"

"Yeah, Sly likes humvees. Go get him the nicest one you can find. And anything else you think would go with it."

Dex grinned. "Are you serious?"

Rocky nodded. "Yep."

Dex snorted. "He really is your kid."

Rocky just smiled. He liked the sound of that.

4

———

Nicole hovered over Sly until he groaned and said he was 'fine.' She knew when she pushed him that far that he was frustrated with her but didn't know how to say back off. It also meant he was feeling better and the pain wasn't as bad as it was the day before.

Nicole settled in her chair with a book, watching Sly more than she read the pages of the book. He stared at the TV, his eyes glazed over.

Until there was a knock on the door.

"Can we come in?" Rocky asked. He was in a wheelchair wearing a hospital gown with a blanket draped over his lap. Behind him was a stunning man with dark hair and skin, and eyes that said she better not hurt his friend.

Ha. If he only knew. Nicole was not the one in danger of doing the hurting.

"Of course," Nicole said, forcing a smile to her lips.

Sly tried to prop himself up on the bed but winced with the pain of moving.

"Let me help you," Nicole said automatically.

"I can do it, Mommy," Sly answered defiantly.

He was growing up. She knew it would happen, but she didn't expect it to happen so quickly. One day he was her little man snuggling next to her in bed, and the next he wouldn't even let her help him sit up in his hospital bed.

She almost cried.

"Hi," Nicole said, extending her hand to the other man once he reached her side. "I'm Nicole. And this is Sly."

"I'm Dex," he said.

Nicole shook his hand and accepted the thinly veiled threat he offered with a nod. She knew enough men like him to know his bark was probably worse than his bite, but she couldn't take the chance that she read him wrong.

"Dex is a teammate and friend of mine. We've known each other a long time. And he came to make sure I follow the doctor's orders about recovery. He also ran an errand for me yesterday," Rocky explained.

He lifted his blanket and pulled out a box wrapped in camouflage wrapping paper. Sly's eyes lit up, and he reached for it.

"What do you say?" Nicole reminded her son.

"Thank you," Sly said automatically, the words nonsense as he lunged to take the gift from Rocky.

Sly tore at the paper as soon as the gift was in his hands. The box filled his entire lap, and as he shredded the paper covering it, Nicole knew exactly what it was.

It was a humvee, like the one Sly was playing with in the waiting room before surgery.

Her gaze snapped to Rocky's, who was watching her instead of Sly. There was a question in his eyes, like he was asking if it was okay. She couldn't tell Sly no, but she also didn't mind. She thought it was sweet that Rocky wanted to give Sly something, even though it made her feel guilty that she didn't have anything for him.

"Wow! This is awesome! I love it! Mommy, look at this! This is the coolest thing ever!"

Nicole grinned at her son's excitement. She hadn't seen him so happy in years. He was a great kid with a lot of joy inside, but he was rarely spoiled. He didn't have grandparents or other family who overwhelmed him on holidays, and he didn't have a big group of friends. Nicole hosted a birthday party for him in first grade after she realized everyone in class had a party, but the cost of it was so high she was still paying for it. She'd already decided not to have a party for him in second grade but felt like the worst mom ever for that choice.

And now his father swooped in with a gift Nicole knew was well out of her price range, and made her feel even worse.

"Is there anything else you want to say, Sly?" Nicole prompted.

Sly looked up at her, and she raised an eyebrow. He nodded like he'd forgotten all about why they were there in the first place.

"Thank you for my new kidney, too. I really needed it. Mommy cried every night and prayed someone would give me one. Now, maybe she won't cry."

Sly looked up at Nicole and smiled. Her cheeks burned with embarrassment. She didn't want Sly to know how hard it was on her to see him sick. She would have done anything for him, but she wasn't a match. If she could have, she would have given both her kidneys, but she felt helpless. Until Rocky showed up.

"Thank you," Nicole said softly to him, avoiding his gaze as tears filled her eyes.

"You're welcome," Rocky said just as softly. Then he cleared his throat and focused on Sly. "Hey, why don't we open this bad boy up and you can show us everything it does?"

"Yeah! Can we, Mommy?"

Nicole nodded and forced another smile. "Of course. You guys start on that. I'll be right back."

Nicole hurried out of the room before anyone could stop her. The chatter she left behind said the three males inside barely noticed she left.

She walked to the end of the hall and turned to the right. She knew the floor made a loop and decided to just walk it, giving herself a break for a few minutes.

Seeing Rocky again was overwhelming, but having him act like they were important to him messed with her head. She told herself he was just trying to be nice to Sly and get to know his son, but the way he looked at her made her think there was more to it.

Their fling was brief, but it was the best weekend of Nicole's life. She was working at a hole in the wall bar in Texas and studying to be a phlebotomist. When Rocky walked in, she zeroed in on him, but she never thought he'd give her a second glance. She wasn't a virgin and had been with enough men to know when a guy hit on her in a bar, it wasn't forever, but her heart didn't want to believe that.

She fell in love with him that weekend. She never said the words, but she loved him. He was passionate and sweet and overwhelmingly sexy. He loved her body, but he also talked to her. He made her feel like she was more than a woman from a bar. She was special.

That was why she left when he was still asleep. She wasn't sure she would be able to say goodbye to him. She wanted to hold on to the memories she had of their weekend together without the tarnished last morning when he would say thanks and disappear forever.

But it wasn't forever. All the memories she held on to for the last seven years rushed over her when she saw him. The way he held her and kissed her and loved her were a comfort in the darkness of night when she was alone, but standing in front of the man with their son between them, the proof of their weekend a living, breathing person who shared a part of him and a part of her, made her question everything.

What would have happened if she hadn't left that night? Would he have asked to keep in touch? Would she have asked him? Would she have known his name so she could tell him she was pregnant? Would that have changed anything?

Would it have made Sly's life easier?

That last question was the one that got to her. It was the one she always asked herself. If Rocky had been a part of their lives, would it have changed her son's?

Nicole learned to live without a man in her life, but she'd sentenced her son to the same punishment. And now that Rocky was back, she wondered if she'd made a mistake.

"No wonder you couldn't let go," Dex whispered once Nicole was out of the room.

Rocky shot him a glare that said *not in front of the kid* and *back off, she's mine*. Dex just laughed.

"I'm just saying—"

"So, how are you feeling, Sly?" Rocky asked his son, ignoring his friend. Dex could wait until they were alone.

"My stomach hurts. But don't tell my mommy. She worries about me."

"That's what mommies are supposed to do," Rocky said with a smile. "And you have a pretty great one."

Sly nodded, rolling his humvee across his lap. "She's the best. She cries a lot, but she tells me it's just because I'm such a good kid. I know it's because she thinks I'm going to die and then she'll be all alone."

Rocky nodded, his heart breaking just a little for the family he should have had. Nicole never should have gone through everything she went through alone. He should have been there.

"What about your grandparents? Aren't they around?"

Sly shook his head. "I don't have grandparents."

Rocky thought Nicole mentioned her parents once, but he couldn't remember. It had also been seven years and a lot could happen in that time.

"Well, hopefully you and your mom aren't alone anymore. And hopefully you start to feel better soon so your mom isn't so scared."

Sly nodded. "Why did you wait so long to come see me?"

Rocky drew back, surprised the kid figured out who he was. They looked similar, but he didn't think Sly would put it together, especially so fast. "Well, I didn't know about you."

"I thought there was a list. Mommy said no one on the list was a match. Were you not supposed to be a match? Like Mommy talked about on the phone?"

Rocky exchanged a glance with Dex, who wore a matching confused expression.

"What do you mean?"

Sly shrugged and slid down his bed a little. "I don't know. Mommy said I was running out of time and she needed someone to help. She told you she would do anything. So, why didn't you come sooner? Did she not give you enough money? Because we don't have a lot of money."

"What are you talking about, Sly?" Rocky asked.

Sly shook his head. "I'm tired. Thank you for giving me a kidney."

Almost that fast, he was asleep. Rocky turned to look at Dex, who asked, "What was he talking about?"

Rocky shook his head. "I don't know, but it didn't sound good."

"No, not at all."

ZEKE MARTIN LOOKED at his phone and grinned. He held up a finger so the boss would know he had to take the call and stepped out of the room.

"Well, if it isn't my favorite client. How are you?"

Nicole breathed a sigh through the phone. He could hear the relief in her voice. "I'm good. So good. And I'm so glad I caught you. We don't need your help after all."

Zeke's smile faded. He moved farther from the door so the boss wouldn't overhear his call. "What do you mean?"

"My son's father showed up. He didn't know about us, so I couldn't contact him, but he turned up on the list. They had their surgery yesterday morning, and it went really well."

"Why are you calling me now?"

"I wanted to make sure everything was good. Before I told you we didn't need the help. Just in case."

"That's not exactly how this works," Zeke growled.

"Well, um, I thought that since we were still talking about everything that it wasn't a big deal."

"It is a big deal. We have an agreement. I don't know if I can get you out of it."

"What do you mean?"

"I have a boss, and he's counting on the revenue from you to cover expenses. He's not the kind of man who's going to say no big deal and let things move on. We had an agreement."

Her voice trembled at the steel in his. Zeke wanted to protect her, but he couldn't do that if his boss killed him. He had a feeling Nicole had no idea what she was agreeing to when they talked, but she said she would do anything to help her son. Even the dollar figure they gave her wasn't too much for her. Zeke was sure that alone would scare her off, but she said okay.

But going back and saying never mind... that never went over well.

"What can I do?"

"Do you have the money?"

"No," she said hurriedly. "I needed it to pay for his surgery. And all the time I have to be off work."

"How were you going to pay for all that if you had to pay us?" Zeke asked. He wanted to kick his own ass for even asking. That wasn't his job. Once they got their money, it didn't matter what happened to the other parties. It wasn't their business, and it wasn't their concern. He never had trouble with that side of things. Before Nicole.

"I was going to figure it out," Nicole admitted, sounding small and defeated.

Zeke breathed a heavy sigh and dropped his head into his hand. He rubbed at the bridge of his nose and told himself not to say the words even as he said them. "Let me see what I can do. I'll try to get you out of this. But I can't make any promises."

"Thank you, Zeke. So much. I owe you."

"Are you sure about this father? Is he decent?"

"Rocky? Yeah, he's a great guy."

"He can't be that great if he wasn't around the last few years," Zeke spat.

"That was my fault. He was a SEAL, and I skipped out on him when we met. I thought it was for the best to walk away instead of have him walk away. For years, it's been my biggest regret. Life could have been so different for Sly if he was in our lives."

Zeke wanted to punch the brick wall in front of him. Nicole was his, not some random ex who wasn't there. But now the son of a bitch got to slide in at the last minute and steal Zeke's hero move and save Nicole's stupid kid.

"Well, I'll see what I can do. We'll talk soon."

"Okay, yeah. Thanks, Zeke," she said before she hung up.

Zeke rubbed the back of his neck and took a deep breath. He was not looking forward to the conversation he had to have next.

He walked back into the office and took a seat opposite his boss's desk. "Well?" Jon asked.

"The father showed up and donated a kidney. She doesn't need us."

Jon's eyebrows jumped together for a second, like he was confused. "So?"

"So, she wants out of her deal."

Jon leaned back in his chair and tented his fingers on his short hair. His biceps jumped, flexing with the subtle move. Zeke was a large man, but Jon made him feel small. Especially when he delivered one of his stares that made Zeke want to piss himself. Like he was doing in that moment.

"Do we go back on deals?" Jon asked as though speaking to a child.

Zeke shook his head.

"So why are we having this conversation?"

"I told her I would talk to you."

"Maybe you should bring her to see me," Jon said, a smile curling his lips up.

"Why?" Zeke blurted. He knew what Jon did to the women who came to see him.

Jon glared at Zeke hard. "Because if her pussy is so good that you're willing to talk to me for her, I think I should have a turn."

Zeke shook his head. "It's not like that. She's not... we're not..."

"She won't give it up for you?" Jon taunted.

Zeke glared back at his boss.

Jon's grin slid from his face, and he leaned forward. "She made a deal. Either she pays me in cash or she pays me in flesh. I don't really care which one."

Zeke wanting nothing more than to put his fist through his boss's face, but the men standing guard at the door would put bullets through his head before Zeke could even think about a second punch. And that would leave Nicole unprotected.

Zeke nodded and stood. Jon turned away from him, dismissing him. Zeke walked out like he wasn't in a hurry at all and went to see Harry.

Harry was in his icebox wearing a fur coat and staring at one of seven monitors. Some of them flickered through the multiple security cameras set up around the property, one played an old sitcom, and one ran a program that Zeke couldn't understand if he tried.

"Can I help you?" Harry asked.

Zeke hated the man almost as much as he hated his boss. Harry was the last person he wanted to go to for help, but he was the only option Zeke had left. He needed to know everything he could about Nicole's ex.

"I need you to find someone. He was matched with a kid on the donor list. I need you to tell me everything you can about him."

"Do you know his name?"

"His nickname is Rocky. He's a former SEAL, maybe current, but I doubt it. He was matched with Sylvester Burke at St. Gerard's."

Harry was already typing, his fingers flying across the keys so fast Zeke couldn't see them.

"How much would you like to know about him?"

"Everything," Zeke said.

5

ROCKY SETTLED INTO A ROUTINE WITH THE HOSPITAL STAFF over the next few days. He ate when they told him to eat, he did his PT when he was scheduled for that, and every minute he wasn't doing something, he was visiting with Sly and Nikki.

Dex was staying at a local extended stay hotel near the hospital and spent the day with Rocky every day. A part of Rocky wanted time alone with Nikki instead of having it always be the four of them, but he couldn't exactly tell Dex to get lost.

"What do you want to be when you grow up?" Dex asked Sly while they all played cards one afternoon.

Nikki sucked in a breath that drew Rocky's attention. "You okay?" he asked softly.

She nodded while Sly told Dex he wanted to drive a big truck and save people. "For a long time, I didn't think he'd ever grow up. I didn't think he'd get to choose a career." She met Rocky's gaze and smiled. "Thank you for that."

Rocky smiled back and grabbed her hand. She threaded her fingers through his and held on to him. The rest of the world disappeared while they stared at each other, holding hands like it was something they did all the time.

"Mommy, it's your turn," Sly said loudly, as though it wasn't the first time he'd issued the reminder.

Rocky pulled his hand back when Nikki let go. Dex raised an eyebrow at him, but Rocky ignored his friend. He didn't know what was going on either.

They played cards and talked until Sly yawned. "Do you need to rest?" Nikki asked, brushing the hair off his forehead.

Sly shook his head, the sandy hair falling right back to where it was. He still wore a hospital gown all day so the nurses could check his incision and help him bathe more easily. Rocky was grateful they'd given him permission to wear his own clothes since his wounds were smaller.

"I'm not tired, Mommy," Sly argued.

"Maybe a little bit of quiet time will help you. It's been a busy few weeks for us."

"But I want to play cards and drive my humvee around. I can rest later."

Nikki looked even more exhausted than Sly. The circles under her eyes had grown darker over the last few days. Rocky knew she wasn't getting a lot of sleep in the chair she pulled out every night into a bed, and she wasn't resting during the day. She was constantly doing something, and Rocky wondered if the downtime was more for her than it was for Sly.

"You know what," he said with a wide yawn, "I'm getting pretty worn out. I think Dex and I are going to head back to my room for a bit so I can rest."

"Why can't Dex stay here with me?" Sly asked.

Dex shook his head. "I need to keep an eye on this one. Your mom is pretty awesome at making sure you do what you need to do, but Rocky doesn't listen all that well. I need to keep him in line." Dex pounded his fist into his opposite hand.

Sly giggled while Rocky glared at the two of them, playing along so Sly would think resting wasn't a big deal.

He yawned and shrugged. "Okay, I guess I'm tired, too. I can try to sleep a little. But can you guys come back for dinner?"

Rocky and Dex both nodded. "Absolutely."

Dex pushed Rocky out of the room, enjoying being the one to treat Rocky like an invalid. He'd insisted he could walk around the hospital and be on his own, but hospital policy wouldn't let him. Besides that, the doctors refused to let him leave since they knew what he did for a living.

When they got back to the room, Rocky flopped onto his bed and Dex settled into the chair. "I need a break from this place. I wonder if they'll let me go on a field trip."

Dex snorted. "Not likely. If they would, you wouldn't be here. You're not going to survive a month of this."

"I don't know why I need to stay a month."

"Although the daily routine isn't all bad," Dex said with a raised eyebrow.

Rocky took a deep breath and nodded. "Getting to know Sly is great. I want to tell him who I am, though."

"Then tell him," Dex said.

Rocky shook his head. "I can't. Nikki has her reasons for not wanting him to know yet. I'm not going to go against her on it. She's his mom. She's the one who's been there with him his whole life. If she thinks it's best to wait, then I'll be patient and wait."

"I would think it was weird if some guy was hanging around all the time," Dex said.

"Like you are?" Rocky joked.

Dex flipped him off. "Whatever. I'm here because your stubborn ass can't leave the hospital."

"Well, I might have some good news about that," Rocky's latest nurse, Bella, said as she walked in with a smile.

"About leaving?" Rocky asked hopefully.

Bella nodded. "The on call doctor came around while you were gone and asked what was going on. I told him you've been going up to see Sylvester and that you have a friend in town who goes with you so you aren't alone. He said if that's the case you can leave."

"Seriously?" Rocky asked.

Bella nodded again. "Of course, you still have to stay in town, and you can't be alone. I wasn't sure how long you were staying..."

Dex shook his head. "I'm leaving tomorrow. But another teammate is coming down so he has company. We didn't think he'd have such amazing people here looking out for him."

Bella's cheeks flushed, and she shook her head. It didn't matter that she wore a wedding ring, not many women were immune to Dex's charms. He could flirt with a telephone pole and make it quiver for him.

Rocky had never gotten that kind of reaction from a woman. Not that he was hurting for companionship, but he wasn't like Dex or Jack. Nikki was the only woman he'd ever known who made him feel like he wasn't just a fumbling fool compared to his teammates.

"I'll have to talk to the doctor again, but if you have someone staying with you, I think he'll let you leave. You will need final approval from Dr. Andrews, but you're clearly not really in need or medical care. You're essentially independent, but you're still a patient since they don't want you going home yet," Bella said.

"That would be great," Rocky said. "No offense to anyone here, but I'd love to be at a hotel instead of here for three more weeks."

Bella grinned. "I understand completely. Let me know when you'll have people here over the next few weeks and where you're staying and I'll talk to them about getting you out of here."

"You're awesome, Bella. Thank you."

She smiled and left the room.

"Already on the schedule," Dex said. "Dunn is sending it to both of us so you can share it with whoever needs to see it. Are you going to be able to pull yourself away from Nikki?"

Rocky shook his head. "I have to eventually. She's not going to leave here, and I..." Rocky paused, the reality of walking away from them hitting him hard.

"You'd leave the team, wouldn't you? If she wanted you to stay?" Dex asked.

Rocky took a breath and met his friend's gaze. "How can I abandon my son now that I know about him? How can I just go back to Niagara Falls like he doesn't exist? What kind of person would that make me?"

Dex didn't answer because there was only one answer. Rocky couldn't leave his kid. Not if he ever wanted to look himself in the mirror again.

Nicole leaned back in her chair and laughed. For his last night in town, Dex wanted to watch a movie and eat pizza. He even approved the menu change with the nurses on Sly's floor and bribed them all with pizzas of their own.

Nicole wasn't sure what to think of him. He was cute, but

he was obviously aware of everything that had happened between her and Rocky. She wondered more than once if Dex was going to tell Sly that Rocky was his father, but he hadn't spilled it yet. As the movie creeped toward the end, she was thankful he and Rocky respected her decision enough to not say anything without her approval.

She felt bad for not wanting to tell Sly yet. The first night, she was about to, until Dr. Andrews walked in. She took it as a sign that she should keep her mouth shut about that part of the truth until she knew for sure that Rocky meant what he said when he made the instant decision to get to know his son.

Rocky definitely impressed her with his repeated attempts to get to know Sly. After the first day, he didn't show up with more gifts, which she appreciated, but he was always there. He played games with Sly and told him stories about being in the Navy. Nicole learned more about the man than she ever thought she'd know.

"You doing okay?" Rocky asked her quietly.

She nodded, glancing at Sly. He was wrapped up in the movie and ignoring them entirely. She was happy he was recovering well, but she still wasn't getting enough rest. And she hadn't taken a real shower in almost a week. She was used to doing everything on her own, but she felt like she was being watched constantly, which put her on edge.

"You sure? You look tired," Rocky said.

Like she said, being watched. She turned to look at him and raised an eyebrow. "You do know when you tell a woman she looks tired she hears you saying she looks like shit, right?"

Dex snorted from the other side of the room. Rocky had the decency to look ashamed. "I just meant that I'm worried about you."

"I'm fine," Nicole said. She crossed her arms and turned back to the movie, ignoring him.

Dex carried on a conversation with Sly through the last bit of the movie. When it was over, he told Sly he was going to miss him.

"Will you come back and visit me?"

Dex nodded. "Absolutely. If I didn't have to go back to work, I'd stick around a little longer, but a friend of mine will be here tomorrow. Mason's a cool dude. You might need a bigger room, though. He's huge."

"Really?" Sly asked, his eyes wide.

Dex nodded again and held out his arms. "I don't think he'll fit through the door. You're lucky he didn't donate his kidney to you. It probably wouldn't fit inside your stomach."

Sly giggled, acting like a six year old. He threw his head back and collapsed against the pillows. Dex tickled him gently, then hugged him. "I'm going to miss you, little man. But you take care of your mom. And this guy. Make sure he drinks his milk and eats his veggies, okay?"

Sly nodded solemnly, taking his duty seriously. "I will."

They exchanged a complicated handshake that threatened to bring Nicole's tears to her cheeks. She forced a smile and drew in a shaky breath.

When Dex stood and turned to Nicole, she wasn't sure what she was supposed to do. She didn't know him and had never had a conversation with him alone, but she felt like she was losing someone important with him leaving.

Dex opened his arms and moved closer. He kissed Nicole's cheek and whispered, "Take care of him."

She nodded against his chest, unsure which him Dex was referring to. Dex held her for a long moment, until Rocky cleared his throat, then chuckled when he pulled back.

"It was really nice to finally meet you."

Nicole smiled at him and wondered if she really would ever see him again. There was no reason to think she would, but a part of her hoped she would. He brought out a side of Rocky that she didn't know existed. There was an easy affection between them, like brothers who'd been through everything together. Seeing it made her wish for things she had no business wishing for.

Rocky said he would see them the next day and said goodnight as Sly yawned and slid under his covers. Nicole nodded and stifled her own yawn, wondering if she'd ever feel like she got enough sleep.

NICOLE WOKE up early the next morning as the sunlight streamed through the too thin blinds in Sly's eastward facing room. Nicole became a light sleeper when Sly was an infant, and she'd never gotten back to sleeping like a normal person with his many illnesses and trips to the hospital.

"Why don't you go get some breakfast?" nurse Rebecca said softly when she checked in on them. "I'll be nearby."

Nicole nodded and took the offer. The cafeteria was quiet before the shift change that would bring a new group of people in to start their day full of caffeine. She ordered an extra large cup of coffee and splurged on a muffin that she ate on her way back to Sly's room.

He was still asleep when she got there. She kissed his forehead and noticed he felt a little warm. She called the nurse in, and Rebecca scanned his forehead.

"Not a fever, but he's warmer than yesterday. I'll make a note of it and pass it on to dayshift so they watch out for him. I know you'll keep an eye on him, too," Rebecca said.

Nicole nodded. She kept an eye on Sly while she folded up the pullout chair and washed her face. She gave up on makeup years ago when she realized between work and home she ended her day without makeup, anyway.

The dayshift nurse came in when Sly was still sleeping. She told Nicole Rebecca had passed on the news that he was a little warm and she wanted to check in.

"I just noticed it this morning," Nicole told her. "I went to get coffee and when I got back, I kissed his forehead."

"A mother knows," the nurse said. She was one Nicole didn't remember seeing before, but the days and nights were starting to run together. "I'm Marie. I was on vacation when you guys got here. I already checked Dr. Andrews' schedule, and he's in surgery this morning, but he's going to come by as soon as he's free. We'll keep a close eye on him until then."

"Thank you, Marie," Nicole said.

Nicole settled into the chair and felt Sly's forehead again. She could have been wrong, but she thought he already felt cooler.

Nicole busied herself with deleting junk emails and paying her bills while Sly slept. She wanted to take a shower, but she didn't want to leave Sly's side.

He finally stirred close to eight and smiled at her when he opened his eyes.

"How are you feeling?" Nicole asked him.

"Good. Is Dex here?"

Nicole shook her head. "No, honey. I haven't seen him. I don't know what time his flight is."

"Oh. Can we call Rocky and ask him? Is he coming today?"

Nicole nodded. "Sure, we can call Rocky. He seems like a nice guy, right?"

Sly nodded. "Yeah. He's really fun. They both are. I hope I like Mason, too."

Nicole grinned. He had never had a man as a part of his life. Dr. Andrews was there when Sly was sick, but they didn't see him outside the office. Rocky and Dex were men Sly could talk to and joke with and call friends.

Family.

"He's awake," Marie said with a bright smile. "How are you feeling, Sylvester?"

"Good. I'm still tired, though. Can I have my truck?"

Marie chuckled and nodded. "Of course. Let me take your temperature real quick. Is that okay?"

Sly nodded and leaned back. Marie scanned his forehead again and smiled.

"Back to normal. Dr. Andrews is still going to stop by. Just to check in."

"Maybe he can see Rocky and me together today."

"Who's Rocky?" Marie asked.

"He was my donor," Sly said simply.

Marie looked at Nicole with a question in her gaze.

Nicole smiled. "His name is Adrian Malone. If it's okay with Dr. Andrews, that would be fine."

Marie nodded and flipped through the screens on her tablet. She narrowed her eyes and shook her head. "Well, it looks like Mr. Malone is no longer a patient here. He was discharged this morning."

"What?" Nicole breathed.

Marie shrugged like it was no big deal, but to Nicole, it meant she was right not to tell Sly that Rocky was his father. He was just another in a long line of people who'd let her down when she needed someone, except this time he let down her son, too.

"Rocky's gone?" Sly asked.

"It's fine, honey," Nicole said.

"But I want to see him. I thought he was going to come back." He started to cry.

Nicole's heart broke right along with Sly's. He wasn't the only one who was disappointed, but she had the foresight to know better than to believe Rocky in the first place. She'd had enough pain in her life to know trusting anyone was only going to end up with tears. She just hated that her son was learning that painful lesson at six.

6

———

Rocky got settled in the extended stay hotel in a two-bedroom suite so there was space for Mason and the others when they came to visit. He still didn't think he needed a babysitter, but when he flopped onto the couch, he realized his incision site was hurting.

He lifted his shirt to check it. Three pink scars had begun to form on his abdomen. The surgical glue the doctor used to close the surface wound had mostly come off already, but whatever stitches were inside were still likely healing. If he had a desk job, it wouldn't be an issue for him to return to work, but it was rare he spent a lot of time at a desk.

Rocky gave himself a few minutes to rest before he claimed a room and unpacked his bag. He expected to be wearing scrubs or a hospital gown, so he hadn't brought a ton of clothes. He saw a store not far from the hotel and knew he would have to make a trip there at some point to get some extra things. There was a laundry room in the hotel, but he didn't want to do laundry every other day.

Once he was unpacked, he felt better. He checked his

phone and saw a missed text from Mason. His flight was delayed. He should still make it that day, but he would be in closer to dinnertime.

Rocky looked around the hotel room and shook his head. It was far too quiet for him to sit there all day. Normally, he'd be in Sly's room playing cards or watching TV and getting to know his son. Visiting hours for the hospital were in the afternoon, and since he was no longer a patient, Rocky figured they wouldn't be able to let him hang out all day.

He worried Nikki and Sly would think he skipped out on them. He thought about calling before he left, but it happened so quickly that he didn't get a chance. When he had time, he realized he didn't have Nikki's number. It was definitely time to call the hospital.

Rocky asked to be connected to Sly's room and waited as the phone rang. He gave it a while, listening to his end ring over and over again. When no one picked up, he looked at his phone like it had done something wrong.

He hung up and wondered if they were taking a walk or something else. It didn't matter. He'd give them some time and call again.

For an hour, Rocky called, and for an hour, no one answered the phone. The next time he called, he asked the person who answered the phone what time visiting hours began.

"In twenty minutes," she told him.

"Good. Thank you." Rocky hung up and grabbed his keys. He thought about stopping by the store on his way over, but he wasn't going to be the kind of father who bought his child's love and affection. Giving him gifts wasn't a bad thing, but he'd seen too many parents who bought gifts every time they upset their child. Rocky was going to talk to Sly and hoped he and Nikki would be willing to listen to him.

At the hospital, Rocky handed over his ID and got a visitor's pass to go up to see Sly. He listened to the directions from the attendant and followed instructions up to Sly's floor. The nurses there smiled when he stepped out of the elevator.

"Well, it's good to see you on your feet. I heard you'd been released," one said, smiling at him.

Rocky nodded. "I have been. But I had to come back to check in on Sly. I tried calling earlier, but they must have had a busy day."

The nurse pursed her lips and raised her eyebrows.

"How bad?" Rocky asked, lowering his voice.

"You should have brought flowers. And candy. And maybe some wine. I'm sure Sly will forgive and forget, but I don't know if Mom will."

Rocky groaned to himself and thanked the nurse. He needed to find out her name and bring her a gift next time he visited. He paused outside Sly's room and pasted on a smile, then knocked on the door and waited for them to say he could come in.

"Come in," Nikki's voice sang out.

Rocky opened the door and peeked inside. His grin was real when he saw the excited look on Sly's face.

"You didn't leave me. You're here!" Sly said.

Rocky pushed the rest of the door open and walked in. He glanced at Nikki, but she was scowling and avoiding his gaze, so Rocky focused on Sly. "I'm not going anywhere. Dr. Andrews said he needed the bed I was using for a belly button transfer, and since mine is not very pretty, he had to throw me out."

Sly giggled and flopped back on the bed. "He's so funny."

Rocky nodded. "He is." He risked another glance at Nikki, and she stood and busied herself putting away things that usually stayed out all day and all night. "What have you two been up to today?"

"Just watching TV. It was boring. Mom asked if you could see Dr. Andrews with me today, but the nurse said you were gone and Mom got sad. I cried because I thought you left without saying goodbye."

Rocky shook his head and sat on the edge of Sly's bed with him. He wrapped his arm around his son and hugged him close. "I'm not going anywhere for a few more weeks, and when Dr. Andrews says I can travel, I promise you it won't be for long. I'll come back to see you. You'll always know where I am."

"I love you," Sly said, hugging Rocky tight.

His throat filled up with emotion and made it hard for him to answer, but he choked out, "I love you, too, Sly."

Nikki snorted, but her back was to them. Her movements were jerky, and she was definitely pissed off.

Rocky wanted to ask her what was going on, but he wasn't willing to put her in that position. Not with Sly sitting there. Maybe he could get some time with her later.

"Oh, you have company," another nurse said, walking into the room. "I apologize. I was going to see if Sly wanted to go to the community room so Mom could get a break for a little while. Maybe even go home and shower and get some things done."

"That sounds like fun," Rocky said, looking at Sly. "What do you say? We give Mommy a break and you and I can hang out for a little while?"

Sly nodded. "Yeah, Mommy, can we?"

Nikki turned and faced them. She focused only on Sly, avoiding Rocky's gaze. He studied her, knowing she was aware of him watching her. She looked tired, but he knew better than to say that again. She also looked hurt. Like him being discharged upset her more than he realized it could have.

"I'm not sure it's a good idea," Nikki said. "You had a fever this morning, and maybe you shouldn't be around other kids."

The nurse stepped forward. "If it makes you feel better, this is a quiet time. That's why I came down. No one is in there right now, and usually during visiting hours, it's empty. It's still your call, but I wanted you to know that."

Rocky watched as Nikki's excuse crumbled and she couldn't find another one, except the one she really wanted to say. She didn't want Sly around Rocky.

"I'm staying at the extended stay a few lights past the hospital. Mason is on his way to town, but his flight got delayed. I've checked into the hotel for the next three weeks. I will give you my phone number and tell you anything you want to know. You can see my license, take a picture of it, whatever. But please, Nikki..."

She studied him, arms crossed over her chest. Her mind worked to find an excuse, but defeat shined in her eyes. She scowled and huffed a sigh and said, "Fine."

"Thank you, Mommy," Sly said loudly.

"But you have to listen to Nurse Marie. If she says you have to come back to your room, you come back. And I'll be back for dinner so we can eat together."

Sly nodded, and Rocky imitated him. Nikki glared at Rocky but didn't say anything to him. She moved toward Sly, hugging and kissing him before she left without a word to Rocky.

"Let's go check out this community room," Rocky said with a smile, trying not to let it bother him that Nikki was so mad. He'd fix it. He had to.

NICOLE COULD BARELY REMEMBER where she parked her car once she got outside. She was so angry with Rocky, and she was hurt and upset, and she was scared. Sly said he loved Rocky. He hadn't said those words to anyone except her. For more than six years, she'd done everything for him, and in a week, a complete stranger swooped in and made her son fall in love with him.

It hurt to have Sly love Rocky so easily. Especially because Nicole understood it. He was the kind of man who made it easy to love him. He was funny and smart and kind. He made Sly feel like he was important. Hell, he made Nicole feel like they were both important.

She knew if she let herself, she could easily fall for him again. But he was leaving in less than a month. He would go back to his life, and she was sure all his promises to visit and stay in touch were nothing more than words. He owed them nothing, and she was sure he'd disappear and never be seen or heard from again.

Nicole made it home without really paying attention to where she was going. She'd driven the route between St. Gerard's and home so many times she could do it in her sleep. When she got home, she unloaded the bags she'd packed up with Sly's and her dirty laundry and carried them upstairs.

Her apartment was nothing fancy or nice, but it was affordable and mostly clean. The neighbors kept to themselves and didn't try to get to know each other. There was a part of Nicole that wished she had friends to talk to, but she knew she wouldn't have time to keep up a relationship like that. Sly was her priority. He always had been, and he always would be. That was the only thing that mattered.

She made it to her door and was fumbling with the key when she heard, "Hey, Nicole. Let me help you."

She peered over the edge of the bags she had and smiled at Zeke. "Hey, what are you doing here?"

He grabbed her stuff and said, "Why don't we talk inside?"

His answer made her nervous. She didn't know Zeke well, but she knew he was the kind of man who could make a person disappear. She also knew he didn't call the shots, and he had a boss to answer to.

"What's going on, Zeke?"

"Let's go inside," he said in a tone that left her no option.

Nicole unlocked her door and stepped inside the apartment she'd called home for the last three years. She flipped on the lamp next to the door and reached to take the bags from Zeke. She set everything on the couch, wanting to know what he had to say before anything else.

"Tell me what's going on," she said, her voice shaky with fear. Zeke had never hurt her, but she wouldn't put it past him to do so.

"We made a deal, Nicole. A deal that says you owe us money. We still need money. And the price is double since it's extra work for us to get it."

"That's not fair. And I don't need the kidney anymore. My son is healthy and alive. Why do I still need to pay you when I'm not getting anything for it?"

"You're getting a healthy son," Zeke said. "He gets to stay alive."

"Are you threatening my son?" Nicole demanded, getting close to Zeke.

"Just reminding you of the situation you're in. How's Sylvester's fever, by the way?"

Nicole went weak, her knees threatening to give out. "How do you know about that?"

"You owe us, Nicole. I'm here to try to help you. I'm here to make this easier on you."

"How is threatening me and making my son sick going to make this easier on me? Why do you think I would trust you if you're risking my son's life?" Her voice trembled with every word. Fear and anger blended together and made her feel sick. The only thing she wanted was to go back to when she first talked to Zeke and never confide in him.

She was on her way to work and stopped to get a coffee. It was an indulgence she only allowed herself when she was feeling particularly depressed. Zeke was in line behind her and started talking to her. He said he hadn't seen her in there before and asked if he could buy her coffee. She thought he was attractive and indulged in a little flirting to go with her drink.

She had a slightly later shift that day and sat down to drink her coffee without having to rush, and on impulse asked Zeke to join her. He agreed to it and said to choose a seat while he spoke to the owner about something. She watched their interaction, wondering even more about it when it didn't appear as though Zeke paid for their drinks.

She joked with him about it, but Zeke didn't explain. They talked and laughed, and by the time Nicole left for work, she was feeling less like a tired mommy and more like a desirable woman, something she hadn't felt like in far too long.

That was the morning she got a call from school that Sly had passed out and needed to go to the hospital.

Zeke gave her his number and asked her to let him know how Sly was. She thought he was just saying it to be nice, so she never called him, but the next time she stopped for coffee, the owner called Zeke and he was standing next to her car when she walked outside.

They developed a friendship over the next few months, and when Sly ended up on the donor list, Zeke said he could help if she ever needed it.

Nicole never thought his help would end with her standing in the middle of her shitty apartment worrying that the man in front of her was going to kill her son as revenge.

"I can help you, Nicole. I can make sure no one hurts you."

"How?"

Zeke shrugged. "Go on a date with me."

"What?" she breathed.

"A date. One date. If you're mine, they won't mess with you."

Nicole's mind tripped over the idea, and she wondered exactly who Zeke was. She always assumed he was danger-ous, but the way he said it made her think he was a lot more dangerous than she ever assumed. "I… I have to focus on Sly right now. He just had surgery a week ago. He's still in the hospital. He will be for another few days, and when he's home, it's going to be weeks of recovery and taking care of him."

Zeke rubbed his jaw, the sound of his rough hands scraping against his whiskers putting Nicole on edge. He tilted his head to the side and said, "Well, I can understand that. I'm not so sure my boss will, though. He wants his money, and if he doesn't get money, he's going to want something else."

Icy cold fear snaked up Nicole's spine. His words left no room for misunderstanding. Either she pay up with money or she pay up with her body.

"What about a payment plan? If I pay you some in the next few weeks and more as I get it."

"That's not how this works, Nicole. Either you pay up, or he takes what he wants," Zeke said. His eyes were dark and menacing. His entire body screamed danger. Nicole wasn't sure what she ever saw in him, but the man in front of her was not the man she found attractive when they first met.

"I think it's time for you to go, Zeke," Nicole said.

Zeke glanced around her apartment. He took his time moving to the door. When he got there, he turned and looked back at her. "Say hi to Malone for me, will ya?"

Nicole sucked in a breath, wondering what the threat meant as Zeke let himself out. Was Rocky involved with him? Did they know each other? Was he in on whatever Zeke did?

Nicole's mind raced with more questions as she hurried through her apartment. She decided she could wash clothes later. The only thing she wanted to do was get back to the hospital and hold her son and never let him go.

And once she knew he was safe, she would figure out what she was going to do about everything else.

7

Rocky and Sly were laughing at the movie they were watching when Nikki rushed into the room. Her eyes were wide with fear until they landed on Sly. She raced to him and hugged him tight, holding on until he squirmed and pushed at her to let him go.

"Sorry, honey," she said with a smile that didn't touch her eyes.

She sat on the edge of the bed and stared at him for a minute. Rocky studied her. She was worried. She had every right to be worried, but there was something else going on. He could feel her anxiety and the tension in her body, and something wasn't okay.

"You weren't gone long," he said, drawing her attention to him.

Her gaze snapped to his. More fear warred with distrust. She had every right to be upset with him after he left the hospital without telling them, but he thought she at least trusted him. She left him alone at the hospital with her son, their son. Now, she was looking at him like he was a threat.

"Was there something you needed to do that I ruined by

coming back so soon?" she asked, her voice dripping with danger.

Rocky tilted his head and examined her closely. Something happened while she was gone. If he didn't know any better, he would think something happened with them, but he was in the community room or Sly's hospital room with him the whole time. He couldn't have done anything wrong.

"Of course not. I just thought you were going to take a shower and get a little bit of rest. We're always happy to have you back with us."

Nikki glared at him, but the fear in her eyes made it less impactful. She was afraid of him.

"Okay, I got cookies and candy, but they were out of the chips you asked for," Mason said, walking back into the room from a snack run.

Nikki threw herself on top of Sly and shielded him with her body. "Stay away from him. Just get the hell out."

Mason finally looked up and realized Nikki had returned. He grinned and took another step forward, but Nikki tensed even more.

Mason's gaze slid to Rocky, and his entire posture changed. His shoulders slumped, and his hands fell uselessly to his sides. He looked at the ground instead of at anyone else in the room. He slowly started to back out.

"Mommy, you're hurting me. Mason brought me snacks. The nurse said it was okay after dinner," Sly said, once again shoving at his mom.

"Who... Mason?" Nikki stammered. She finally looked at Rocky. He smiled, trying to look reassuring and normal about her flipping out because a friend of his walked into the room.

"We talked about Mason coming to stay for a while. He got here shortly after you left and has been hanging out with us. Sly wanted snacks, so Mason offered to go on a search so I could stay here. They're for after dinner," Rocky said, his words slow and clear.

Nikki smoothed a hand down her pants and forced a smile. "Sorry," she told Mason.

He shook his head and forced a smile of his own. "Don't worry about it. I get that reaction a lot."

Rocky knew Nikki didn't understand his comment, but it definitely wasn't the time to tell her that Mason spent time in jail for killing his own wife. It was an accident, but it still happened. He did his time, but he never forgave himself for it. Rocky guessed he never would.

Mason set the snacks down on the tray Sly used for his meals, then hovered near the door. The chair he was sitting in before Nikki returned was on the far side of the bed, which would mean walking past Nikki and Sly. He looked like he was getting ready to make a break for it.

"Mason, you have to see this part," Sly said, already laughing at what was going to happen on the screen. "Come here."

Mason gave Nikki a look, and she tried to smile again. When she nodded slightly, Mason moved closer. He didn't settle as close as he was before, but he didn't make a run for it either, so Rocky took it as a good sign.

Mason and Sly laughed at the movie and talked through the rest even though Mason was clearly uncomfortable. Rocky took his time watching Nikki, trying to figure out what changed. Every sound in the hallway made her jump. Every burst of laughter from Mason made her jump. Even when Sly shifted positions and sat up quickly, she jumped.

"I need to stretch my legs," Rocky announced, standing up and making a show of moving around. "Want to join me?" he asked Nikki.

Nikki shook her head.

"But what if he gets hurt, Mommy?" Sly asked. "You tell me I can't go for a walk by myself because I might get hurt."

"You're the patient I worry about," Nikki told him. "Rocky isn't a patient anymore, and he has Mason here if he needs someone to go with him."

"Uh, yeah, I can go," Mason said, lurching to his feet. "We'll be right back."

Mason followed Rocky into the hall, neither of them happy about it. They fell into step together, no destination in mind.

"Did you tell her about me?" Mason asked after a few minutes.

Rocky shook his head. "We told them they would love you. Dex told Sly you would need to turn sideways to get in the door, and maybe duck. This... something happened when she left. She's acting like someone is after her."

"Do you know for sure someone isn't?"

"She's a single mom with a sick kid," Rocky said as a way of explaining.

Mason shrugged. "What I hear is a woman with money problems who would do anything."

"Dammit," Rocky breathed.

They walked silently for a few minutes.

"Sly said something to Dex and me last week that we couldn't figure out. Something about paying money for me to donate. We thought maybe he was misunderstanding something, but she's acting like something's wrong. We to figure out what's going on," Rocky said.

"We can get her phone records, but that doesn't always tell the whole story. I'm assuming this walk was an attempt to get her alone so you could ask her what happened?"

Rocky nodded.

"Sorry about that. Maybe tomorrow I'll stay at the hotel and let you try to talk to her."

Rocky shook his head. "I don't think that will work. She doesn't look like she's willing to leave Sly's side."

"You can just ask her what happened," Mason suggested.

Rocky snorted. "She doesn't tell me anything, but she tells me even less with Sly around."

"Too bad Lily isn't here. She can get anyone to talk about anything."

Rocky laughed. "Maybe we should hire her to interrogate people."

Mason snickered. "I've wondered why you guys never did."

They were almost back to Sly's room. "Nikki is completely on her own. She's done everything for Sly. I can't blame her for being careful with all of us. Maybe I'm over-reacting."

Mason shrugged. "Maybe. I don't think you are, but I don't know her. Give it a few days and we'll go from there."

When they walked back into the room, Nikki was standing over Sly, blocking the nurse from giving him medicine. She was demanding to know what it was, what all the side effects were, and who ordered it.

"What's going on?" Rocky asked, moving between the two women.

"Dr. Andrews asked me to give Sylvester an antibiotic just in case his fever was something else," the nurse explained.

"May I see it?" Rocky asked her.

She held out the bag and showed him the name. It was a standard antibiotic, nothing that would cause any issues. And it was a low dose, something that would go through his IV in about an hour.

"I think it's fine," Rocky said, glancing at Nikki. She rolled her eyes. "Can we speak to Dr. Andrews first, though? It's been a tough day."

The nurse shrugged and set the bag down. She scanned through the tablet until she found what she was looking for, then lifted the phone next to Sly's bed and dialed.

"Sorry to bother you, Dr. Andrews," she said after a minute. "I'm with Sylvester Burke, and his parents have a few questions about the antibiotics."

After a few seconds, the nurse extended the phone to Nikki. She asked Dr. Andrews about the medicine and if Sly really needed it. After a minute, she thanked him and hung up. She smiled at the nurse and said, "Okay."

The nurse nodded as though patients' mothers questioning her skills was a normal thing and no big deal. She went through the motions and was out of the room in a few minutes.

Then Sly asked, "Why did she say you're my parents? Is Rocky my dad?"

So much for telling him when Nikki was ready.

NICOLE OPENED her mouth to say something, but no sound came out. Rocky stared at her, allowing her to answer the question. She wanted to give Sly more time before she told him, and she definitely didn't want to tell him like that, but she knew lying would be worse than just not admitting the truth.

"The nurse just made an assumption," Rocky said finally, taking the reins since Nicole was clearly incapable.

"So, you're not my dad?" Sly asked him.

It was Rocky's turn to flounder. He was obviously feeling

the same things as Nicole. Not admitting the truth was one thing, but lying was another.

"Do you remember when I told you that I cared a lot about your dad but that he couldn't be with us?" Nicole asked, drawing Sly's attention back to her.

Sly nodded as she sat on the edge of the bed. Nicole took his hands in hers and smiled.

"Your dad was in the Navy. And I didn't know how to get in touch with him when I found out I was going to have you. We met years ago, but he had to go back and defend our country. I told you many times that if he knew about you, he would be here, right?"

Sly nodded again.

"The problem is Rocky has a life in Niagara Falls. He wants to be a part of your life, but he has a job and people who count on him there. For now, he's here with us to make sure you're okay, but eventually, he needs to go back to New York."

Tears formed in Sly's eyes. "You told me my dad would be with us if he knew, but Rocky's my dad and he doesn't want to be with us. You lied to me!"

Rocky stepped forward and said, "She didn't lie. Your mom has always done everything for you, and that includes telling you that I would be here if I could. I didn't know about you. But now that I do, I'm not leaving. I can't. I haven't talked to your mom about it yet, but I'm going to stay here so I can be a part of your life."

"Really?" Sly asked, his tears drying up instantly and a smile replacing his frown.

Rocky glanced at Nicole and nodded. "If it's okay with your mom, yes."

Nicole closed her eyes. She couldn't tell him no because then she would be the bad parent. The one who kept him from his father. But telling him yes would mean letting him into her life. After the conversation she had with Zeke, Nicole wasn't sure she could do that.

"Mommy, can Rocky move in with us?" Sly asked.

Rocky chuckled, saving her from having to answer. "I would get my own place, Sly. Somewhere close to you so we could get together all the time."

"But my friends who have both a mommy and a daddy said they all live in the same house together. Why wouldn't you want to live with us?"

Rocky opened his mouth and closed it again, looking to Nicole for help on that one.

"We'll figure it all out," Nicole said. It was her standard answer for anything that she didn't have an answer for. Moving Rocky into their apartment wasn't an option, and she couldn't afford anything bigger. Of course, she didn't know much about what he did for a living or what he would do when he moved, so she didn't know what he could afford. But it would all happen eventually, assuming he actually moved like he said he wanted to. It was just as likely he would skip town and never see them again.

"Can I call you Daddy?" Sly asked Rocky.

Rocky swallowed roughly and glanced at Nicole. She kept her face neutral but inside it broke her heart how quickly and easily he latched on to Rocky.

"I would be completely okay with that," Rocky finally said.

Sly extended his hand to Rocky. Rocky slid his much larger one over Sly's and they shook. "Nice to meet you, Daddy."

Rocky grinned and pulled Sly into his arms, holding him tight against his chest. "Nice to meet you, too, son."

If Nicole was the sentimental type, she might have found

the situation heartwarming. Instead, she just worried. She was setting her son up for heartbreak, the kind of heartbreak a kid never recovered from.

WHEN THEY GOT BACK to the hotel that night, Rocky still felt like everything was going to be okay. That was, until he faced Mason and saw the stormy look on his face.

"What?"

"Are you really going to move here?"

Rocky sighed. "I can't turn away from them. Not now that I know about him."

"You should have asked her first. She did not look happy."

Rocky nodded. "I know. I meant to, but it all happened so fast. I knew she didn't want to tell him yet that I'm his biological father."

"Do you still think something is going on with her?"

"Yeah. I don't know what, but the way she was acting with the nurse and the meds, plus the way she reacted to me moving here... Something isn't right."

"Do you want to reach out to Dunn? See if we can get her phone records?"

Rocky shook his head. "Not yet. I want to try to talk to her first. I want to give her a chance before I start digging into her life. She has a right to not trust me. She doesn't know me. Hopefully, I'm being ridiculous, but if not, we need to figure out what's going on."

"Agreed. And you need to tell Dunn you're not coming back."

Rocky groaned. "I'm not looking forward to that."

"Have you thought about asking them to move to Niagara Falls?"

Rocky shook his head. "I can't. I mean, yeah, it would be great, but they have a life here. Sly's doctors are here, and his friends and school, and Nikki's job. I can't ask them to throw all that away and move to be closer to me."

"Sure you can. But it's a conversation. Instead of demanding they move, tell her you want to be a part of their lives and ask if she'd be interested in considering a move. What does she do?"

"She's a phlebotomist."

Mason chuckled. "You know Lily would get her a job in a heartbeat."

"I know, but it's a lot to ask someone."

"So is moving into their home so you can be close to your son."

Rocky laughed. "I didn't suggest that one."

"No, but Sly adores you. He's going to be tough to resist. I saw Nicole's face, though. She did not like the idea."

"And we're back to her not trusting me and something being off."

"Talk to her. Ask the questions. See if something is going on. And if she won't tell you, we'll find out on our own. We have ways of doing that."

Rocky nodded. "For now. I'm going to have to find something else to do if I move here. I am not looking forward to that."

"We'll figure it all out," Mason said.

Rocky nodded again. "I hope so."

8

———

NICOLE BARELY SLEPT OVER THE NEXT FEW DAYS. EVERY TIME someone walked into Sly's room, she wanted to ask who they were and why they were there. If Zeke was able to make Sly sick, there had to be someone helping him. One of the nurses who'd been caring for her son.

But Nicole sounded like a crazy person. She couldn't tell someone that. Not even Rocky. She wanted to trust he was there for the right reasons, and he genuinely looked shocked when she told him Sly was his son, but she didn't know anything about him. For seven years, he'd been a ghost, a figment of her imagination. If it weren't for her son, she wasn't entirely sure she could bring Rocky's image to her mind all those years.

She definitely never expected him to stick around, and that concerned her. Was he a part of Zeke's plan? Was he the one who made Sly sick?

Nicole groaned and dropped her head back against the chair. Sly was still asleep, which was normally when she would try to get coffee and take a break, but she wasn't willing to leave him alone again. Not when anything could happen to him.

Nicole stood and stretched, trying to work out the last of the sleep clinging to her. She hadn't pulled the chair out into a bed last night and she was paying for it already. Her neck was stiff and her back screamed in pain. Dr. Andrews said he was hoping to send Sly home, so Nicole took the chance that she would only have to spend one more night in the hospital and then could go home to her own lumpy mattress.

She groaned again. That didn't hold much more appeal.

A nurse walked in a little while later with a smile and a clipboard. "Dr. Andrews is going to be here around eight to check in on you guys. I already have the discharge papers ready for you to sign. Assuming he's okay with it all, you will be on your way home today."

Nicole breathed a sigh of relief and nodded. She took the clipboard from the nurse and started reading. She said she'd be back in a little while to get them from Nicole and left quietly again.

Nicole was just about to sign them when there was a soft knock on the door. She expected it to be Dr. Andrews there a bit early and said he could come in. She did not expect Rocky's face to appear in the open doorway.

"Good morning," he said with a smile. "Can I come in?"

Nicole nodded and set the clipboard to the side. She'd been uncomfortable around him since Zeke's visit, but when Sly was awake, it was easier. Sly carried the conversation and asked Rocky tons of questions. Nicole was able to sit back and listen, cataloguing everything he said in case she needed it later.

"I brought you guys breakfast, if that's okay. I see someone isn't up yet," he added in a softer voice. "Sorry."

Nicole smiled and gratefully accepted the cup of coffee he handed her. She took a sip and was surprised to find it was perfect, exactly how she liked it. She opened her eyes in surprise and found Rocky staring at her.

"Good?"

She nodded and licked her lips. His gaze followed her tongue and darkened. Was he really...? No, there was no way.

"What's the clipboard for?" Rocky asked, pulling himself out of whatever trance he appeared to be in.

"Discharge papers. Dr. Andrews is hoping to send us home today."

"Great news. I'm glad I showed up when I did. I can help you get there and get settled in."

Nicole immediately shook her head. "No. No, we're fine. You don't need to do that."

Rocky tilted his head. "I want to, Nikki. I told you, I want to get to know him. I meant what I said about moving here, too."

"I'm not sure that's a great idea."

Rocky nodded slowly and met her gaze. "You are the one who told me he's my son. I'm grateful that you did, but did you really think you would tell me and I'd go back to my life and forget about you two?"

"You can be a part of his life. You can talk and visit and get to know him. But relocating to a new city isn't something I expect from you."

"You didn't ask. I want to be near him."

"You have a life in Niagara Falls. You have friends and a job and I don't know what else. What would you even do if you moved here?"

Rocky shrugged, and for the first time, looked less than sure about his decision to move. "I don't know, but I'll figure it out. What kind of father would I be if I didn't try to figure it out? What kind of man would I be?"

Nicole was surprised by the pain behind the questions he asked, as though he was asking himself instead of voicing rhetorical questions. He was moving there out of some misguided guilt, not because he wanted to be there. And Nicole was not willing to put her son in the middle of that. If Rocky moved, they could get together, but she was not about to turn her son over to a man who was little more than a sperm donor.

"Nikki, listen—"

"It's Nicole," she said firmly. Nikki was what she introduced herself as years ago. A lifetime ago. She was Nikki back then. Carefree and fun without any concern for the rest of her life. Spending the weekend with a stranger was fun. It was reckless. It was something Nikki did.

But Nicole? Nicole was a mother. She was a woman who put her son first. She was professional and proper and not willing to back down when a man tried to tell her what she could or couldn't do.

Especially not the man who donated the other half of her son's DNA.

"Nicole, sorry," Rocky said, looking hurt by her correction. "I know I don't have everything figured out yet, but it's been less than two weeks since I found out I have a son. It isn't enough time for me to plan out everything. But I want to be in his life, and I want to help the two of you out. If you want me to buy a house near you, I need to know where you live. If you want me to buy a house big enough for the three of us, you need to tell me where you want him. I would prefer—"

"No, this is too much. I can't... No."

Rocky made a move to get closer to her, and Nicole

flinched. He froze, staring at her, then took a step backward. "You're afraid of me," he stated.

Nicole couldn't speak.

SEEING the fear in her eyes was the worst moment of Rocky's life. Maybe second worse. The worse moment of his life was getting the call that his father was up on the roof of Rocky's childhood home, patching a section Rocky himself promised to fix before he left for boot camp, and fell. His father never woke up, and Rocky never forgave himself for not being a better son.

He was not about to fail as a father, too. But Nikki, no Nicole, was afraid of him. She thought he was going to hurt her in some way.

Rocky backed up to the door and tried to figure out why she feared him all of a sudden. He didn't think she felt that way when she sat down next to him and told him the kid he was there to donate a kidney to was his son, but something had changed in the past two weeks. She'd changed. All the time he spent getting to know Sly was meaningless unless Nikki was willing to let him be a part of their lives.

But everything changed the night he stayed with Sly and she left the hospital. He had to find out what happened that night.

"What happened that you think I would hurt you?"

She shook her head, too quickly prepared to deny it.

"Nik-cole, talk to me. Three nights ago, you left the hospital to go home and take a break. You came rushing back in here like you thought something happened. You were terrified when Mason walked in and yelled at him to stay away from Sly. You are acting like you're scared of something. What is it? I can help you."

She shook her head again. "I don't know what you're talking about. I'm a single mom, so I'm protective of my son. A strange man walking into his room should scare me. That's not irrational."

Rocky wanted to argue with her, but he could see she wasn't willing to tell him anything. He simply nodded. "I apologize for that. You're right. You should protect your son. But he's my son, too. I'd like you to know you can trust me to protect him also. I know you don't know me anymore, but you can ask me anything and I will be honest with you. Always."

She opened her mouth like she was going to say something, then snapped it shut again. She nodded, dismissing him.

Rocky blew out a breath and left the room. He would get through to her, but she wasn't ready yet. Which meant he had some work to do. And he needed help.

ROCKY CALLED Mason to dig deeper into what happened that night, and by the time he made it back to the hotel, Mason had a full report from English, the team's computer expert. English found Nikki's home address easily enough and ran a credit report and got her phone records. There weren't any calls the night she left the hospital, which meant whatever scared her was an in person meeting.

"Is it possible to get footage from around her apartment? Something that could show us if someone met her there?" Rocky asked. He didn't like looking into Nikki behind her back, but he tried to talk to her. He asked her what happened. If she wasn't going to tell him, he didn't think they had a choice but to figure it out so he could make sure Nikki and Sly were safe.

Mason shook his head. "English already looked. It's a pretty rough area from what he said. No cameras anywhere nearby."

"Probably something whoever met her knew."

Mason nodded.

"Did the phone records help shed light on anything?"

Mason shook his head again. "Still going through everything, but so far no. School, work, and friends. Nothing out of the ordinary."

"Dammit," Rocky exclaimed. "There's something there. We just have to find it."

Mason nodded. "We will. Maybe you should go visit them tonight without me. She seems more willing to talk to just you."

Rocky shook his head. "I don't know. She basically told me she doesn't want me in their lives. I think showing up at their home without her telling me where they live might be pushing it."

"They're listed. It's not like you couldn't look her up in the phone book."

Rocky drew in a breath and let it out slowly.

"If you really think something is going on, you need to stay close to her. If someone is after her, or them, I don't get the feeling she can protect herself."

Rocky remembered her throwing herself across Sly's bed to protect him when she thought Mason was a threat. If that was all she could, or would, do, it wasn't enough.

Rocky sighed. "This would be so much easier if she would open up to me. If she would tell me what's going on."

Mason shrugged. "People aren't always willing to share

details with strangers. You have to remember that's what you are to her. She doesn't know you, and it sounds like she never really did."

Rocky glared at Mason, and Mason held up his hands in surrender.

"No judgement," Mason said quickly. "I know she left. But if you were the one who insisted on a first names only weekend, she knew you were going to leave. She was protecting herself."

"If I could go back…"

"Would you really change your life? Would you walk away from the Teams for them?"

Rocky thought about it for a minute and shrugged. "I guess I would have liked to know. I keep thinking things would have been easier on her if she wasn't going through all this alone. If I'd been here to help her."

"And that's why you want to be here now?"

"Partly," Rocky admitted. "She's already dealt with so much, and Sly is only six. I don't think it's fair for her to go through all of it by herself."

"Can I offer you advice?" Mason asked, his brows darting up.

Rocky nodded.

"Don't tell her that."

"Why not?"

"Because it sounds like you think she's incapable of handling everything. Like if you were here, Sly might not have gotten sick. Like you're the savior they've been waiting for."

"I didn't mean—"

"I know," Mason said with a hand up to stop Rocky. "It's just how it sounds. Especially if she's fragile and tentative about your relationship. I think she needs to know you trust her and think she's a good mom before she'll be willing to trust you."

Rocky nodded slowly, then looked up at Mason. "How the hell do you know all this?"

Mason grinned. "I've done a lot of work studying people and psychology."

Rocky chuckled. "You continue to surprise me."

Mason laughed. "Part of my charm. You need to get ready to go see your family. Flowers, a gift, jewelry. Something. You need to smooth over the fact that you're showing up uninvited."

"I have a feeling I'm going to be doing a lot of that when I move here."

"I still can't believe you're pulling up stakes and relocating."

"Family is important. Always has been, always will be."

Mason nodded. The shadows in his eyes said he was thinking about his wife. Rocky hoped he never knew that kind of pain.

He headed to the room that was his and did his PT for the day. He agreed to keep up with it after he left the hospital. Even though it wasn't nearly as hard as his usual workout, Rocky knew it was all his body could handle at the moment.

When he was done, he took another shower and read through everything English had sent about Nikki and Sly. It wasn't as comprehensive as most of their reports, but Nikki was a pretty average person. No criminal history, stable work history. She didn't seem to have a lot of skeletons in her closet. Rocky hoped that meant he was overreacting to her behavior. It wouldn't be the first time one of them thought something was happening that wasn't. Paranoia was a hazard of the job.

Rocky made sure Mason knew where he would be and headed out. He stopped by a store and picked up another toy for Sly and flowers for Nikki. He considered jewelry, like Mason said, but he hadn't noticed her wearing any and decided that might be going too far.

He followed the directions to her apartment complex and whistled when he found a parking spot. The place made rundown look like an improvement. Some of the cars in the lot had more rust than paint, and the buildings looked like they could crumble at any minute.

The first thing Rocky was going to do when he moved there was get Nikki and Sly the hell out of that place.

He made his way to the third floor, holding his side against the discomfort. It reminded him he still wasn't one hundred percent. He paused when he got to the top and looked around, scanning for which way he needed to go.

He figured it out and made his way, watching the numbers increase until he found their apartment. Rocky stood in front of the door, feeling like an idiot. He wasn't sure if it was considerate or creepy that he found out where they lived and went to visit. He brought gifts for them. He wasn't sure if that helped or not.

He lifted his hand to knock and stilled at a muffled sound inside the apartment. He paused. Something crashed.

Rocky knocked hard on the door, pounding more like. "Nikki!"

Silence answered him.

Rocky waited half a second before he slammed his palm against the door. He didn't give up until he heard a sound on the other side and the door swung open.

A large man stood in front of Rocky. His shoulders were wide and his neck bulged with muscles. He looked like Mason on steroids. And three times meaner.

"Who the hell are you?"

Rocky glared up at him. "Who are you?"

He smirked. "A friend."

"Is Nikki home?"

The guy shook his head. "She's all yours."

He pushed past Rocky and walked down the narrow pathway, his hip bumping the rail when he moved to the side to let someone pass.

A whimper drew Rocky's attention from the man leaving into the apartment. Nikki was cowering in the corner, curled up in a chair. Tears streamed down her face. She stared at the door, but it didn't look like she actually saw Rocky.

He closed and locked the door, then set the gifts he brought on a nearby table and went to her. He crouched in front of her. "Nikki?" He touched her thigh.

She jumped. Her gaze finally landed on him. Her eyes slid closed and her shoulders slumped. She curled in on herself. "What are you doing here?"

"I... I wanted to see you again. Are you okay? Who was that?"

Nikki shook her head. "He was my last hope before you showed up."

"What does that mean?" Rocky pressed.

She tried to smile. "It means I made his boss a deal, and he doesn't really care that I don't need his help anymore. He wants what he asked for. And if I don't pay him twenty thousand dollars, he's going to get it another way from me."

9

NICOLE WATCHED AS ROCKY PROCESSED HER WORDS. IT WAS clear he understood exactly what she meant. Hell, until he pounded on her door and stopped Zeke's partner from taking the first payment, she really was convinced he was a part of the entire thing.

She should have known better. It didn't matter that she hadn't seen him in seven years and had only spent a few days with him, he wasn't that kind of man. He was the kind who watched out for the people he cared about.

"What deal did you make with him, Nikki? Sorry, Nicole."

Nicole finally pushed herself to stand, ignoring Rocky's outstretched hand. Her legs were shaky and her breath still ragged, but she had to stand on her own two feet to prove to herself she still could physically even if mentally she wasn't quite there yet.

She drew in a breath and met Rocky's gaze. Everything would change when she admitted the truth, but she had no choice after what he heard. "I agreed to pay them ten thousand dollars for a kidney that matched Sly. And now I have to pay double because I haven't already paid them and want out of the deal."

Rocky blew out a breath and ran a hand down his face. Gone was the carefree man she knew the weekend they spent together, and gone was the open and honest man who'd spent the last few weeks getting to know them. The man in front of her was all badass, and he was pissed off. At her.

"Why would you do something like that, Nikki?"

"Because I was desperate! My son was going to die. Do you have any idea what it's like to sit back and watch the person you love the most in the world suffer and know there is nothing you can do to stop it? To see the pain in his eyes and know you're useless? To watch him slowly drift away as he weakens and not be able to do anything? Because unless you do, you can't even begin to imagine what I went through the last few years."

Rocky drew a shaky breath and nodded. "I do know what that's like, Nikki. And I'm sorry you've had to go through that."

She looked up at him, tilting her head to the side in question. Judgement and disappointment, she expected. Understanding? Never even considered it.

"My dad died when I was in training. He went up on the roof to patch something I said I would take care of, and he fell. He never woke up. My mom and sisters took him off life support while I was away. They told me not to come because my dad would have wanted me to stay where I was and finish. My mom never blamed me, but it was my fault. I saw it in her eyes when I visited her the next time. My sisters, too. They weren't dying, but they were wishing I'd been the one who had."

"That wasn't your fault anymore than this is mine," Nicole said.

Rocky huffed a mirthless laugh and shook his head. "That's not really true. That was my fault, but this isn't yours. But I still understand the need to fix it."

"I didn't think there was another option."

Rocky nodded. "When my dad died, I wanted to sign up to be a donor, like he was, but I was afraid to do it before I went overseas. When I finally left the Teams, I still wrestled with the choice. I should have signed up sooner so you didn't have to go through all of this."

Nicole shook her head. "You can't think that way."

"I never should have insisted we didn't exchange info that weekend. I should have told you who I was."

"And then what? Would we have kept in touch? Would you have written to me and asked me to write to you? Would you have spent your limited calls on me? If I'd never gotten pregnant, we would never have seen each other again. We're strangers, Rocky. Two people who barely know each other. I wasn't anymore ready for something than you were when we met. I had plans for my life. Big plans."

"Like what?" Rocky asked.

Nicole looked around her rundown apartment with the stained carpet and the dumpster furniture. She never decorated even though they'd been living there for years. She worked a job with a normal schedule and kept to herself. If she died, no one would notice or care.

She snorted a laugh and gestured to her home. "Doesn't this place look like the stuff dreams are made of?"

Rocky looked around and wisely kept his mouth shut.

"Who wouldn't want to live here?" Nicole asked him. "You can totally see why Sly asked you to move in with us. It's so spacious and welcoming, isn't it?"

"Are you okay?" Rocky asked.

Nicole huffed a laugh and shook her head. "No. I'm not okay. I've been trying to keep it together for Sly, but I'm cracking. And now Zeke's buddy shows up. And you're here. I... I can't do it all."

NIKKI STARTED to crumble right before his eyes. It took Rocky a second to figure out what was happening. He stepped forward before she collapsed and caught her. He guided her to the couch and sat with her, holding her against his chest while she sobbed uncontrollably. He wondered how long she'd been holding all that in and realized probably since she found out she was pregnant.

He hated himself again for not being there for them. He should have been. He should have helped her. A part of him knew it wasn't possible, but that part was silenced by the irrational part of him that just wanted to erase Nikki's pain. At any cost.

When she finally stopped sobbing, she kept holding on to him, her arms around him as she whimpered and hiccuped. He kissed the top of her head and held her close. Her scent infiltrated his senses and wrapped around him. The way her breasts pressed against his side made him more aware of her as a woman. She sucked in a sharp breath, her entire body shifting against his side, and he hardened.

Her fingers glided across his chest, not in a seductive way, but questioning, exploring. His entire body tightened in anticipation, readying for whatever she wanted, needed.

His hand slid gently down her spine then back up, his

thumb dancing across her cotton covered skin. He wanted to feel her, to touch her, to remember her.

She lifted his shirt and splayed her hand on his abdomen. She froze for a long moment, her hand blazing against his bare skin.

"Nikki," he groaned, needing to see her eyes. He had to know she was as gone as he was.

She tilted her head to look at him.

"Mommy?" came from the hallway.

Nikki jumped off the couch so fast Rocky was sure he imagined the entire encounter. Nikki ushered Sly back to bed before he made it to the living room and saw Rocky on the couch.

Rocky leaned forward and rested his head on his hands. What was he thinking? Nikki was a mom, a single mom, to his son. She was lonely and scared, and he was pawing her like a teenager at prom.

His erection wilted at the thought of taking advantage of her, and Rocky added his behavior to the long list of things he'd done wrong. He went there to check in on them, not to fuck her.

He heard her footsteps coming back down the hallway. She paused before she stepped into view. Rocky took a breath and stood.

Nikki looked up at him, all the desire he imagined her feeling erased from her beautiful face. Instead, there was just resignation. "Was there a reason you stopped by?"

He shook his head, then remembered the gifts he brought. Rocky grabbed them from where he'd dropped both on the table to get to her and handed her the mostly smashed flowers. "Sorry."

She smiled and accepted them, her gaze snapping to his when their hands touched. She pulled away quickly and turned away from him to go to the kitchen. "I'll just put these in water."

Rocky waited until she filled a plastic pitcher and added the flowers before he held out the gift for Sly. "I need to figure out what he likes. I'm hoping all kids like superheroes. He's always been my favorite because Captain America is a soldier, someone who volunteered to protect the country. He gave up everything he knew to give back, at any cost."

Nikki smiled softly. "He's Sly's favorite, too. I think it has something to do with what I told him about his father."

Rocky breathed a laugh. "I really wish I'd been here for you, Nikki. But I am now. I want to help you. Let me give you the money."

She shook her head. "No. You've already done too much. I'll figure it out. I always do."

"I know, but you're not alone anymore."

She smiled sadly and looked around. "I was never alone. I have my son."

Rocky nodded once. "Yeah, but I have—"

"Thanks for stopping by," Nikki interrupted him and moved to the door. "I'll tell Sly you're sorry you missed him."

"Can I come back sometime soon?" If she wasn't going to let him pay, he at least wanted to know he could be there.

Nikki closed her eyes for a minute and nodded. "I won't keep you from him."

Rocky stepped closer to her and lifted her chin so she met his gaze. "And I won't take him from you."

She smiled and swallowed roughly.

"Good night, Nikki."

"Bye, Rocky."

When Rocky made it back to the hotel that night, he told Mason everything that happened at Nikki's and everything Nikki told him.

"Fucking hell," Mason groaned.

Rocky nodded. "Pretty much. We need to find out who these guys are."

"Agreed. Any chance you know a name or any information? Did you take a picture of the guy?"

Rocky shook his head. "All I was worried about was making sure they were okay. Sly wasn't in the room, but Nikki was terrified. The only name she mentioned was Zeke."

"Let's go through the phone records and see if that name comes up. We might get lucky. We'll loop Dunn and the others in tomorrow."

Rocky nodded and started going through the phone records English sent them. They divided up what they had, starting with the most recent calls and going back months. For hours, they searched the records, crossing off numbers they identified. The list of numbers they couldn't find was short, but too long for them to trace all of them before they crashed.

"I'm beat," Rocky admitted. "I need to get some sleep. I have a checkup tomorrow at the hospital."

"You head to bed. I'll be up for a while. I'll see what else I can get through tonight."

Rocky nodded and thanked Mason, then shuffled to his room.

It wasn't long before his internal clock was going off and Rocky was waking up. He showered and got dressed quietly in case Mason was still asleep, then went out to the kitchen to get breakfast.

Mason was staring at the computer screen in the clothes he wore the day before.

"Did you go to bed at all?" Rocky asked.

Mason shook his head. "No. I found something right after you left. One of the numbers was registered to a corporation."

"So?"

"It's a corporation that has more than a few shady things happening. I figured a single mom isn't likely to have a lot of friends who work at a big corporation, so I started looking into them. I found a lot of dirt without much digging. I think this is our guy."

"You found Zeke?"

Mason shook his head. "No, no one named Zeke, but the company website is full of pictures of people who don't actually exist at all, so why would they advertise their real names?"

"Dammit," Rocky breathed. "What the hell is she involved in?"

Mason shook his head. "I don't know, but it's not good. Any chance we can pay it and she'll be safe?"

Rocky shrugged. "I offered, but she said no. I get the feeling she doesn't want any help."

"Even to keep her son safe?"

"They aren't threatening Sly, just her. They want her." As Rocky said the words, bile rose up in his throat and threatened to come out. He couldn't even stomach the thought of someone else touching her, let alone forcing themselves on her.

"Does she really think she can handle them?"

"I don't fucking know," Rocky shouted. As soon as he yelled, he closed his eyes and took a breath. "I'm sorry. I... This sucks."

"Yeah, it does. And if something happens to her, you're going to blame yourself, so I'm looking for options to keep her safe."

Rocky felt his phone buzz and looked at it. "I need to go. If I don't leave now, I'll be late for my appointment. Thank you for looking at all this. And for being here. I'm just..."

"Yeah, I know," Mason said. "You go see the doc. I'm going to get some sleep. We'll come up with a plan later. I've already sent a bunch of stuff to Dunn. We'll see what they can find out."

Rocky nodded. "Thanks."

Rocky thought about what Mason said on his drive to the hospital. He wasn't willing to manipulate Nikki into doing what he wanted, but he wanted to keep them both safe. And the only way to do that was to get the people who were after her to stop.

Nikki was strong, but she was no match for the man Rocky saw at her apartment. That man would tear her to shreds if he wanted to. There was no way in hell Rocky would sit back and let that happen.

His appointment with Dr. Andrews was quick and easy. The doctor said he was healing well and could resume all normal activities except his job.

"Really? I can lift and run?"

Dr. Andrews nodded. "Unless there's a reason you don't think you can. You might still be sore, but that could linger for a long time. Months. If you push yourself too hard, you could tweak something, but there's no reason you can't ease your way back into a routine. I'm assuming you do something."

Rocky nodded. "Yeah. I've been taking it easy, but I was definitely sore last night after a few flights of stairs."

"Like I said, that's to be expected. If you do those stairs today, you should feel a little better."

"That's great news. Thanks."

Rocky stood and pulled his shirt down over his abdomen. He looked up at the doctor when he realized he hadn't moved.

"Doc?"

"You're Sly's biological father?"

Rocky nodded, wondering where the questioning was going.

"Are you heading back to New York soon?"

Rocky shook his head. "I was thinking of sticking around here. I don't feel right asking Nikki to uproot her world, and I can't walk away from my son."

Dr. Andrews's brows jumped up. "That's pretty commendable. Especially knowing what you do. Do you think you'll find work here?"

Rocky shook his head. "I don't know what I'll end up doing. Nikki doesn't seem thrilled with me hanging around."

"Nicole has been on her own since I met her. She's a strong, stubborn woman who doesn't like to ask for help. I married a woman like her, so I know the type well."

"Yeah? Any advice?"

"It depends on what you want the advice for. Getting to know your son or getting to know them both?"

Rocky smiled and thought of the way he responded to Nikki the night before. "Both."

Dr. Andrews chuckled. "I know that look. For Sly, be there for him. He's never had a man in his life, and he already looks up to you. Don't let him down. For Nicole, anticipate what she needs and do it. If you wait for her to ask you, she's already done it herself."

Rocky nodded, thinking the advice was exactly what he needed to hear. "Good to know. Thanks, Dr. Andrews."

He nodded. "Good luck. I'll see you back here in two weeks, and I can hopefully clear you to return to New York so you can start your life here."

Rocky nodded. He wanted to be near Nikki and Sly, but leaving Niagara Falls was not what he wanted to do. The more he talked about it, the less he was convinced it was the right move for him. But he meant what he said when he told people he wasn't leaving his son and he didn't think it was fair to ask Nikki to move.

So, he was going to have to start making plans. He needed to find a place to live and a job and tell Dunn he was leaving.

Just when he thought things were settling down and he'd found where he belonged, everything changed.

10

"Sly, wash your hands! It's almost time for dinner," Nicole called toward the living room.

It was a quiet night at home, and Nicole was hoping it would stay that way. She hadn't heard from Zeke or his partner since the visit from the man a few days earlier, but she was still on edge. She knew they weren't likely to just let things go and not try to get the money from her.

The truth was, she didn't have that kind of money. She made the agreement without it. She had more than half of it, but she used a lot of that for the transplant Sly did have. Zeke's boss jacked up the price for the inconvenience of having to get it out of her.

She almost laughed at that. If she wasn't willing to part with the original ten grand they agreed to, why did he think she was able to hand over double the amount?

Sly walked into the kitchen slowly, staring behind him at the TV as he moved. Nicole shook her head. She thought he might have had enough TV in the hospital when all he could do was sit there and watch, but she was clearly mistaken.

"Why didn't you pause it?" Nicole asked. They didn't have cable so whatever Sly was watching was recorded.

He shrugged and rushed to the sink. He stepped up onto his stool and stuck his hands under the water, then squirted a drop of soap on and rinsed it off almost as quickly. Before he could get down, she stopped him.

"Wash them well, stinky boy," Nicole said with a grin.

Sly giggled when she tickled him and stuck his hands under the water again. He used a little more soap and actually worked his hands into a tiny bit of a lather before he rinsed and ran off, rubbing his hands on his shorts.

Nicole just shook her head.

She pulled the enchiladas out of the oven and set the pan on the stovetop to cool for a few minutes. She carried the rest of what they needed to the table and made sure it was ready for dinner.

"Come on, Sly. Turn off the TV so we can eat."

He did as he was asked without arguing at all, something she loved about him. She had too many coworkers who complained that their kids fought them on turning things off. Nicole was happy she didn't have that problem.

She'd just set the pan down on the table when there was a knock on the door. She froze, staring at it like it would explode and some movie villain would be standing behind it, ready to take her away.

"Nikki, it's me. It's Rocky," Rocky's voice came through the door. He knocked again.

"Can I get it, Mommy?" Sly asked.

Nicole nodded and busied herself with fixing the table even though nothing needed to be done. She hadn't seen Rocky since the night Zeke's partner came either. She told herself it was a coincidence, but deep down, she was sure he was gone. There wasn't really a reason for him to be there. He said all the right things, but when she admitted what she'd done, she knew whatever could have possibly been happening between them was over. Rocky was a former SEAL. He was honorable. He was perfect. He was not going to be involved with someone like her. Someone who made so many mistakes.

Sly opened the door and hugged Rocky. "Thanks for my Captain America. He's awesome. He's the best superhero."

"He's my favorite, too. I was hoping you would like him."

Nicole tried not to stare at them, but it was hard. Sly looked like a mini-me standing next to Rocky. Same dark hair and eyes. Same general build, just much smaller. Even the way they stood was similar.

Of course, Rocky stirred something inside her she thought was long dead. The way his gray tee stretched across his chest made her mouth water. And the way his jeans cupped him and hung low on his hips made her want to nudge them down and remember what was beneath them.

Heat pooled between her thighs at the memory of him. She hadn't been with anyone since him, and it seemed her body had forgotten less than her mind had. She wanted him again. Badly.

"Hey, Nikki," Rocky said finally, looking up and meeting her gaze. His eyes were unsure, but his stance was all confident alpha. He was a man in control of everything in his life, but when they were in bed together, he let her take control a few times.

It had been a rush to tell the powerful man what to do, but he'd listened to her every word. And she loved every single minute of it.

"Are you staying for dinner?" Sly asked, tugging Rocky toward the table.

Rocky looked up at Nicole. She smiled and said, "We have enough if you'd like to."

"I didn't come here for dinner, but if you're sure, I'd love to stick around."

He was asking her even though he was making it clear what he'd like.

She nodded. "Of course you should stay."

Rocky smiled at her, and Nicole's insides turned to mush. She wasn't sure she could survive another evening with him. Not after she admitted to herself she still wanted him. He was a special blend of potent that most men she knew couldn't even dream of being. He was strong and powerful, but also caring and passionate. He was everything she hoped to find in a man one day, and exactly why she'd never tried dating after Sly. She knew men like Rocky existed, and she wasn't willing to accept anything less, so why bother?

Rocky glanced at the table and tilted his head. Nicole followed his gaze and realized they only had two chairs and two plates. They never had guests over, so a third chair was never something they needed. Until Sly's father walked back in.

"Where's Mason?" Sly asked.

Rocky glanced at her and she knew Mason was keeping his distance because of the way she treated him. "He had some work to catch up on."

"Can he come tomorrow night? Mommy is making meatloaf, and it's really good."

Rocky looked up at Nicole and smiled. "We'll see."

"Hey, Sly? Why don't we eat on the couch tonight since Rocky is here?"

Sly looked up at her. "Can we watch TV, too?"

Nicole shook her head. "I don't think so. But you can sit on the floor if you want."

"Really?"

Sly loved sitting on the floor. Nicole had no idea what the fascination was, but he always wanted to sit on the floor to eat dinner. A lot of the time, he wanted to do it with the TV on, but even sitting on the floor and eating at the coffee table was a treat for him.

Nicole nodded, and Sly cheered. "Fix your plate first and then you can sit."

Sly accepted a plate and held it while Nicole added one chicken enchilada to his plate. She topped it with extra sour cream and cheese and put a fork on the side of his plate.

She handed the second plate to Rocky while Sly went to sit. He moved closer to her and lowered his voice, "I'm sorry I just barged in on your dinner."

She shook her head. "It's fine. This is one meal that always has extra."

"Still. I should have called. I wasn't sure you would answer, though."

"Why not?"

"Because I haven't been here in two days."

She scoffed. "You aren't obligated to see us daily. You have a life."

Nicole started to walk away to get another plate, but Rocky caught her around the waist and held her still. She froze, her body plastered to his. She could feel all the muscles beneath his clothes and the heat she felt earlier intensified. Her breath became shallow, and her whole body flushed with desire.

"Nikki," he groaned, sounding as though he was feeling all the same things she was.

She looked up at him and swore she saw desire in his

eyes. Why? She was a single mom, wearing no bra and sweats. Her hair was up in a messy bun. She had no makeup on and wasn't even sure if she showered that morning. There was nothing desirable about her.

"I want to see you as much as possible," Rocky said after a long moment. "Both of you. I was working, and yesterday I had an appointment with Dr. Andrews."

"Is everything okay?" she asked, the man's name alone causing a cold sweat. She wondered if that would ever go away.

Rocky nodded. "Just a follow up. I go back in two weeks and then I'm cleared to go. Yesterday's appointment was to allow me to return to all my normal activities, besides work."

Did his tone drop when he said *normal activities*, or was it just her imagination that there was a dark, sexy tone that said he wasn't just talking about exercising? She licked her lips, realizing when she did that she could feel every inch of him against her. And she wasn't the only one affected.

Nicole pulled free of his arms and cleared her throat. "Um, I'm going to get another plate."

She escaped to the kitchen and gave herself a minute to breathe. He was dangerous. He made her think she could have things she couldn't have. It was not smart for her to start imagining them as a family unit. They weren't and never would be. He would be a part of their lives, but any lingering feelings between Nicole and Rocky were just that... lingering. They would fade eventually. Just like her hope that he would magically appear seven years ago even though he didn't know her last name.

By the time Nicole made it back out of the kitchen, Rocky was sitting on her couch and talking to Sly. She ignored their conversation and fixed her own plate. She was hoping to have enchiladas for lunch the next day, but when she counted how many were left, she knew that wasn't an option. Ramen noodles would have to do.

Nicole took a breath and made her way to the couch. Rocky was sitting close to the middle so he could put his plate on the table, which meant when Nicole sat down, her thigh brushed against his. She jerked away and shifted away, but she could still feel him.

She was losing her damn mind.

Nicole ate quickly, letting the two of them talk while she ate her food. She barely tasted anything, too distracted by the timbre of Rocky's voice echoing around inside her. The way he spoke to Sly reminded her of the way Dr. Andrews did. No question was ridiculous. They talked and laughed and Rocky made Sly feel like he was the most important person in the world.

When Nicole was done with dinner, she picked up everyone's dishes and carried them to the kitchen. She rinsed them and loaded it all into the dishwasher. She scooped the food that was left over into a container and stuck it in the fridge. When she admitted she couldn't do anything else to stay away from Rocky, she swallowed hard.

She took a moment before she left the kitchen to compose herself. Her panties were wet and her entire body felt like it was on fire. Just having him there was turning her on, and she needed to change that.

She wasn't willing to keep Sly away from Rocky, but that didn't mean she couldn't stay away from him.

Nicole walked back into the living room and stood near the TV, waiting for Sly and Rocky to stop speaking. Rocky noticed her and looked up with a smile.

"Are you running out or can you stick around for a little while?"

"I don't have anywhere I need to be. Why?" Rocky asked.

"If you don't mind, I was going to jump in the shower."

Rocky nodded, his gaze slowly trailing down Nicole's already steaming body. "Of course." There was that gravelly voice again.

Nicole nodded. "Thanks." She disappeared before either of them said anything else that would make it harder for her.

Her bedroom had access to the bathroom from inside, but there was another door to the bathroom from the hall. Nicole locked her bedroom door and the outside bathroom door, then turned on the shower. She stripped out of her clothes and let her hair down. She avoided looking at her body in the mirror, knowing she'd only find more reasons for Rocky to not be interested. She could think about that later. Right now, she needed to believe he was feeling the same way she was.

Nicole stepped into the shower and let the heat from the water soak into her. She washed her hair, luxuriating in the feel of her fingertips on her scalp. She closed her eyes and let her imagination begin to work.

She showered with Rocky one time during their weekend together, and he insisted on washing her body. As she added body wash to her loofah, she let her hands linger the way his did, adding a little dirty to her clean. She stayed under the hot spray of the water and let it slide over her body, following her curves all the way down.

She slid her hands over the same curves, lifting one of her breasts and rolling her taut nipple between her fingers. She moaned softly, letting her eyes fall closed as she teased herself.

She toyed with her other breast and let her right hand fall between her thighs. The slick wetness coated her fingers instantly, making her groan. She couldn't remember the last time she felt relaxed enough to even think about trying to come, let alone the last time she did.

Her body was tight with need. She drew the moisture from her entrance up to her clit and swirled around the sensitive nub. She ran her finger over it, pinching her nipple at the same time. A louder moan escaped her, but she bit her lip to stop it.

Nicole already knew she wasn't going to be able to stop with one orgasm. The longer she drew it out, the louder she was going to get, and in an apartment with paper-thin walls, she couldn't afford to make noise.

Especially with Rocky in her living room.

"Rocky," she whispered.

She stroked her clit, and her entire body trembled, letting go of the first one. She wasn't anywhere near done, but she had to hurry before her body demanded more than she could deliver.

She pumped her finger inside herself and groaned at the feel. The only thing that had been inside her lately was tampons, and that was nowhere near as much fun. Maybe she should get a waterproof dildo? She pumped her fingers in again and withdrew, slipping them up to her clit once more.

The slickness spurred her on and she was coming again quickly. She gasped, trying to hold back the louder noises. More, more, more, her body demanded.

She didn't bother with her channel again, just focused on her clit. She let the water stream down her front and soak her flesh, aiding her in her ministrations. One more. Then two. Oh, yes, three.

Nicole's knees nearly gave out after the last one, her

body deliciously spent in a way she hadn't felt in far too long.

The water was already turning cold. Nicole made sure all the soap was off her, then she shut off the shower and stepped out. She wrapped in a towel, her limbs still quaking from the effort.

She padded into her room and debated on what to wear. Rocky had seen her in nothing many times, and just had dinner with her braless, but Nicole still wanted to pretend there was a line between them.

She grabbed a sports bra that was old and stretched out, which meant it was soft and comfortable. She added a cotton tank top and a pair of cotton pajama pants. She dried her hair with the towel and brushed it, then pulled it back into a loose braid so it was out of her face.

She hung up her towel and unlocked the bathroom door. She left through her bedroom, pausing one more minute to make sure her debilitating desire was under control.

Nicole was good. She'd gotten it out of her system. She could be around him and not feel like she couldn't breathe unless she jumped him.

Then she walked into the living room. Rocky was sitting on the couch next to Sly. They were watching a show on TV, but Rocky wasn't looking at it. He was staring at her.

There was no mistaking the desire in his eyes or the bulge in his jeans. He looked like he was barely keeping himself together.

Nicole nibbled her lip. There was no way he knew what she just did. He couldn't possibly. He was just sitting there, his cock pressing against his zipper, for no reason.

She walked over and sat down on the other side of Sly.

She tried to relax and watch the show, and was almost there when Rocky said, "Did you enjoy your shower?" in a tone that left zero hope that he didn't know exactly what she was doing.

So much for thinking a few solo orgasms were enough. She was right back to where she started, needing him all over again.

Dammit.

11

———

Rocky could barely keep himself on the couch when Nikki walked out. Her wet braid clung to her neck and teased its way inside her shirt. Her tank hugged her curves and made his mouth water. He wanted her. Especially after he heard his own damn name.

Sly was watching TV when Nikki got in the shower, but the moment Rocky heard her moan, he forgot all about whatever show was on the TV. He'd never been so thankful for thin walls in his life as he was listening to Nikki get herself off. And when she gasped his name, he nearly came with her.

Fucking hell.

"Are you okay, Mommy?" Sly asked, barely pulling his gaze from the TV.

"Yeah, sweetie. Why?" Nikki asked him. Her cheeks were red, and it wasn't from the shower.

"We heard you call for Rocky. He thought maybe there was a spider in the shower, but I told him you're the best spider killer ever and that wasn't it. I wanted to knock on the door, but he didn't let me."

Nikki's gaze snapped to Rocky's. He knew she knew. He couldn't hide anything about it. Even the throbbing erection threatening to burst through his zipper. He was using all of his strength to keep his ass on the couch instead of grabbing Nikki and tossing her over his shoulder and having his way with her, consequences be damned.

"I was fine. And, um, I didn't call Rocky's name. I'm not sure what you heard."

"You did. It was quiet at first, but you got louder, like you wanted him to come to you."

Nikki laughed in a rusty, uncomfortable way. Rocky clenched his jaw and swore something popped. He forced himself to take a deep breath and blew it out slowly.

"Well, I don't know. But I think it might be time for you to get ready for bed. It's getting late."

"But I want to finish this show," Sly whined.

It was the first time Rocky could remember him acting like a kid and not like a small adult. He was the most well-behaved and respectful kid Rocky had ever seen, and it was all thanks to Nikki being a great mom.

Just the thought softened his desire for her a little. It wasn't just sex that he wanted. He was looking for a connection. He had one with her years ago. It was something he'd never known since, and something he looked for in every woman he was with. For most of them, it was obvious when they met the connection wasn't there. A few gave Rocky hope, but none were Nikki.

"How long is the show?" Nikki asked.

Sly picked up the remote and hit a button. "Seven minutes."

Nikki sighed and nodded. "Then right to bed, mister."

Sly nodded and grinned, getting sucked into the show instantly again.

Nikki chewed on her lip like she wasn't sure what she should do. Rocky had the same thoughts. He wanted to spend as much time as possible with them, but he didn't want to overstay his welcome. He showed up unannounced and not only ate their food but hung around for hours. He still couldn't bring himself to leave.

Nikki finally sat on the couch, at the far opposite end from Rocky, curled in on herself so there was no risk of them touching. She stared at the TV, ignoring him. It almost made him smile.

Rocky watched her while she watched the TV. She was stunning, and from so close, he could smell the light, flowery scent of her shampoo or body wash. She was like waking up in a field of flowers. Not that he'd ever done that, but it reminded him of The Wizard of Oz. Without the psychedelic effects.

The second Sly's show was over, Nikki was up off the couch and herding Sly toward the bathroom. "Time to get ready for bed. Rocky's going to leave."

"But I want him to read to me."

"I don't know if we're going to read tonight. You stayed up extra to watch the show."

"Yeah, but you say reading is one of the most important parts of our day."

Nikki closed her eyes for a moment and sighed heavily. "You're right," she gave in. "I don't know if Rocky can stay, though."

She looked at him and pleaded with her eyes for him to say no. He opened his mouth to do what she wanted and heard himself say, "I can stay. There's nowhere else I'd rather be."

Nikki's shoulders drooped in defeat as Sly cheered. He

hurried to the bathroom and brushed his teeth. Nikki followed him, and Rocky hung back.

He'd never gotten into a routine with anyone. He'd never spent enough time with another person to know how they got ready for bed at night. The weekend he spent with Nikki was the closest to it, and she always closed the door, saying it wasn't sexy to watch someone else brush their teeth.

After seeing his teammates fall in love and hearing the way they talked about their women, Rocky thought seeing someone brush their teeth was quite possibly the sexiest thing he could imagine. Not because teeth were hot, but because it signified a level of intimacy and trust that people only had when they were that close. The idea made him wish he had it with someone.

Once Sly was done getting ready, Nikki helped him change into pajamas and tucked him into his bed. She made a move to lie down next to him but stopped when she reached for the book.

"Sorry. I forgot."

She sat back up and smiled sadly. Rocky figured it was the first time she'd ever been sidelined, and it obviously hurt her. She stiffly walked to him and handed him the book she had in her hand.

"Why don't you stay with us? You can help me with the big words."

Nikki laughed softly and nibbled her lower lip. Rocky's eyes fell to that spot and he hardened again. Something as simple as a lip should not make him so horny.

It wasn't simple, and it wasn't just a lip. It was Nikki. It was everything that made up Nikki. It was being close to her and seeing her, it was spending time with her, it was knowing how amazing she was as a mother.

He was rushing things, but he wanted them in his life.

He already loved Sly after just a few weeks, and Nikki... well, he thought maybe he fell in love with her years ago and never stopped. Even considering walking away from them made him want to rip out his own heart because they owned it. They owned him.

Nikki finally nodded and moved back to the bed. She sat at the foot and let Rocky sit up closer to Sly so he could see the pictures.

Rocky started reading, his throat rough and scratchy with all the emotions running through him. He wanted to do that every night. Read to Sly and be with Nikki and spend time together as a family. He wanted to be a family.

As Rocky read the book that was clearly a favorite, Sly read along with the parts he knew. After a little while, he settled against Rocky's arm. His breathing grew deeper and his weight was heavier. Rocky kept reading, not wanting the moment to stop.

When Nikki shifted and made a move to get off the bed, Rocky looked up at her. "He's asleep. We can go."

"The book's almost over," Rocky said quietly. "Why don't I finish?"

Nikki hesitated, then settled onto the bed again. Rocky kept reading, his voice soft so he didn't wake Sly. When he finished the book, Nikki got up quickly and took the book from him. She put it back on Sly's shelf and waited for Rocky to get up. She leaned over and kissed Sly, whispering something Rocky couldn't hear.

They were a team, a unit. It had been the two of them against the world, and Rocky was interrupting and messing up their lives. He didn't want to mess them up, but he did want to be a part of them. He was not looking forward to walking out the door and not coming back until the next day or the day after that. He wanted to go into her bedroom and be there, be a part of it. He wanted to make them breakfast the next morning and spend the day together. He wanted it all.

Nikki moved toward the door, and Rocky stepped closer to Sly. He leaned down and kissed the boy's head. He couldn't resist telling Sly he loved him, and he meant it, too.

Nikki turned off the lights and pulled Sly's door mostly closed, then headed toward the living room. Rocky followed her, knowing his time with them was coming to an end.

She stopped before she made it to the door and faced him. Her cheeks were flushed again, and her eyes unfocused. "Did you mean what you said?"

"About what?"

She swallowed roughly. "That you love him?"

Rocky smiled and nodded. "I do. I've only known him for a few weeks, but I can't imagine not having him in my life. I know that's not fair because you've raised an amazing kid and it means you have to allow me to be a part of it, but I want to spend time with both of you. I want to be in your lives."

She nodded, fear and love and uncertainty on her face. "It's always been us. Just us. When I found out, my parents... they weren't okay with me having him. They said it wasn't right because I wasn't married, and they tried to convince me to 'take care of it.' That's how they phrased it. I couldn't do it, and I knew I couldn't raise him around them. I haven't spoken to them in years, and I know it was for the best, but I'm protective of Sly. Probably more than most parents because it's just him and me."

"I wish I was there for you," Rocky said. "I don't blame you, and I hope you know I never would. I think you're the strongest person I've ever known. You've raised an amazing son, and you've taken care of him. You're... thank you."

Nikki drew in a shaky breath and laughed quietly. "Most of the time, I think he's just a great kid. I don't think I've done all that well for him."

"Oh, Nikki, no. You're an unbelievable mom. You get to take all the credit for who he is because you're the one who's made him who he is."

She smiled softly and looked up at him. They were standing close, speaking quietly, and just how close they were hit Rocky all of a sudden. He could almost feel her breath on his face. The heat from her body warmed his.

He reached for her hand and threaded their fingers together. She looked down at their hands, her hair falling over her shoulder, then tossed it back and met his gaze. Her cheeks were pink again.

"About earlier... um, when I was in the shower..."

Rocky swallowed hard and stepped closer to her.

"I was... I mean..." She groaned.

"If you think I haven't thought about you when I made myself come, you're insane, Nikki. You've been my favorite fantasy for seven years."

"What?"

He moved their joined hands behind her back and pulled her closer to him. Her free hand braced against his chest, and he stepped into her personal space, letting her feel the effect she had on him.

Her eyes widened as she gasped. "Rocky."

"I'm not asking you for anything, Nikki. God, I want to. I want you so badly, I can barely restrain myself right now, but I'm not here for that. I'm not here to pressure you or push you, but we're tied together forever. I'm not going anywhere. And I want you to know that if you're ever interested, you don't have to question if I am."

She narrowed her eyes. "What about in a year? Or two? Or five?"

He chuckled. "Baby, it's been seven years. Seven years since I've been dreaming about you and fantasizing about you and jerking off to memories of you. Seven years since I've even seen you, and I'm gone. Everything is in your hands, Nikki. Everything."

NICOLE NEARLY CAME JUST LISTENING to him talk. He said things she only wished someone would say to her. Not just about wanting her, but about being there. She'd never been able to count on anyone else.

She wasn't silly enough to think just because he spent a few weeks with them and found out he had a son that everything was going to be easy, but it was a start. He hung around longer than Nicole expected.

She drew in a shaky breath and licked her lips. She wanted him. She could tell herself she didn't, but she did. He was the only man she'd considered letting into her life in years. And the only one she really wanted in her life.

Nicole looked up at him and shifted closer. He sucked in a breath, dragging his chest against her sensitive nipples. The clothes she wore weren't doing much to block the feel of him against her body, but she felt like clawing them off so she could press her skin to his.

She lifted on her tiptoes, meeting Rocky halfway. He groaned at the first touch of their lips, sending a shockwave of desire through her. Every cell in her body pulsed with need. It was too much and not enough at the same time.

Rocky thrust his tongue into her eager mouth and tangled with hers. She slid her hand up his chest and wrapped it around his neck, holding on to him. She couldn't get close enough. He groaned like he was just as frustrated as she was.

Rocky released the hand he had trapped behind her back and slid both his hands down to cup her ass. He teased and kneaded her flesh as he probed her mouth with his tongue. Every move he made sent her pulse higher and higher.

Nicole dragged her hands down his chest, wanting to feel the contours of his muscles. She loved his body when they were together, and it had only improved if his clothes were anything to go by. Nope, her hands verified it. He was even more muscular, and she wanted to taste him.

She slid her hands under his shirt and lifted it up. When she exposed his chest, she dragged her mouth from his and bent to taste him. She knew he enjoyed having his nipples teased and sucked hard on one, nipping it before she kissed and licked her way across his chest to the other one.

Rocky brushed the hair that fell from her braid out of her face, and when she looked up, he was watching her. He'd stripped off his shirt and stood in her living room in only his jeans. She wanted those off, too.

"You're so beautiful," he whispered.

She chuckled softly, knowing it was just something he said. He hadn't seen what pregnancy and childbirth had done to her body. She was always curvy with larger than standard breasts and wide thighs and hips, but she swore everything got bigger after Sly. Her old jeans never fit again, and her thighs always felt like they rubbed each other more than before.

Her body didn't bother her, but she also didn't flaunt it. She didn't walk around in skimpy or tight clothes and show off how much extra she had. And she hadn't had sex since Sly.

Letting Rocky see her was a challenge, one she suddenly wasn't sure if she was ready for. Would he expect the twenty-four year old body of the woman he slept with before, or would he be okay with the mom-bod she'd honed since then?

"What happened?" he asked softly. "Did you hear Sly?"

Nicole looked up at him. He was staring toward Sly's room, his gaze narrowed on the door. Nicole shook her head. She'd all but forgotten about Sly sleeping in the next room while she stood in their living room and stripped his father naked.

She took a head clearing step back and drew in a breath.

Rocky nodded once and reached for his shirt. He was about to put it on when Nicole said, "I haven't been with anyone since you."

Rocky stilled, his shirt hovering over his head. He drew a breath and pulled his shirt on, taking away the best view she'd ever had from her apartment.

"I'm not... I don't know. This is a lot for me."

"I told you, Nikki, you're in charge. You say stop, I'm going to stop. Like right now."

She shook her head. "I don't know if I want you to stop."

Rocky groaned and reached for her. He held her against his chest and rested his chin on top of her head. "I don't want to make you feel like you have to do anything."

She snorted. "I was masturbating in my shower and thinking of you. I clearly want you."

Rocky chuckled and squeezed her tighter. "When Sly said I should go check on you, I thought I was going to die."

"I still can't believe you could hear me."

"I'm glad I could. I never would have told you how much

I wanted you. Nikki, this is all up to you." He pulled back and looked at her. "I'm here if you want me to be, and I'll go if you want me to. It's all up to you."

She stared up at him and knew there was really only one choice. "I don't want you to go."

The words were barely out before his lips were on hers again. "Thank fuck," he whispered.

She felt the same way.

12

——————

Nikki's body molded perfectly to his. She had more curves than the last time they were together, but he thought they made her more beautiful, more sensuous. He couldn't stop touching her body, sliding his hands up and down her curves.

Together, they stumbled toward her bedroom. She didn't make a move to turn on a light, but with Sly's door partially open, it didn't surprise him. He broke free from her and turned to close her door instead of kicking it closed like he wanted to do. Letting her go was painful, but it was temporary as he quietly closed and locked the bedroom door.

When he turned back to her, the moonlight shining through her cheap, upturned blinds highlighted her skin and made him think she was an angel made just for him.

"God, you're beautiful," he breathed.

She ducked her chin, hiding herself from him even in the darkness.

Rocky took a step closer to her, bringing her back into his arms. "I don't know what you're thinking right now, but I'm not saying anything that isn't true, Nikki. You're stunning. And I can't wait to peel these clothes off of you and kiss every inch of your body again."

Her sharp intake of breath told him his words had the desired effect. She might be second guessing herself, but she was turned on. "I look a lot different from seven years ago. My body has changed."

Rocky started to pull away from her. "Then we need a light on so I can see all those changes."

"No!" she gasped. "Um, I..."

Rocky stopped and went back to her. "You can have your way this time. Next time I get my way."

"Next time?"

Rocky nodded. "Hell, yes, Nikki. There will be a lot of next times if I get my way."

She sank into him, her body turning liquid. He wrapped his arms around her and let his desire take over.

He kissed her slowly, savoring the taste of her lips. Her hands slid up his chest and around his neck before she sighed happily. He caressed her curves again, wanting to touch her everywhere at once but wanting to take all night to love her the way she deserved to be loved.

Seven years. She hadn't been with anyone in seven years. He hadn't slept his way through the country, but he definitely hadn't refrained either. Of course, he wasn't a single parent like she was.

He had a lot of making up to do.

They moved toward the bed, one of the only pieces of furniture from what he could tell. When her legs hit the mattress, she pulled back from him and bit her lip, glancing at the bed.

"What?" he asked, stroking her cheek while she debated something.

"I was trying to decide if it was better to take my clothes off now or wait until we were on the bed."

He groaned. "Always now. Always. You should just walk around naked all the time."

She chuckled, the husky sound sending a jolt through him. He was the luckiest son of a bitch on earth because he got to hear that. He got to make her laugh.

Then she reached for the edge of her shirt and peeled it off, and he amended his thought. Nope, he was the luckiest son of a bitch because he got to have her.

He stood, gobsmacked, as she quickly undressed. Shirt, bra, pants, and panties all fell to the floor as though she was racing to get out of them. The second she was naked, she reached for the covers and yanked them back, keeping them in her hand.

"Oh, no. We're not doing that," he said.

"Doing what?" she asked, continuing her move.

He trapped her around the waist and pulled her back flush to his fully clothed front. His arms locked around her and he splayed his hands wide to touch as much of her as he could reach.

She moaned softly and melted against him, the security of her bedding forgotten for a moment.

Rocky kissed her neck, licking and sucking on her until she dropped the covers and surrendered to him. He was not going to let her hide in her bed. He wanted to see her. All of her. And touch her.

One hand cupped a breast and teased her hard nipple. She shivered against him. His other hand slid south, meeting tight curls.

She stiffened. "I... I don't shave anymore. Sorry."

He shook his head and whispered, "You're perfect, Nikki." He teased his way through her curls, letting her relax again while he lazily caressed her. His cock ached to slide into her, but he was a patient man. He'd waited seven years for her, he could wait a few more minutes.

She let out a shaky breath and parted her thighs just slightly. He took it as a good sign and moved his fingers between her legs. He bit her neck when he felt how wet she was, how ready she was.

"Fuck, Nikki."

She leaned back and wrapped her arms around his neck, stretching her body. He kissed her cheek and moved his hand to her other breast, watching his fingers pinch and roll her nipple.

Between her thighs, he dipped lower until he could push a finger into her wet entrance. She dripped onto her thighs, her tight channel ready and waiting for him. He wasn't sure he would be able to wait once he felt how tight she was.

"Spread your thighs, baby," he whispered against her ear. "Let me in."

She did as he asked and moaned instantly when he thrust his finger hard into her.

"Rocky," she whispered.

"I'm right here, Nikki." He pumped his finger in and out, letting her body get used to the feel of him. She was tight, gripping his finger. He teased her nipple and stroked her inside, feeling her body relax and open for him with every second.

She spread her thighs wider and leaned back, letting him take more of her weight while she enjoyed the orgasm heading for her. He added a second finger, earning a moan from her. Then he pressed his thumb to her clit and held her tight while she shook with an orgasm.

"Oh, God," she breathed.

"My thoughts exactly," he whispered. "Give me another one, beautiful."

"I don't know if I can."

He thrust hard into her and she tightened around his fingers. "You can, Nikki. Ride my hand."

"I'm not sure I can be quiet enough."

"I got you. Bite my arm. When you feel it coming, just grab my arm and bite as hard as you want. Scream into me."

"I might hurt you."

"It'll totally be worth it," Rocky insisted. "I need to feel that again."

He didn't wait for her to agree before he stroked inside her again, rubbing over her clit quickly. She whimpered and moaned. Her knees weakened, and she barely stayed on her feet. Rocky held her up, taking all of her weight so she could let go.

Then she grabbed his arm like he told her to. He let her take it, clamping it across her mouth. She bucked her hips and rode his hand, biting hard on his arm. The pain kept him from coming with her as she let go, coming with a scream he was sure would have woken Sly and half her neighbors if she'd let it out.

He eased his fingers from her, making her tremble once more as he did. She couldn't stand on her own, so he helped her onto the bed and was rewarded when she didn't bother reaching for the sheet to cover herself up.

Rocky couldn't resist touching her legs while he threw his clothes on the floor with hers. He grabbed a condom from his wallet and rolled it on, then joined her on the bed, lying down next to her instead of on top of her.

"Are you okay?" he asked.

"Never better," she said with a smile. She reached up and cupped his jaw. "I thought maybe I'd dreamed you up all these years. That maybe the weekend we spent together wasn't as great as I remembered it being but that I'd sensationalized it because it was the last time I was with anyone."

"And now?" he asked, kissing her palm.

"Now, I don't think I sensationalized it enough."

He chuckled.

"We haven't had sex yet and I'm already a wet noodle."

"We don't have to," Rocky said, feeling disappointed but willing to walk away if that was what she wanted.

Nikki shook her head. "Not a chance, Rocky. I want you. Just don't break me."

He leaned over and kissed her softly. He gently pried her lips apart and held her cheek while he kissed her. She let her hand rest on his side tentatively.

"I've missed you," he admitted.

She nodded. "Me, too."

He pushed himself up and kissed her nose, then settled between her thighs. She stretched them wider to accommodate him. He stared at her, holding her gaze while he pushed inside, slowly so she could get used to his size.

When he was buried deep in her, they both groaned. "You're the only person who has ever felt this good," she said quietly.

He let his weight press her into the mattress and kissed her lips. "For me, too."

Her arms went around his neck as he started to move. Rocky kissed her, alternating between kisses and strokes until they were both panting and dangerously close to losing their minds.

"I don't know how I walked away from you," she whispered.

"It doesn't matter. We're together now," he said, thrusting

hard into her. "I'm not going anywhere, and now I know your last name so you can't disappear on me."

She chuckled with him and moaned again when he thrust deep inside her. "Oh, yes."

He kept going, the harder strokes pushing him closer. He could feel her tightening around him and ached to let her come first, to have her body lock around his. Again and again, he crashed into her, unable to separate her from him. Her need was his, her desire was his, and her orgasm, thank God, was his.

She let out a loud moan that threatened to wake Sly. Rocky held himself on one hand, continuing to charge toward his own orgasm, and pressed his forearm against her lips. She opened her mouth and bit down hard on him.

"Fuck," Rocky bit out, the pain sending a jolt through him.

He couldn't stop, pounding hard into her as she pulsed around his cock. His throat tingled and his body broke out in a cold sweat, then everything released.

"Fuck, Nikki," he growled, burying his face in her pillow. He jerked and emptied into her, biting hard on the pillow as he groaned his way through the best orgasm of his life.

Sex had never been that good before, even with Nikki.

He laid on top of her until she squirmed just enough to tell him he needed to move. He pushed up and looked down at her, brushing the hair from her destroyed braid back. She smiled at him.

"Did I crush you?" he asked.

She shrugged. "It's okay. You were trying to make sure we didn't wake our son."

His dick pulsed with her words.

She raised an eyebrow. "That turns you on?"

He shrugged. "Our son. You haven't said that. You said mine or yours, but never ours."

"Well, he is."

"This... whatever this does or doesn't become, will not change my relationship with Sly," Rocky said.

She nodded. "I know. You would have been a great father if you'd known about him. I'm sorry about that."

He kissed her forehead. "I was the one who made that stupid rule. I didn't think I'd be able to walk away from you. From the first time I saw you..."

"Don't," she said, her voice soft and shaky.

"Don't what?"

She shook her head. "Don't say things you don't mean. Not now. I know all this is... whatever, but we don't know each other. The sex is amazing, and I think you're a great guy, but I can't just think about myself. I have to think about what's right for Sly. Which means he can't know about this, and we can't start talking about things until we know for sure."

"But I do—"

"Just...let's take all this slowly. We can get to know each other again and see if we're compatible, but I can't go into this thinking it could last and have it all fall apart."

"What if it doesn't?"

She shrugged. "Then it'll be a good surprise."

"So, you're counting on this not working?"

She laughed mirthlessly. "I haven't had a lot of things work out in my life, Rocky. It's not easy for me to expect the best."

He tried to understand that, but he didn't. Losing his dad was the worst thing that ever happened to him. He'd faced challenges and hard things, but everything always worked out, one way or another.

"Maybe I'm wrong, but there are a lot of things we need to figure out. You don't have a job or a place to stay. Have you told your boss you're not coming back?"

"Not yet," he admitted.

"You're still recovering from surgery, and I'm on leave for another few weeks until Sly can go back to school. This isn't all tied up in a neat little bow."

Rocky took a breath and realized she was right. He didn't like it, but he had to accept it.

She made a move to push him off her, but Rocky dropped his weight onto her and held her hands still when she tried to fight him.

"You said your peace, now I need you to hear mine."

She scowled at him. He raised an eyebrow, and she said, "Fine. What is it?"

"I wasn't here for you, and I'm sorry. I wish I had been. But I'm here now. I will figure out everything with my job and a place to live. I want you to help me find someplace because I want you two to move in with me."

She opened her mouth to argue, but he leaned down and kissed her before she could say anything.

"Let me finish."

She opened her mouth again, and he kissed her once more, sweeping his tongue through her mouth until she moaned.

"Are you going to let me talk?"

She rolled her eyes and nodded.

"We can get a place with three bedrooms so you have your own. I'm not saying we have to sleep in the same room. But I want to be with you two every day. I can help you. It'll be easier. My second condition is that I want you to give us a chance. A real chance. This isn't just sex for me, although that was spectacular. I want to know you. And that means I want you to let me in. Talk to me and tell me when things aren't okay. I want to know you."

Rocky looked at her and raised an eyebrow when she didn't say anything.

"Am I allowed to talk now?" she asked.

He tilted his head and glared at her. "Yes."

"Thank you. First, it's not your fault you weren't here. I was never mad at you about that, and you shouldn't be either. You can be mad at me for walking away, but if I'd known... I'm sorry. And everything else... I'll think about it."

Rocky rolled his eyes and shook his head. "I guess I'll take what I can get."

She smirked. "You're going to have to."

He kissed her again and hardened inside her. The urge to have her again was strong, but he wasn't going to push his luck.

He broke from their kiss and looked down at her. Her eyes were closed, and she looked deliciously sated. He did that. He wanted to do it again.

"Do you have another condom?" she asked him quietly.

He breathed a laugh and nodded. "One more."

"I think maybe you should get it."

"With pleasure," Rocky said.

WHEN HE FINALLY PULLED HIMSELF AWAY from Nikki, Rocky knew he'd never be able to walk away from her. The woman he'd known years ago was still there. She was just shielded by the tough mama bear who'd been raising their son.

"I'm glad we didn't wake Sly."

"He's a really heavy sleeper," Nikki said as she wrapped a robe around herself to walk him to the door.

"That's good since I intend to make you scream again soon."

She shivered at his words, and his cock twitched at the sight.

"It's not easy to walk away from you."

She chuckled. "I know the feeling."

He smiled sadly at her. He wanted to ask why she left that night, but they had a great time and he didn't want to ruin it by bringing up their past.

"Hey, Rocky?" she said softly.

"Yeah?"

"Thank you for being here for us."

"Thank you for letting me be. You didn't have to tell me who he was at the hospital. I never would have known."

She shrugged. "That didn't feel right to me. None of this ever felt right to me."

He wrapped an arm around her. "This feels right to me."

She smiled at his cheesy line and nodded. "Me, too. But we're going to go slow."

He smirked and kissed her neck. "I like slow. All night long kind of slow." He groaned and licked her salty flesh.

She moaned and leaned into him. She let him kiss her neck and work his way to her lips. Only when he slid his hands under her robe and cupped her bare ass did she pull back.

"Nope, you need to go. You're far too tempting for me."

"The feeling is mutual," he said, letting her feel how hard he was.

She pushed at his shoulders. "I need another shower."

"Now you're just being cruel," he said with a groan.

She laughed softly. "Go to your hotel. Get some sleep. We'll see you tomorrow. And tell Mason he can come, too. I won't threaten him again."

Rocky smiled. "Thank you. I'll see you tomorrow." He stole another kiss and let himself out, waiting until he heard the lock click into place before he walked away.

He spun his keys around his finger on his way down the rickety stairs. The complex was quiet in the middle of the night. Even the road out front was quiet. Everything was quiet, except the car running at the far side of the small lot.

Rocky tried to see who was inside, but the windows were too dark. The inside was dark, no dash lights or anything helping to illuminate whoever was watching Nikki's building.

Rocky tried to judge where Nikki's apartment was compared to the car. A cold chill slid down his spine. It looked like the car could be staring right at her living room and bedroom windows.

Or it could be another resident talking to a friend instead of waiting to go inside.

There was no plate on the front of the car, but Rocky made a mental note of the look of the vehicle, without being too obvious, so he could look it up later. It wasn't the nicest car, but in a neighborhood like Nikki's it looked brand new and fancy.

Rocky shook his head and tried to convince himself he was being paranoid, but in his line of work, paranoid wasn't always wrong.

He thought about going back upstairs and talking to Nikki, but the driver of the car started it up and slowly pulled out, like there was nothing out of the ordinary happening. They waited until they were on the street to turn on their headlights, which meant Rocky couldn't see the license plate.

It had to be nothing. He'd check, but he was sure it was nothing.

Well, almost sure.

13

Zeke slammed his front door and stalked to his fridge. He grabbed a bottle of water and ripped the top off. He drained what didn't splash on the floor, then threw the empty bottle against the wall and screamed.

"Fucking bastard," he growled.

He went to Nicole's to watch her place. When he heard Mikey had paid her a visit, Zeke knew she was in even more danger than he first expected. He thought he could pay the debt for her and no one would notice, but if the boss had Mikey going to see her instead of Zeke, it was a bigger issue than he realized.

Then that fucker showed up. The asshole reminded Zeke of Nicole's kid, always in the way. But Zeke knew how to get rid of obstacles. He'd been doing it his whole life.

"Is everything okay, honey?"

Zeke spun and nodded. "Yeah, Grandma. Go back to bed."

"I heard you yell. What happened?"

Zeke shook his head. His grandma was the only person who'd ever believed in him. She took him in when his mom was too high to care and his dad was too worried about the next person he could stick his dick in. It took Zeke a little while, but he found a way to make both of them care about him. Just before he made sure they knew what it cost them. They both died begging for his help, but he ignored them the same way they'd ignored him his whole life.

"Nothing," Zeke grumbled.

"I thought you were going out with your girlfriend tonight. I didn't think you'd be home."

Zeke shook his head. "Nicole had other plans. I didn't realize she was busy."

"That's too bad. Maybe you can see her tomorrow."

Zeke nodded and stroked his beard. The raspy feel of stubble would leave a mark on her skin. It was why he kept his beard short. He was going to mark her, in more ways than one, and make sure she, and every man who ever thought about touching her, knew who she belonged to.

"I will definitely see her tomorrow."

"That's good, honey. I'm going back to sleep. Make sure you lock up."

She patted his cheeks, then shuffled back to her room. Zeke was still until he heard the snick of her door shutting softly. He held his breath a few more minutes to make sure she was in bed.

He checked the doors and windows even though he knew none of them would stop anyone who really wanted to get in the house. He went to his room and pulled up the pictures he took on his phone. Nicole's blinds were open just enough to see inside when she walked around her room after her shower.

He zoomed in on her breasts and licked his lips. He unzipped his pants and sat on the edge of his bed. Nicole was his. That bastard who left her house in the middle of the night was going to pay for hanging around. But Zeke wasn't thinking about him. All he was worried about was Nicole, and how good it would feel when her lips replaced his hand.

"Soon, baby. Soon."

NICOLE WOKE up early the next morning like she always did. Ever since she found out she was pregnant, she'd become an early riser. Before that, she could spend half the day in bed and not think twice about moving, but everything changed when that stick turned blue.

She stripped the sheets off her bed and inhaled them, letting herself remember the feel of Rocky inside her again. It was the same, but everything with him was different. Sex meant more to her now. She didn't jump into bed with him because he was hot and she was horny. She did it because she liked him. Because he was safe. And yeah, maybe a little because he was hot and she was horny.

She smiled at herself and grabbed clean sheets from her closet. The sheets were clean and fresh, but she admitted to herself she preferred the smell of Rocky and sex on the other ones.

Okay, maybe she was a lot horny.

With the bed changed, Nicole took the dirty sheets and put them in the wash. Then she started breakfast and getting ready for the day. Sly had schoolwork to catch up on, and she needed to check in with work.

Sly stumbled into the kitchen just as Nicole finished his breakfast. Eggs and bacon with toast. He was still half-asleep and rumpled, which was Nicole's favorite. He always let her hug him a little extra and kiss his hair a little longer when he wasn't fully awake yet.

Sly started with his toast. He nibbled on it and let her hug him. She knew by the time he was done, he would want her off, so she took one last sniff of his hair and poured him a glass of orange juice.

"Where's Rocky?" Sly asked.

"Um, he went back to his hotel after you went to bed. Why?"

Sly shrugged. "I thought maybe he would be here."

Nicole smiled at her son. "He's going to see us today. And Mason. But we have school to do."

Sly groaned. "I don't want to do school."

"Sorry, bud, you don't have a choice. You're going to fall behind if you don't get your work done. You've already missed a lot."

"I don't care. School is stupid."

"Where is this coming from?"

Sly shrugged, which told Nicole there was something going on that he didn't want to tell her. She'd get it out of him eventually, but she wasn't going to push now.

"How about you finish breakfast, take a shower, and we can go do some schoolwork at the park? Get out of here for a little while?"

Sly shrugged again. Nicole bit her lip to keep from sighing.

"If you get schoolwork done early, maybe we can do something fun today, too."

"Like what?"

Nicole shrugged. "Anything you want to do."

"Anything?" he asked, his eyes wide.

Nicole was sure she was going to regret it, but she nodded. "Anything."

"Can we move to New York to be with Rocky?"

Nicole opened her mouth, then snapped it shut again. She bit down hard on her lip and tilted her head. She stretched her neck to alleviate some of the instant tension. It didn't work.

"I have a job here, Sly. And Dr. Andrews is here. I can't just pick up and leave."

"But I don't want to stay here. I don't like it here."

"Since when?"

"Since no one wants to play with me because I'm always sick."

Nicole's heart broke for her son. She did everything she could to shield him from every pain imaginable, but he still got hurt constantly. She wanted to march down to the school and tell his classmates to stop being little assholes, but she knew that wouldn't solve anything. And running away wouldn't change it either.

"I'm so sorry, honey," Nicole said, wrapping her arm around Sly's shoulders and pulling him to her. He fought her, pushing her away far too soon.

"Why can't we move to be with Rocky?"

Nicole sighed heavily and closed her eyes. Rocky insisted he was going to move there, but he hadn't made any plans to move. She couldn't help but wonder if he said something to Sly about moving to New York instead.

"Where is this coming from? Why are you asking to move all of a sudden?"

"Because I want to be near my dad. Everyone at school has a dad, and I never did. But now I do, and I want to live with him."

Nicole swallowed the pain that rose up. He didn't say he hated her or he didn't want her. She understood him wanting a father. Especially a father like Rocky. He was smart and strong and funny and kind. He was the kind of person who made you feel safe and cared for. She wanted to be around him, so she couldn't blame Sly for wanting the same.

"We'll see," Nicole finally said, hoping the non-answer would suffice for a little while.

Sly huffed and went back to his breakfast, ignoring Nicole.

She poured herself a second cup of coffee and added a spoonful of sugar. She leaned against the counter and tried to figure out if Sly came up with the idea to move on his own or if he had help.

Nicole still hadn't figured out the answer to that question when she was getting out of the shower. Sly was in front of the TV, and she was getting ready to go so they could head to the park before the grocery store. It might not be the answer to her concerns at the moment, but it was the best she had.

Sly wanted her to invite Rocky to the park with them. She told him she'd think about it, and was still debating when she walked into the living room, dressed and ready to go.

"Is Rocky coming?" Sly asked excitedly.

"I don't know yet."

"Did you call him?"

"No. Did you get your school stuff together?"

Sly groaned and pushed off the couch. He was almost to his room when he grumbled something Nicole couldn't hear.

"What was that?"

"Nothing," he said.

Nicole shook her head. She was losing her son, the only person she had in her life. Sly was growing up, but she knew it was more than that. It was having a shot at a relationship with his father that was changing him. Bringing to light all the things he didn't have that he'd missed out on. She understood, but it hurt that suddenly she wasn't enough for him.

He trudged back into the living room with his backpack over his shoulder. He tossed it on the floor with a thud. "Got my stuff."

"Come here and sit down," Nicole said, moving to the couch.

Sly looked at her and followed after a minute. She wasn't sure she would handle him being a teenager if he was already acting that way as a six year old. Six year olds should be happy and cheerful, not sullen and annoyed.

"Are you feeling okay?"

He shrugged.

"Does anything hurt?"

He shrugged again.

"What's going on? I've never known you to act like this."

"I just want to know my dad," he said. His lip trembled and his eyes filled with tears. "You said he would be here if he could be, and now he can be. But I don't want to be here. I'm not sick anymore. I don't want to be the sick kid. No one wants to play with me or be my friend. I just want to live with my dad."

Nicole took a breath and pulled Sly in for a hug. She'd helped create this mess by telling her son his father would be around. She made him believe in a fantasy that wasn't likely to happen. And she was the one who was hurting him. If things didn't work out with Rocky, it would be her fault for getting Sly's hopes up.

"Are you going to marry my daddy?" Sly asked after a minute.

Nicole laughed and shook her head. "No, honey."

"Why not? He's my dad, and you always told me you loved him."

"I do love him. But I love him because he helped me create you."

"What does that mean?"

Nicole drew a deep breath and let it out slowly. "It means Rocky gave me a special gift, and that gift was a part of you. And if I hadn't known him, I never would have known you. But Rocky and I aren't in love. We're not getting married."

"But why not? Everyone at school has two parents that are married."

"I just—" Nicole's phone rang and interrupted her. "Hold on," she told Sly. She hurried to answer her phone before it stopped ringing. It was already in her purse, ready to go to the park. She dug it out and turned it over. Her boss's name was lit up at the top. She slid to answer but was a second too late.

"Shoot," Nicole said. She didn't realize what time it was. She should have called into work by now. She unlocked her phone and went to her phone app to call, but it rang again.

Without thinking, Nicole answered the blocked call. "Hello? Amanda?"

"Amanda? Nope, this isn't Amanda," a man's voice said.

"Who is this?"

"You don't need to know my name. What you do need to know is that the next time someone comes to visit you, he won't be leaving empty-handed."

Nicole trembled at the deadly tone of the voice. "What do you want from me?"

"You know what I want, Nicole. And I always get what I want. Say hi to Sly for me. I'll see you both soon."

"No—" The line went dead.

Nicole lowered the phone, every cell in her body shaking. She stared at it, as though the man was going to come through the phone and hurt her.

She looked around her apartment and felt exposed. They'd already been there once. The man on the phone made it clear they would be back. He knew about Sly.

Her gaze landed on his backpack at the door. Leaving... no, leaving wasn't an option. They couldn't go out. Not in public. Not alone.

"Mommy, are we going?"

"No!" she shouted. "I mean, why don't we stay here for today. We can have a quiet day at home."

"No school?" Sly asked.

Nicole forced a grin. "No school. Let's just watch movies and be together."

"Yay!" Sly said.

Nicole moved Sly's backpack in front of the door to slow down anyone who tried to get in. She double checked that it was locked. She turned all the blinds in the living room so no one could see in.

"It's like a movie theater," Sly said.

Nicole smiled at him, thankful he hadn't picked up on her terror. "Why don't you pick out a movie?"

Sly grabbed the remote and started flipping through. Nicole looked around the apartment for other ways someone could get in. She was not going to sit around and wait for danger to arrive.

Her phone buzzed, and Nicole nearly dropped it. She stared at it, struggling to register there was a voicemail from her boss. She couldn't listen. She couldn't do anything.

Nicole held down the power button and waited until her phone turned off, then she sat it on the table and curled on the couch next to Sly and tried to forget the outside world.

ROCKY TRIED CALLING Nikki all day and kept getting her voicemail. She was avoiding him. He shouldn't have pushed her the night before. He should have just pretended he didn't hear her in the shower and left when she came back out.

That was the last time he was going to let his dick do the thinking.

"Still nothing?" Mason asked when Rocky tried to glance at his phone without it being obvious.

Rocky shook his head.

"Maybe we should go over there. Make sure they're okay."

"I'm sure they're fine," Rocky said.

"Okay, but what if they're not?"

"They are."

"Then explain to me why she's not answering your calls or texts."

"Because I slept with her, okay?" Rocky yelled. He got up from the couch, ignoring the ache in his side.

Mason looked up at him with one eyebrow raised. "You do have a kid together, so that's not news."

Rocky sighed heavily. "Last night. I slept with her last night."

Mason leaned forward and chuckled. His chuckles turned to full-blown laughter, and he shook his head. "You're one messed up dude."

"Yeah, I know. I should have kept my dick in my pants. I was stupid. And now she won't talk to me, and she's never going to let me see my son, and I messed everything up."

Mason looked up at Rocky. "I'm not going to argue with the first half of what you said, but the second half? I'm not buying it. Nikki told you Sly was your kid. She could have pretended she didn't know why you were there, or ignored you entirely. She could have easily never spoken to you. But she did. She wanted you to know about him. I don't think she would have done that if she intended to take him away from you."

"Yeah, well, she also didn't plan on me dragging her to bed."

"You forced her," Mason growled, rising slowly off the couch. The man moved like a jungle cat and was just as deadly if he needed to be.

"No. Fuck no. I would never."

"Then what did you mean?"

"When I went over there last night, I didn't intend to sleep with her. I just want to get to know Sly. I really do. But Nikki..."

"She's the one that got away?"

Rocky ran a hand over his hair and gripped the back of his neck. He nodded after a minute. He'd never admitted to himself how much he missed her, but Mason was right. He'd compared every woman he'd been with to her, and all of them fell far short. He wanted to find her, but he didn't have a chance to. She was it for him. She always had been.

"So, tell her that. Tell her it wasn't just sex for you. Tell her you want both of them in your life. Women need to know that shit."

Rocky shook his head. "I can't. If I spooked her already, I can't make it worse by telling her I'm in love with her."

"Are you?"

Rocky drew in a breath and shrugged. "I don't know. Maybe? I could be."

"Make sure you know before you start talking. Because 'maybe' or 'I could be' aren't good ways to tell a woman you love her."

"I'm not going to tell her anything. Especially if she ignores me forever."

"Okay, let's put your ego aside for just a minute and think about everything rationally. Yes, you slept with her last night, but she's also been threatened by someone else."

"And there was the car outside her building," Rocky remembered.

"What car?"

"Shit. I forgot about it this morning when I got up. When I left last night, there was a car in her lot. I told myself it was nothing, but I don't know."

"Did you get a plate? Make and model? Anything?"

Rocky sighed. "No. The lights were off until they pulled out of the lot so I couldn't see the plate. It was dark. Black SUV. New. It was definitely less than five years old. Maybe a Toyota."

Rocky was already running a search. "No one who lives there drives a black Toyota."

"What about something else? Mazda, Honda, Hyundai?"

Mason shook his head. "Nothing new and nothing black. There are a few blue ones, but they're older. Most of the residents in her building drive cars or pickups."

"Fuck. What if something else is going on?"

"We need to go over there," Mason said. "Now."

14

———

Rocky's heart pounded in his chest the entire drive to Nikki's. He couldn't believe he was stupid enough to think this had anything to do with him. The woman he loved and their son were in danger, and he convinced himself she was just upset that they slept together.

Mason insisted on driving, which left Rocky with nothing to do but wait. It was the right call, and he knew it, but it still pissed him off to sit there and not race through the streets. When Mason parked, Rocky was out of the SUV and on his way up the stairs before Mason even got out.

He pulled up short at Nikki's door and knocked on it, resisting the urge to pick the lock and let himself in.

Rocky strained to hear something but inside was quiet. He pressed his ear to the door to listen for something, anything. He knocked again and swore he heard a gasp or some other soft sound.

"Nikki. Nikki, it's me. It's Rocky. Are you guys okay? Let me in."

Mason caught up to him and raised an eyebrow in question. Rocky shook his head and waited.

"Her car is here," Mason said.

Rocky glanced at the parking lot and saw her blue sedan. He closed his eyes and said a prayer that they were okay and knocked again.

"Nikki, please. I need to see you guys."

He held his breath and nearly collapsed when he heard movement inside and the door unlocked and swung open.

There she was, standing in front of him, wearing her pajamas like she'd just gotten out of bed. Her hand was on top of Sly's head, holding him to her side. Her gaze flickered behind Rocky to Mason, then to the ground.

Relief flooded his system. He couldn't have stopped himself from wrapping her in his arms if he tried, but he didn't try. He needed to hold her and convince himself she was okay. That they were okay.

"I was worried about you," he whispered in her ear. "Don't shut me out, okay?"

She nodded against him and slid one arm around his waist, still holding Sly with the other. Rocky put an arm around Sly and held both of them to him, his heart throbbing with love for them.

"Are you okay?" he asked when his own shaking subsided enough that he could feel hers.

She nodded and pulled back. She kept her face from them and stepped back to let them inside. Rocky stepped in first, tickling Sly as he moved into the apartment. Sly said hi and hugged him, then high-fived Mason.

"Dude, I think you got bigger since I've seen you," Mason told Sly. He held his hands torso height apart. "Last time I saw you, you were only this big."

Sly giggled and shook his head. "That's because I was in bed."

"You lazy thing. Why were you laying in bed all the time? You need to be up. No wonder you're so much bigger."

Sly laughed with Mason and grabbed his hand, dragging him to the couch. Mason sat gingerly on the edge of the sofa that looked fragile enough for him to break with his massive frame. He nodded at Rocky to go see Nikki.

He didn't need to be told twice. She was in the kitchen, staring into the fridge.

"I tried to call you," Rocky said.

Nikki jumped but tried to hide it. "I turned my phone off. After... um, everything, I wanted a day with Sly. We've spent a lot of days with doctors and me working and school and everything. We don't have a lot of time just the two of us."

Rocky nodded. "I understand. I was just worried about you guys."

"Why?" she asked, her voice hesitant.

Rocky crossed his arms and leaned against the counter. "Because I care about you."

Nikki held his gaze for a long moment. She finally drew a breath and smiled, but it looked forced. "We're fine. Sorry I worried you." She ducked her head again and turned back to the fridge.

Rocky could tell something wasn't right, but he knew she didn't want to talk to him about whatever it was. Maybe he wasn't off-base thinking she was avoiding him. And instead of giving her her space, he showed up and beat down her door and demanded to be let in.

"I forgot to go to the store today," Nikki said after a minute. "I promised Sly meatloaf, but I don't have everything I need. Crap."

Rocky chuckled. "I'm sure he'll understand. Why don't we all go out?"

Nikki snorted and gestured to her clothes. "I'm not exactly ready to go out anywhere."

Rocky's gaze slid down her body, and he hardened. He remembered every moment of their night together and was more than willing to help her get ready to go out or stay in or do just about anything. Especially if it meant getting her naked again.

"Nope," Nikki said, breaking into Rocky's mind. "Not going there."

Rocky looked up at her and raised an eyebrow at the blush staining her cheeks.

"I don't have anything for us to eat here so I guess going out is our only option, but I'm getting dressed without assistance. You can sit in the living room with the other men."

Rocky grumbled but didn't argue. He did wait for her to try to sneak past him and caught her around the waist. He pulled her in close and pressed his nose to her throat. "You smell amazing."

She snorted. "It's just my soap. It's nothing special."

"You're special, Nikki."

She tilted her head back and gave him a look that said the line missed the mark completely.

Rocky chuckled and forced himself to let her go. He didn't want to, but pushing too hard wouldn't get him where he wanted to be.

Nikki hurried to her room, and Rocky joined Mason and Sly on the couch. It creaked when he sat down, and Mason gave him a look. A new couch was definitely in order for them.

"What are we watching?" Rocky asked. He wasn't up on shows that kids liked, so he had no idea who the characters were.

"They're dogs who save the people in their town," Mason provided. "Each dog has a special talent, and the kid helps them."

"And the dogs talk?" Rocky asked.

Mason nodded. "Of course."

Rocky grinned back at Mason and settled in to watch. He figured Nikki would be awhile and didn't want to be impatient with her. He was surprised when she was back out right at the crucial part of the episode.

"Mommy, can we wait and see the end?" Sly asked, never taking his eyes off the TV.

Rocky, on the other hand, couldn't take his eyes off Nikki. She'd changed into a pair of jeans that hugged her curves. Her tan sweater slid off one shoulder to reveal a black tank underneath. She had black booties on and had brushed and fluffed her hair. He was fairly sure she added a little makeup, too, although he didn't think she needed it.

"Sure," Nikki said after she looked at the three of them. Her gaze slid over Rocky like she didn't want to look at him.

Rocky forced himself to look away instead of continuing to stare at her. He was starting to worry himself with all the ways he was watching her.

Sly was wrapped up in the show, and Nikki disappeared into the kitchen again. Rocky wanted to go in and talk to her, but he had nothing to say. He just wanted to be close to her.

As soon as the credits started for the show, Rocky was on his feet and ready to go. He called out to Nikki so he could get his eyes on her again. He was gone, and it was painfully obvious. He was sure he was going to send her running.

"Come on, little man, let's head out," Mason said to Sly.

"Grab a jacket," Nikki called.

Sly snagged a zip up hoodie from the hooks near the

front door and followed Mason out of the apartment. They waited on the walkway while Nikki locked the door, and they all walked downstairs together.

"Where do you guys want to go?" Rocky asked just to make conversation.

"Cheeseburgers!" Sly shouted.

"Sly," Nikki said in that stern mom voice.

"I like cheeseburgers," Mason said. "I like pretty much everything."

"Do you like milkshakes?" Sly asked.

"Oh, yeah. Chocolate is the best."

"Nuh-uh. Vanilla."

"How about Oreo?" Mason asked.

"Yeah, yeah," Sly agreed, his eyes wide with excitement.

"Sly, come with me," Nikki said when they made it to the parking lot.

"We can all ride together. We have an SUV," Rocky said.

Nikki shook her head. "He has to be in a booster seat."

"Can we move it to the SUV?"

"Yeah, Mommy, can we? Please?" Sly joined in.

"It's not easy to get in and out of the car," Nikki said.

"Why don't I do that?" Mason suggested. "I've done it a few times."

Rocky gave him a questioning look, but Mason didn't elaborate.

Nikki finally huffed a sigh and shook her head. "I guess I have no choice."

Mason and Sly hurried to Nikki's car to retrieve the booster, but Rocky hung back. "You always have a choice," Rocky said quietly.

She breathed a laugh. "Really? With the three of you?"

Rocky stopped her in the parking lot and turned her to face him. "Yes, Nikki. Always. I want to spend time with you two, as much as possible. I'm pushy when I want something. I should probably back off and give you a break, but I don't want you to slip away."

Her brows went up. She crossed her arms and leaned back. "So this is because I left that night."

"What? No. What are you talking about?"

"You just said you don't want me to slip away. Like I did seven years ago?"

"I didn't mean it that way. I just mean, I know you have a life. You have a job and Sly has school and I'm inserting myself into your world. I feel like I need to force my way in, but doing that makes me feel like I'm pushing too hard. But I can't seem to stop because I don't want to lose either of you."

Nikki drew in a breath and closed her eyes. She nodded and said, "I'm sorry. I'm not used to anyone wanting to be a part of our lives. No one has yet, and it's not easy for me to let someone in. Even you. Maybe especially you."

"Why especially me?"

She chuckled and gestured to him. Rocky looked down, but he didn't see anything that would explain what Nikki wasn't saying. "You're a badass. You're strong and gorgeous and smart and kind. You're the dream dad, the parent every kid wants to bring to school for career day because all the other kids will be jealous that their dad is something stupid like a doctor or a lawyer or something. Sly is already in love with you, and your friends, and I'm just Mommy. I'm no one special."

Rocky moved closer and licked his lips. "You think I'm gorgeous?"

Nikki laughed. "All that, and the only thing you got out of it was you're gorgeous?"

Rocky shook his head. "Not even close, but I just want to

make sure I heard that part correctly. Next, we're going to talk about how special you are. And then maybe I can find out if I'm your dream instead of just Sly's."

Nikki sucked in a ragged breath that lifted her chest to Rocky's. Her breath huffed out, drifting over his face. They were close enough that he could kiss her without moving far, and he wanted to. He wanted to throw her over his shoulder and carry her back upstairs and tell Mason to take Sly out to dinner because he was having Nikki instead.

But before he could do anything, a car pulled into the lot and reminded Rocky of everything that sent him to her door that evening.

NICOLE SAW the change in his eyes before he took a step back. She was grateful for it, but she didn't like it. She wanted him close, to feel his breath on her face and know she was safe with him around. As long as safe didn't mean she wasn't risking her heart.

If that was the case, she would never be safe with him.

The car drove by and pulled into a parking space at the far end of the lot. A young couple got out and reached into the back for bags of groceries. Rocky watched them like he was waiting for them to turn and attack. His body was tense until the girl laughed and shoved the guy's arm and they headed for the stairs.

"Are you okay?" Nicole asked. The car scared her, too, but Rocky's fear almost made her feel like hers wasn't as bad. She wasn't sure about leaving the apartment, but being with Rocky and Mason gave her courage. No one would mess with her with them around. She hoped.

Rocky drew a breath and shook his head. "Sorry. I'm

fine. Do you know anyone who drives a black SUV. Maybe a Toyota? Something fairly new. Do you have a neighbor with a vehicle like that?"

Nicole shook her head, unable to picture the vehicle in her mind. "I'm not really sure. Why?"

He tapped something on his phone and turned the screen to her. She shook her head slowly, then paused. Zeke drove something that looked like that.

"You recognize it?" Rocky asked, picking up on her hesitation.

"Not exactly. I don't know. Why?"

"Someone who lives here drives a vehicle like this?"

She shook her head before she thought better of it.

"Nikki, talk to me."

"There's nothing to talk about," she insisted, brushing past him. She knew he could easily grab her arm and force her to talk, but that was one of the things she liked most about him. He let her have her space, even when she wasn't sure she wanted it.

All morning, between bouts of fear, she was trying to figure out what happened between them the night before. It wasn't just hormones. She was grown up enough to admit that to herself. But she didn't jump into bed with men, ever. He was important to her, and even more important to Sly, and she couldn't sleep with him again.

And the only way she would be able to follow through on that was if she put space between them and kept it that way. She couldn't fall into him again and let him soothe all the sore spots inside her. She needed to fix the mess she'd gotten into on her own, and not get Rocky in the middle of it.

And if that meant lying about recognizing Zeke's SUV without knowing why Rocky was asking, and not telling him about the phone call she got earlier, she would have to deal with that.

By the time she reached the SUV, Mason had Sly buckled into the backseat. She opened the door to sit next to him, but he stopped her.

"No, Mommy, I want Daddy to sit with me."

His simple request about ripped her in two, but she was doing all this for her son. She was resisting the man she wanted more than she wanted a breath of fresh air so her son could build a relationship with him. She would make it work, and she would not stand in their way.

Nicole sidestepped Rocky and sat in the front. She wanted to run back upstairs and hide from all of them, but she wasn't that trusting yet.

Rocky slid in the back next to Sly and immediately started asking him questions and making him laugh. Nicole stared out the window and smiled at her son's joy. Things were simple for a six year old, especially for a six year old who wasn't sure if he would make it to seven not that long ago. He wanted to enjoy whatever life handed him, and he lived life that way.

Nicole wished she could have an ounce of his innocence and pleasure. She'd never been so free in her life. Even as a kid, she always knew her parents judged her. They wanted what was best for her, but their version of what was best. That was why she left when she was pregnant. Her dad's first reaction was to slap her for getting pregnant. Her mother comforted him for being so upset instead of Nicole for being hurt.

She packed her things that night and left the town she called home for good. She never looked back and never regretted that decision, but she also never got over it.

Parents were supposed to protect their children and love

them unconditionally. She was determined to raise her son in a home where that was the rule instead of the exception. And she had.

But a part of that meant letting him go when he needed something she couldn't give him. Like a father.

"Rocky's a good guy," Mason said quietly. "He'll be a great dad."

Nicole looked at the massive man next to her and saw a kindred spirit in his eyes. He'd known pain, deep, unfathomable, never-ending pain. She hated it for him because he seemed like a gentle man, the kind of man who wouldn't hurt anyone unless it was truly called for. She was happy to have someone like him there and watching out for her.

"Thanks."

He nodded and turned his focus back to the road. She stared out the window and watched the world go by as her son got to know his father. He had a life in New York. Friends, a job, a home. And he was giving it all up so he could move and be a part of their lives.

But what kind of life did they have in Tennessee? Nicole's job was only good enough to pay the bills, Sly apparently hated his school, and they had no family or friends. Did it really make sense for her to ask him to move?

Or should she seriously consider Sly's idea and move to New York? Where Rocky, and his friends, would be there to keep them safe from the man on the other end of the phone.

15

———

THE HOSTESS LED THEM TO A SEAT AND TOLD THEM A SERVER would be right over. Nicole was glad they were at a table instead of a booth, until Sly asked to sit next to Mason and Rocky.

"You don't want to sit next to your mom?" Mason asked.

Sly shook his head. "No, I want to sit next to you and my daddy."

Both men looked at her as though asking permission, but Nicole just shrugged and forced a smile. It wasn't like she could throw a fit in the middle of the restaurant because her son was attached to the new men in his life.

Nicole opened her menu and looked at the options. Immediately, she turned to the kids' menu and tried to figure out something Sly would want to eat. Once she decided on an option for him, she scanned through and chose something for herself.

Their server came over and took drink orders. When he walked away, Rocky asked Sly what he was going to eat.

"Pizza," Sly said.

Rocky looked at Nicole for confirmation. "Pizza is fine,

but you need to eat some vegetables, too. How about broccoli?"

"Yuck," Sly said. "I don't want vegetables."

"You don't like vegetables?" Mason asked. Sly shook his head. "You're missing out. Vegetables are delicious. They get a bad rap because they're healthy, but being healthy is pretty awesome. You should eat more vegetables."

"Really?" Sly asked.

Mason nodded. "We eat a ton of vegetables. All of us do. They give you energy without a crash later and they make you strong." Mason flexed. "Do you think I could get these muscles from cake?"

Sly giggled.

"He's right," Rocky added. "I was going to get a big salad for dinner with a cheeseburger. I thought we came here because you wanted a cheeseburger and now you're going for pizza."

Sly nodded, his eyes wide as he took in everything the men said. Nicole almost laughed at how easy it was for them to convince him to eat his veggies. If they only knew.

"I want a cheeseburger and broccoli," Sly announced.

"Sounds good," the server said as he passed out the drinks. "Should I write that down, dads?"

Nicole raised an eyebrow at Rocky when he looked at her. She crossed her arms and leaned back in her seat.

"Um, yeah," Rocky said. "That sounds good."

"Okay, what can I get everyone else?" the server asked.

When they were done ordering, Rocky asked, "Do you guys come here a lot?"

Nicole shook her head. "We don't go out a lot."

"Mommy always says we don't have enough money."

Nicole's cheeks burned with the truth. They didn't. She barely scraped by most of the time, and facing Rocky with that truth was hard. She felt like she hadn't done right by their son by not being better off.

"I'm sorry," Rocky said softly.

Nicole shrugged and ignored him, pulling out a small coloring book and a bag of crayons for Sly to keep himself busy. She learned a long time ago that if she didn't have something for him to do, he would want to watch videos on her phone.

Sly found a page and opened the bag and started coloring without question. Mason grabbed a crayon and asked if he could color with him. Sly nodded and moved his arm out of the way for Mason to have space.

They spoke softly to each other, quiet enough that Nicole couldn't hear every word of their conversation over the restaurant noise. She hadn't been out in so long that she felt uncomfortable, like people would know she wasn't supposed to be there.

"What do you guys normally do in the evenings?"

Nicole shrugged. "Watch TV and eat dinner. If he was in school, he'd work on homework."

"How late does his school day usually go?"

"He's done at three, but I work until five, so he's in an after-school program."

"Is he on a break from school right now?"

She shook her head and drank her water. It was easier on the budget, and she allowed Sly to drink something else since it was a treat to go out. "With the surgery, he's out of school for a while. Dr. Andrews wants to make sure he's doing well before letting him go back. Although, he was telling me today that he doesn't want to go back because he hates school."

Rocky glanced at Sly, who was still distracted by his coloring, and asked, "What's going on?"

Nicole shrugged. "I guess he gets picked on. I had no idea. He said the other kids don't like him and don't want to be friends with him. I just…"

Rocky covered her hand with his and squeezed it until she looked up at him. "You're an amazing mother. God, you've raised him to be polite and respectful. He's a happy kid. You should be very proud of yourself, and of him. All kids get picked on at some point."

"I don't know if I believe that."

Rocky nodded. "All I know is I did, and so did my sisters."

"You have sisters?"

He nodded again. "I do. I'm the oldest, but I have two sisters. And they got picked on when we were younger. Kids are mean, and sometimes those mean kids grow out of it and sometimes they're just mean. But that's about them, not about the person they're picking on."

"Yeah, well, as a mom, I don't care who it's about. I don't want my son to go through it."

"Have you thought about changing schools?"

Nicole shook her head. "I can't afford it. We would either have to move or I'd have to take him to school every day."

"Maybe I can buy a house in the district you want him to be in. Then he can use my address, or you guys can just move in with me—"

"Yeah, I want to do that," Sly said, looking up at them. "Can we, Mommy, please? Can we move in with Daddy? If we don't move to New York, can we move in with him since our apartment is too small?"

"Moving to New York? What is he talking about?" Rocky asked.

Nicole shook her head. "He asked me earlier if we could move to New York since he doesn't like his school here."

"Is that what you want to do? I would never ask you to do that."

Nicole shrugged. "I don't know. All of this... I don't know."

The food was delivered, giving Nicole a reprieve. She focused on her dinner instead of on where the conversation ended up. She was never that woman who moved across the country for a guy, but the guy was never her son before. She'd already said goodbye to one hometown for her son, and even though she'd never felt at home in Knoxville, she wasn't sure she was ready to move again.

THE REST of dinner mostly involved getting Sly to eat his broccoli and keeping him from bouncing out of his seat instead of talking to each other. Rocky wanted to ask Nikki more about moving to New York, but he could tell she didn't want to talk about it in front of Sly.

When they got back to her apartment, Sly asked if both Mason and Rocky could come up.

"It's late, Sly," Nikki told him. "You need to get to bed soon."

"Yeah, but maybe they can come up and we can all watch a movie, and then they can read a book to me or something."

Nikki didn't look like she wanted to agree, but she looked even less like she wanted to argue with Sly. Rocky wanted her to agree, so he didn't help her come up with an excuse for them not to go upstairs. Even though Mason would be there, he still wanted a little extra time with Sly and Nikki.

"A short movie," Nikki said sternly.

Sly nodded and whooped, racing up the stairs first. Nikki made him change into his pajamas and brush his teeth before he bounced onto the couch to watch a movie.

Mason chose a spot on the floor, and Sly slid off the couch to sit next to him. Nikki sat on the edge of the couch and flipped through the family movies on the screen, going right past all of Sly's choices as they came up.

She finally selected something and pressed play. Rocky thought she might get up again and go do something to avoid being around them, but she settled back against the couch and tucked her feet under her.

He watched her more than the movie, observing as the tension eased from her. She stared at the screen and relaxed more and more with each passing second. He wished he could take all her tension away, but he didn't know what she needed.

When the quick movie ended, Sly was half-asleep and leaning against Mason. "Rock," Mason said softly, drawing Rocky's attention to them.

"Is it okay if I pick him up?" Rocky asked Nikki.

She started to nod, then stopped. "Can you be lifting that much weight?"

Rocky nodded, choosing not to remind her that he lifted her up the night before.

Nikki nodded and said, "Thank you. I usually have to wake him up to get him to go to bed. I can't pick him up anymore."

"I got him," Rocky said as he hoisted Sly into his arms. He burrowed against him and snuggled in like they'd been doing the same thing Sly's whole life. In that instant, Rocky saw all the things he'd missed out on. First steps, first words. Sleepless nights and his illness. He looked up at Nikki and found her watching them, tears in her eyes. Rocky kissed the top of Sly's head and resisted the urge to sit down on the couch and just hold him all night.

He hated how much he'd missed.

He took a breath and stepped over Mason's leg and carried Sly to his room. He laid him down on the bed and covered him up with the blankets. Sly looked up at him, then turned onto his side and hugged the blankets to his chest. Rocky rested his hand on Sly's back and drew in a breath. He held it, then let it out slowly, feeling for Sly's breaths at the same time.

"I don't know how you do it," Rocky said softly, knowing Nikki was watching them. "I don't know how you live with this much love inside you. I've only known him a few weeks and I can't imagine my life without him. How did you survive him being sick?"

"It wasn't easy," Nikki said softly, her voice cracking.

Rocky looked up at her and drew another deep breath. The lights from the living room framed her, making her glow with the harsh backlighting. Her hair glistened the same way the tears on her cheeks did. She just stood in the doorway and watched them.

Rocky finally lifted his hand from Sly's back and went to Nikki. She didn't move from the doorway as he walked closer. When he reached her, he slid an arm around her waist and pressed his forehead to hers. "I love him so much, Nikki."

She nodded. "I know."

"I can't imagine a life without you two in it."

"He'll always be in your life if you want him to be."

"And you?"

She shrugged. "I'm not going anywhere."

"Except maybe to New York."

She let out a sigh and shrugged. "It was something Sly

said earlier. He doesn't like his school so he wants to leave, and he's latched on to this idea that we can just pick up and move to New York because that's where you are. But I don't know if you're staying there or if you want us there or if I even want to move there. There are a lot of questions."

Rocky pulled her closer so their bodies touched. He needed to feel her against him. He wrapped his other arm around her neck and held her tight, finally taking a breath when she slid her arms around his waist and held him.

"First, I want you wherever you want to be. If you'd rather move to Texas, I'll be there. If you're thinking Wisconsin, sign me up. Nothing here is about what I want. You're in charge, Nikki. With all of it. Second, I'm out of the Navy. I work as a civilian now, and I work with other former SEALs, but I choose where I live, not the US Government, so, if it weren't for you guys, I'd be staying in New York. But I want to be near you. And that means I'm moving wherever you want to be."

She nodded against his chest and inhaled deeply.

"Third, and most importantly, like I already said, you're in charge. If you don't want to move, I'll come here. If you want to try New York, I'm good with that, too. If you want to go somewhere else, I hope you'll let me come with you. I don't want to interrupt your life. I want to be a part of it, but I don't want to mess it up."

"All you've done is make my life better," she whispered. "You gave me the best thing in my life. You gave me Sly, and then you saved him when I should have lost him. I owe you everything."

"No, baby, you don't," Rocky said softly, tilting her face up to look at her. "You don't owe me a thing. I thought I was donating to a stranger, and you gave me the best thing ever by telling me who he was. You've already given me more than I could have asked for."

She smiled and closed her eyes when he swiped at her tears.

"Nikki, I—"

"Ahem." Mason cleared his throat loudly.

Rocky wanted to punch the guy. He was seconds from telling Nikki he loved her, the words halfway out of his mouth, and Mason chose that moment to interrupt.

"Sorry, but we need to head out," Mason said, holding up his phone.

"What's going on?"

"Dunn needs us to call him."

"Now?" Rocky asked.

Mason nodded. "Yeah, he said something about the case they are working on. He needs a few more eyes on something. We have to head out."

Rocky sighed heavily and turned back to Nikki. The emotional walls were back up, and she was pulling away again. The moment was gone.

"It's fine," she said. "This is what I'm talking about. You have important work to do."

"I meant what I said, Nikki. You're in charge. You choose what you want to do. And until you decide, I'll be here."

Nikki nodded and walked them to the door. She thanked them for dinner and for spending time with them, then closed and locked the door.

Rocky let his mind replay the night over and over again on the drive back to the hotel. He couldn't walk away from them. Yes, he got a rush when Mason said Dunn called and they needed to go, but it was nothing compared to the rush he felt when he picked Sly up and carried him to his room.

Or the rush he felt when he slid into Nikki and felt her come around him.

He finally knew what the other guys were talking about when they said love replaced everything else. Rocky didn't think twice about leaving F-BOMB. Not if it meant he had Nikki and Sly in his life.

They made it into the hotel room, and Rocky went to the computer in the dining room. Mason went to the fridge and grabbed a beer.

"What are you doing? I thought we needed to call Dunn?"

Mason shook his head. "I lied. You just needed to get the hell out of there."

"What are you talking about?"

Mason raised one eyebrow and spread his feet wide, ready for a fight. "You were about to tell her you love her, weren't you?"

"What the hell business is it of yours?"

"It's not, but I know a thing or two about women. And one of the things I know is that when you say I love you, it has to be for all the right reasons. Telling a woman that isn't for her. It's usually for you, because you can't keep the words inside any longer."

Rocky grumbled, neither confirming nor denying Mason's statement.

"You told her she was in charge, that she was going to make the decision about where you guys all end up. Then you were going to tell her that you love her."

"Why is that wrong?" Rocky asked.

"Because this is a woman who's been on her own for years. She has no one in her life. Her son is choosing you and me over his mother. Her parents aren't here anymore. She has no support system, no friends or family. For all intents and purposes, she's starved for love and affection. She's a lonely woman. And you're going to tell her you love her."

Rocky closed his eyes as Mason's words sank in. "I'm not trying to manipulate her."

Mason shrugged. "I didn't say you were. All I'm saying is you need to think about what you say and when."

"So, you think I should wait until after she makes a decision to tell her I'm in love with her."

"I can't tell you what to do. What I can tell you is that when you're on your own, and you feel like you have no one in the world you can count on, it's hard not to latch on to the first person who's nice to you."

Rocky narrowed his gaze and focused on Mason. Mason drank his beer and sat on the couch. He turned on the TV and effectively ended the conversation.

But Rocky knew he didn't need to say anything else. Mason got his point across. If Rocky really wanted Nikki to make the best decision for Sly and herself, Rocky needed to keep from influencing her with his emotions. And that was going to be easier said than done.

16

———

THE FOLLOWING MORNING FELT LIKE GROUNDHOG DAY FOR Nicole. Another argument with Sly about school and more questions about why they couldn't move to be with Rocky. The only change was she didn't get any phone calls that threatened them. She figured it was going to be a good day.

Since Sly was still fighting her on getting school done, she told him they would go to the grocery store when he was done and he could pick out anything he wanted for dinner. She learned her lesson about leaving things too open the day before.

"Anything?" he asked again.

Nicole nodded. "Yes. Anything. For dinner."

"Okay," Sly said simply before he started doing his work.

Nicole breathed a sigh and tried not to feel guilty about bribing her son. She felt like a bad parent for not being able to encourage him without giving him something, but she was out of options and figured it wouldn't be that bad.

She was wrong.

"This is what I want," Sly said later, standing in front of the steaks.

"Steak? You want steak? Why in the world would you want steak?"

"Because Rocky said he loves it. I thought we could cook it for him and maybe he'll love us and want to move in with us."

Her heart broke right there in the middle of the grocery store. Nicole was trying her hardest not to fall in love with Rocky, and Sly was jumping in with both feet. Blindly. Happily.

"He already loves you, Sly. You don't have to worry about that."

"Maybe he'll love you, too, if you cook him this."

Nicole smiled at him and hugged him to her side. "Why is that important to you?"

"Because if he loves you, he'll marry you and then we can all live together and you won't be alone."

Nicole sucked in a breath and smiled at her son. If only it was that simple.

Nicole bought the steaks and cut a few other things from her list so she could afford them. Sly grinned the entire time and was riding high when they walked outside into the bright fall sunshine.

Sly helped her put the groceries in her trunk, then wanted to push the empty cart to the corral. It wasn't until they were walking back to her car that they noticed the man watching them.

He parked right next to them and got out of his vehicle when they were walking over. "Hey, Nicole. Hi, Sly."

Sly hugged her side. Nicole looked at the man and asked, "Do we know you?"

He shook his head and leaned against his bumper. She could get around him, but it would mean getting very close to him, and she wasn't willing to do that.

"We've spoken before, but we've never met. I figured it was time to see what Zeke was so obsessed with." His gaze took a slow glide down and back up her body. "Now I understand."

Nicole's skin crawled, and the voice clicked in her head. "You're his boss."

The man grinned. He pushed off the bumper and extended his hand to her. "It's nice to finally meet you in person."

She noticed he didn't say his name. Sly squeezed her tighter. She ignored the man's hand. "What do you want?"

He finally dropped his hand and smiled again. "Just wondering what my best option is. We had an agreement, but I think we can amend it. You can work it off, directly for me."

"That's not going to work for me," Nicole said.

He laughed mirthlessly and shook his head at her. "You make it sound like you have a choice, Nicole."

Fear and dread slithered down her spine.

"What are you going to do? Tell the police? I wouldn't recommend that."

"She's going to tell my daddy," Sly said boldly.

The man looked down at Sly as if he just realized he was there, and wasn't happy about it. His scowl made Nicole want to piss herself.

"Adrian Malone is of no concern to me," the man hissed. "And neither are you."

"Stay away from us," Nicole said firmly. She led Sly to the other side of the car and hurried him inside, telling him to buckle up. She raced around the front and pulled away without putting on her own seatbelt.

In the mirror, she watched the man watch them. She

knew he wasn't out of their lives, but she needed to put physical space between them.

She finally stopped checking her mirrors when she pulled onto her street. It didn't matter where she went or what she did. He knew a lot about her, maybe everything. And he wasn't backing off.

They carried their groceries upstairs and put everything away. Only then did Sly ask about the man.

"Who was he?"

"He's my friend's boss."

"I didn't like him. He wasn't very nice."

Nicole shook her head. "No, he wasn't. Are you done with everything for school?"

"Yeah, can I watch TV?"

"Sure," Nicole said. She needed a break, and even though she couldn't get one, letting him watch TV would help a little. She was really winning mom of the year. First she bribed him, then she let the TV babysit him.

Nicole went to her room to get her computer and brought it back to the dining room so she could do some paperwork. She was supposed to go back to work in less than a week, and she needed to make sure everything was in order.

When her phone rang, Nicole jumped. She didn't remember turning the ringer on, and after the call yesterday and the visit, she was extra jumpy.

Until she saw Rocky's name. "Hello?"

"Hey, it's Rocky. How are you guys today?"

"Good," Nicole lied. "How are you? Did you take care of whatever you were doing with work last night?"

Rocky mumbled something she couldn't hear, then said, "All good. Hey, so, Mason leaves tomorrow and was wondering if we could get together later."

"Um, yeah, sure. We actually have food to cook for dinner if that works for you guys."

"You don't have to do that," Rocky said.

Nicole grinned. "We already bought food. Sly wanted to cook tonight. We don't usually go out to eat a lot."

"Well, what can we bring? You don't need to feed us all the time."

"Wine," Nicole said instantly.

Rocky barked a laugh. "We can do that. Anything else? Salad, pasta, something?"

"Yeah, any of that works. Whatever you think."

"Okay. We'll head to the store and be over soon. Thanks, Nikki."

Nicole nodded and smiled. "See you soon."

"Is Rocky and Mason coming over?" Sly asked.

"Are Rocky and Mason coming over?" Nicole corrected him. "Yes, they are. They going to run to the store and get some vegetables for dinner and then they'll be here. Why don't you take a quick bath?"

"Do I have to?"

Nicole nodded. "Yes. Come on. It can be quick. Let's go."

"Can I take a shower instead?"

Nicole shrugged. "Sure. As long as you clean yourself."

"I can do it myself," Sly insisted.

"Really?"

Sly nodded and tried to close the bathroom door between them.

"Sly, let me in. I won't mess with you, but I need to know you're clean."

"Fine," he huffed.

Nicole went through the motions of getting the water ready and helped Sly in since it was slippery. He knew how to wash, but she still wanted to be there in case he needed help.

He was done, and in his room getting dressed when Rocky and Mason knocked on the door. Nicole told Sly to hurry up while she went and answered the door.

"Hey," Rocky said, looking like something she dreamed up. He wore a tight navy blue tee with jeans faded in all the right spots. But the best part was the heated look in his eyes that instantly lit Nicole on fire.

"Hi," she breathed, leaning toward him instead of stepping back to let him in. She pressed her lips quickly to his, taking advantage of his hands being full. She hadn't allowed herself to think about how much she missed him, but staring at him in that moment, she was overwhelmed with how much she had.

"Let me set this down so I can do that properly," Rocky said, his voice dropping low and sexy.

Nicole finally took a step back and let him in, her cheeks burning when Mason was right behind him and clearly witnessed everything. He just grinned at her.

Rocky and Mason went to the kitchen and set everything they brought on the counter. She wondered what it all was since it seemed like enough food to feed all of them for a week, not just something for dinner.

Before she could ask, Rocky looked around and asked, "Where's Sly?"

"He's getting dressed. He just took a shower."

"Come here," Rocky said in the next second, wrapping an arm around her waist and cupping her jaw with the other hand. He didn't give her a moment to resist, and she didn't need one.

Nicole felt safe in his arms, like Zeke's boss couldn't hurt her. She shivered as Rocky's lips touched hers. He gently teased them apart and slid his tongue inside. He kissed like he wasn't worried at all about her stopping him. Like he knew she was barely hanging on by a thread.

She held him and kissed him and felt that thread snap. Everything that kept her from falling for him was gone, and she was sunk. The father of her child was kissing her like he had every right to do it forever, and she couldn't deny that he did. That he was the only one who'd ever owned her that way.

He gentled their kiss and pulled back when there was a noise in Sly's room. By the time he opened his bedroom door, Rocky was ready to turn around and scoop him up.

Nicole fell for him even more. He wasn't just trying to get into her pants, or her heart, he was there for Sly, too. He was doing everything she always hoped would happen if she met the right guy.

"How was your day?" Rocky asked Sly, holding him on his hip so they were eye-to-eye.

Sly shook his head and scowled. "I didn't like Mommy's friend's boss. He wasn't very nice. He scared me."

Rocky's brows went up and his gaze swung to Nicole's. "You didn't tell me about that. What happened?"

ROCKY'S PULSE roared in his ears. He didn't give Nikki much time to tell him anything with his tongue down her throat, but he thought she would have mentioned something on the phone or when he arrived. Instead, he had to hear it from Sly.

"It wasn't a big deal," Nikki said.

Rocky wasn't buying it. Sly was scared, and Nikki didn't look like she was much better. If she wasn't going to tell him, Rocky was going to have to ask someone who would. "What happened, Sly?"

Sly told him everything, from negotiating for school to Sly wanting steaks, and everything the man said when he was talking to Nikki.

Rocky hugged Sly to him and kissed the side of his head. "I'm so happy you're okay. I'm sorry he scared you."

"It's okay. I wish you were with us. Mommy wasn't scared, though."

Rocky looked at Nikki and saw the truth on her face. He set Sly down and said, "Why don't you show Mason your room? Read him your favorite book."

Mason took the hint and reached for Sly's hand, letting Sly lead him to the bedroom.

Rocky reached for Nikki again. "Why didn't you tell me?"

She turned away from him and busied herself unloading the bags they brought with food for dinner. "I handled it."

"I'm not saying you didn't," Rocky assured her. "But I want to know what's going on."

"I fucked up, okay? I never should have tried to get him a kidney that way. I should have waited and trusted that everything would work out."

She was nearly in tears and shaking. Rocky hated seeing her like that, and hated himself for making her feel that way.

He stepped up behind her and wrapped his arms around her waist. He curled his body around hers, covering her. He rested his chin on her shoulder and kissed her cheek.

"You are an amazing mother. You were doing what you

needed to do to save your son's life. I would never question that. You did not fuck up, Nikki."

"I did," she breathed. "I shouldn't have gone to them. I shouldn't have tried to do something illegal. I knew there was a risk with it, but I—"

"You thought you were out of options. I get it. I would have done the same thing if I were you. Nikki, I need you to understand something." Rocky backed up and tugged at her until she turned in his arms. He cupped her jaw and waited until she met his gaze.

"What?"

"I want to know about your day because I want to be able to keep you safe, baby. I will never blame you for those sons of bitches thinking they can come anywhere near you two. That is not your fault. But I want to know. I hate the thought of you being in danger. These people are dangerous. I don't like them threatening you. I don't like anyone threatening you. If you tell me what you know about them, we can help you. We can take care of this. It's what we do every day."

She swallowed roughly and a single tear slid down her cheek. Rocky pulled her into his arms and kissed the top of her head. "I was so scared," she whispered.

"I've got you, sweetheart. I'm not going anywhere. I'm here, Nikki. I... I'm here."

He held her tight while she cried in his arms. It gutted him to know how strong she'd been for so long and to have her think she did anything wrong. She was the strongest woman he'd ever met, and she was an unbelievable mom.

Mason cleared his throat loudly, giving Rocky a warning that they were on their way back. Nikki pulled away from him and turned her focus to the counter and the food they brought. Sly effectively ignored her and asked Rocky if he could show him something.

"I was going to help your mom get dinner ready," Rocky said.

"I'll help Nikki," Mason said. "I'm a better cook than you, anyway."

Rocky didn't like walking away from her when she was still upset, but it was clear she didn't want Sly to know she was crying. Reluctantly, Rocky let Sly lead him into the living room.

Rocky tried to focus on Sly, but the whole time, he was trying to listen to Nikki and Mason. Mason talked, sometimes making her laugh. The wall that enclosed the kitchen stopped him from watching their interaction, but even without seeing them, Rocky knew Mason was helping Nikki feel better. He also knew Mason's advice not to tell her he was in love with her was right. She needed time to get used to him being there before he could let that tidbit out.

"I love you, Daddy," Sly said suddenly, throwing his arms around Rocky's neck and pulling him from his thoughts.

Rocky drew in a breath and pressed his nose to Sly's freshly washed head. "I love you, too, Sly. So much."

Sly pulled back after a few seconds and went right back to playing like nothing had happened. For him, maybe it hadn't, but for Rocky, his entire world shifted. The two people who lived in that small apartment were his whole world. They had been since he found out about them, but he knew, without a doubt, that every choice he'd made had brought him to them and made them a part of him.

His phone buzzed in his pocket, and Rocky hurried to dig it out. He smiled when he saw Archer's name on the screen trying to FaceTime him.

"Hey, man," Rocky said, answering with a grin.

"Hey! You're still alive! We've been worried about you. How's Tennessee?"

"Good. Real good."

"Awesome. Everyone wanted to say hi and make sure you're still doing well down there. We haven't heard from you much."

Archer turned the phone to show Rocky to everyone. The entire group was at Slade's house, piled onto couches and waving.

"Hey, everyone," Rocky said.

"Who's that?" Sly asked.

Rocky leaned over and put Sly in the picture. "Everyone, this is Sly. Sylvester. Sly, these are my brothers."

"Whoa," Sly breathed. "I didn't know I had so many uncles."

Rocky chuckled with the rest of them. "You do. If you ever need anything, you can call any of these people and they will all be there for you."

"Hey, Sly," Dex said, taking the phone from Archer.

"Hi, Dex!" Sly said excitedly. "I miss you."

"I miss you, too, buddy. But Mason's awesome, isn't he?"

Sly nodded. "He is. Are you coming back?"

Dex chuckled softly and shook his head. "Not soon. But I'll visit you again sometime. Make sure Rocky is behaving for me, okay?"

Sly nodded. "I will. He kissed my mommy."

Dex's gaze slid to Rocky. "Did he? Are you okay with that?"

Sly nodded. "I told Mommy I wanted to buy steak today so Rocky would fall in love with us and marry her. It worked."

A laugh burst from Dex, but he covered it with a cough. "Good plan, dude. Very smart."

Rocky closed his eyes and thanked God he and Sly were on the same page. Then his eyes popped open when he realized what he just hoped for.

"Hey, Lily wants to talk to you," Dex said, making it clear Rocky needed to find a place to talk alone.

Rocky nodded and told Sly he'd be right back. He got up and went into the hall while Lily took the phone from Dex. "Archer said you're not coming back. Is that true?"

Rocky drew a breath and nodded. "Yeah. I can't leave them."

"Why the hell can't you bring them back with you?"

"Because they live here. It's not fair of me to ask them to move."

"You men are always so stupid," Lily huffed. The rest of the room groaned. "I'm serious. You're assuming she wants to stay where she is instead of move. Talk to her, give her the choice. Don't just assume you know what's best."

"I—"

"No, not I. This isn't about you."

"Give him a break, Lil," Archer said softly, the edge of his face coming into view.

"I will not give him a break. I need to know what kind of woman is going to make him move to Tennessee instead of coming up here where you have a job and family and a life. I know you've been pining over her for years, but does she have a magical—"

"Lily!" Archer shouted, clamping a hand over her mouth.

She fought him off and focused on Rocky again. "I'm just saying..."

"She's going to miss you," Archer said for her. "We all are. But we're happy for you."

Lily scowled into the camera but didn't argue.

"Thanks. I'm going to head back to Sly. I'll talk to you guys later."

Rocky hung up and turned around to go back to the living room, but Nikki was blocking his way and not looking happy about everything she just overheard.

17

———

Nicole had no idea who the woman on the phone was, but she was definitely someone important to Rocky, and someone who had a lot of opinions about his life. Nicole wanted to ask him a hundred questions about the woman, like why she got any say in what he did and if she was telling the truth about Rocky pining for her, but she had no idea where to start.

"Nikki," Rocky said on a sigh, like he was sorry she overheard the conversation. Maybe he was. Maybe he didn't want her to know he had another woman in his life.

"I was just coming to tell you dinner is ready."

"Nikki, wait," Rocky said, but Nicole didn't. She turned and walked away, hurrying so she made it into the living room before he took the few steps to catch up to her.

She forced a smile for Sly and asked if he washed his hands.

"Do I have to?" Sly asked.

Nicole nodded. "Yes. Go in the kitchen and wash your hands."

"Nikki," Rocky said again.

She ignored him and followed Sly to make sure he washed his hands with soap instead of just rinsed them off.

Rocky was standing at the doorway to the kitchen when she turned around. She refused to meet his gaze and put her hands on Sly's shoulders to make their way past Rocky.

"This isn't over, Nikki," he said softly.

She still didn't look at him. Or respond.

Nicole stood next to the table and started putting food on a plate for Sly. They all sat on the couch and floor again since she still didn't have four chairs. If entertaining was going to be a regular thing, she would have to get more, but she wasn't sure of anything from one day to the next.

Mason carried the conversation through dinner, asking Sly questions and talking about life in Tennessee. Sly made it clear to Mason he didn't like living there and was hoping to move to New York. For all the times Nicole thought about it, there were just as many that told her she was being crazy for thinking about following a man. And after the phone call she overheard, she was even more convinced that moving was the wrong choice. She was not going to insert herself into his world. Whoever the woman on the phone was, she clearly had a close relationship with Rocky, but he'd never mentioned any women when he talked about New York. Nicole didn't get the feeling they were involved, but she still didn't think invading his life was a good plan. She had some level of pride.

When dinner was over, Nicole cleaned up the table. Rocky offered to help her, but she told him she was good. She rushed to the kitchen, and as she did, she knew she'd made a mistake.

Rocky followed her and cornered her. The small galley kitchen was barely big enough for two people, and with only one doorway, she was stuck inside with him.

Nicole crossed her arms and leaned against the sink, waiting for Rocky to say what he wanted to say.

"Lily said I should ask you to move," Rocky said.

Nicole raised an eyebrow. "Is that you asking me?"

He shrugged. "I guess, yeah."

She turned to the sink. "No."

"That's what I told her you would say."

Nicole whipped back around. "You really thought I would uproot my life for a guy I barely know? That I would move to a new city to be near you? Especially after I hear you talking to her?"

"Talking to who? Lily?"

Nicole turned away again. She was done talking to him. She just wanted to wash the dishes and get rid of Rocky and Mason.

Rocky moved closer, making the already small kitchen feel tiny. He cocooned her in, blocking her view of anything beyond him. "Lily is married to one of my teammates. She's like a mother to the rest of us, or at least a sister. She refuses to keep her nose out of everyone's business. I've learned to accept it and don't think twice about it, but I'm sorry it sounded as though there's more going on than I told you about."

"You didn't tell me about anything, Rocky. I don't know a thing about your life. I've met two of your friends, and I know you used to be a SEAL. That's all I know about you."

He sighed heavily and took a half step back. "What do you want to know?"

"Nothing," she said quickly. Too quickly.

"Nikki, you can ask me anything, and I'll tell you. Anything."

"What did she mean that you've been pining for me?" she blurted.

Rocky's eyes widened for half a second, the move so quick, Nicole would have missed it if she wasn't watching him. He drew in a breath and blew it out slowly. "You've been the woman I measure all other women against. The weekend we spent together... I was pissed when you disappeared. I was hurt. I wanted to stay in touch and maybe see you again. But I had no way of knowing how to reach you."

"We—"

"I know. We agreed it would be that way, but by the end of the weekend, I didn't want a fling. I wanted to know more about you."

"I wasn't sure I'd be able to walk away without asking you for more if I did it when you were awake," Nicole admitted.

Rocky huffed a breath and moved into her space, sliding an arm around her waist and tilting her face toward his. "Why didn't you tell me that?"

She shrugged. "Because you're still a stranger to me. I barely know more about you at this point. I've thought about you a ton over the years, but that doesn't mean I know you. You mentioned two sisters and I know your dad died, but I don't know much about what you guys do, or the name of the company you work for. I don't know where you live, if you've been involved with anyone, if you have any pets. I don't know what you want to do with your life or what you want from me. I know nothing about you."

Rocky kissed the tip of her nose and nuzzled against her cheek. The stubble from his unshaven face bristled against her skin and alerted every nerve in her body that there was a sexy man in close proximity. They all stood up and sighed.

Rocky turned her toward him, pressing his body to hers and dotting her face with lingering kisses. By the time he made it to her lips, she was panting for him and anxious to seal her lips to his.

He tightened his grip on her the second their lips touched. He licked his way into her willing mouth, pulsing his tongue between her lips and turning them so her back was pressed against the countertop. He grabbed her thighs and lifted her up onto it, then ground himself against her core.

Nicole moaned softly, forgetting all about the reasons they were talking. None of it mattered when he was kissing her, which was the same problem she had years ago. He had the ability to eliminate all her defenses and excuses for keeping him at a distance.

He pulled back just enough to run his tongue down her throat and up to her ear. Then he whispered, "My company is called F-BOMB. We essentially do the same thing we did in the Navy, but we're civilians. It's mostly guys from my old team. We help people who are in bad situations, which is why I keep asking you about taking care of the situation you're in. I love my job, but I'd walk away from anything for you and Sly because you matter more to me. My sisters are both younger than me and married. They live near my mom. I feel responsible for my dad's death, so I don't visit them much. I live in a house that I rent with Dex. He's a good friend and has been a good friend since before I met you. He was the one who was there for me when I was trying to get over you. It never worked. I'm not involved with anyone and haven't been in anything serious in a long time. Being in the military makes it tough to meet someone, and I didn't really have it in me to find someone that wasn't you. I don't have any pets and never have, although I've thought about getting a cat or a dog. My team is my family at this point. We work together and we hang out together. There's a lot of history between us, but it's made us closer. I would love for you to move to New York, but I'd never ask you to uproot your entire life for me, no matter how well we know each other. The most important things to me are you and Sly, and that means doing what's best for you two."

Nicole couldn't breathe by the time he finished speaking. She needed to escape, to get away. She needed a clear head to think about everything. She asked for the truth from him, but the truth was she couldn't ask him to give up his life for them. And she needed to find a way to tell him that.

She pushed him away and took advantage of his surprise and ducked out of the kitchen. She went down the hall and was in her bedroom with the door closed and locked before the tears started to fall.

It took Rocky a minute to figure out what happened. One second, he was pressed against Nikki in the kitchen, and the next, she was gone.

He tried to play everything back in his head to find out what he said that upset her, but he had no clue.

He looked out into the living room, but Mason and Sly were oblivious to what happened. Rocky wanted to chase after her and demand she talk to him, but he needed to calm down first. Making demands never got him very far, especially with women.

Rocky focused his energy on cleaning up the kitchen. He washed all the dishes and opened cabinets until he found where everything went. He cleaned up the countertops and wiped down the stove. He even cleaned the sink and wiped off the table.

Through all of it, Nikki stayed gone.

When Rocky walked back into the living room, Mason looked up at him. Rocky shrugged. Mason tapped his wrist, and Rocky realized how late it was.

"Hey, Sly, why don't you get ready for bed? Mason and I can read you a story."

"Where's my mommy?"

"She's in her room. She needed to lie down for a few minutes."

Sly nodded and let it go. He didn't argue about getting ready for bed, something Rocky already knew meant he was exhausted.

Sly was out before they made it halfway through the book they were reading. Rocky and Mason kept reading until the end, their voices getting softer as the story went on. When they were done, they quietly left the room and closed the door so Sly could sleep.

In the living room, Mason asked Rocky what happened with Nikki. Rocky shrugged. "I don't know. She said she didn't know me, and she was worried about who Lily was, and then when I answered all her questions, she ran off."

"Did you tell her something stupid? Something like you were going to tell her yesterday?"

Rocky shook his head. "No. I know you're right."

Mason nodded. "Good. Then whatever it is will work out. Are you staying here tonight?"

Rocky looked around and nodded. "I was hoping to. I don't like the idea of someone threatening them. They've already been to the apartment and cornered her at the store. I don't think leaving them alone is the best idea."

"I tried to get some info out of her while we were cooking. She doesn't have a lot of details, but I got a little bit from her. I'm going to dig into this tonight. Want me to reach out to the team?"

Rocky nodded. "Probably not a bad idea. When do you head home?"

"My flight's at noon. I think Archer and Lily are trying to come instead of Slade and Kyra."

Rocky groaned.

"Maybe it'll be a good thing. Nikki can meet Lily and know there's nothing going on."

"Yeah, but you know how subtle Lily is."

Mason chuckled. "About as subtle as a Mack truck."

"Exactly."

"Maybe it won't be that bad."

Rocky snorted.

"Okay, fine, maybe it won't be worse."

Rocky shook his head. "I can only hope."

"You going to be okay here?"

Rocky nodded. "I'll sleep on the couch. It'll be fine."

"All right. I'm going to head out. See what else we can find out about these guys. Talk soon."

"Thanks, Mace."

Mason left, and Rocky locked the door behind him and turned off all the lights. He settled onto the couch in the darkness and debated turning on the TV when he heard a door open down the hall.

Nikki's soft footsteps padded across the hall to Sly's room. His door creaked open quietly, then a minute later eased closed. Rocky waited for her to return to her room, but her footsteps came toward him. He wasn't sure if she knew he was there or not, so he waited silently for her to discover him.

She went straight to the kitchen and turned on the light. He couldn't see her, but he could hear her. She spoke softly to herself in words he couldn't quite make out. But she sounded surprised.

She got a glass of water and stayed in there for a long moment. He listened as she set the glass in the sink. She turned the lights off again and was on her way back to her bedroom when she stopped. She moved to the kitchen again, and he heard a knife gliding out of the drawer.

"Nikki, it's me. I'm sleeping on your couch so you're not here alone," Rocky said quietly.

"Jesus, Rocky. What the hell? You gave me a heart attack."

"I'm sorry. I was trying to stay out of your way."

"Why the hell are you staying here?"

"Because I only just got you back in my life. If you'd let me pay this guy off, you would be safe, but you refused. We're trying to figure out what's going on and who's behind all this, but no matter what, I'm not about to lose you again."

"Rocky, you can't say things like that to me."

"Like what?"

"Like I matter. Like I'm important."

"You are," he said, wondering why she was upset.

She shook her head, something he could see through the darkness. She wore light clothes, a tank and shorts if he had to guess, that highlighted her curves. Years of working in the dark had given him better than normal vision in darkened rooms, and with the nightlight in the hallway, he could see almost all of her.

"Why do you think you aren't important?" Rocky asked.

"Sly is your son. I know that means you love him, but I'm not really anything. I'm just his mom. You don't have to be involved with me because of him."

Rocky stood and walked across the room to her. "I would never get involved with someone because of something else, or someone else. Yes, I love Sly. But you're important to me, too."

"Rocky, you don't have to do this. We had a great weekend years ago, and we had a great night the other day, but that can be the end of it."

"Why do I feel like you're trying to end things with me before we really get started again?"

"Because nothing ever works out for me," she said firmly. She drew a ragged breath and shook her head. "My parents have never met Sly because they were so disappointed in me for getting pregnant. Every man I've ever met bolted when they found out I had a son. I don't even really have friends because my coworkers are all single or married and there's no space for a single mom."

"What does any of that have to do with me?" Rocky asked.

She laughed mirthlessly. "You don't have a choice. You have to be here for Sly. Or at least, you feel like you have to be. You're the kind of man who isn't going to abandon his kid. But saying things about me being important... I'm not going to keep you from Sly. You don't have to pretend you care about me."

He laughed and shook his head. "Pretend I care? I don't have to pretend I care? Nikki, I love you. I know I shouldn't be telling you this, and I know it's too soon, and I know it's likely to make you bolt, but none of those things make it any less true. I love you. I'm here tonight because you and Sly are the two most important people in the world to me. You two are everything. And I'm not willing to risk anything happening to either of you."

She shook her head and took a step back. "No, you can't. That's not true." Her voice shook and tears slipped down her cheeks. "Don't say things like that."

Rocky stopped his advance and took a step back. "Please don't tell me how I feel, Nikki. If you don't feel the same, I understand, but it pisses me off to have you tell me I don't actually love you. I was going to tell you yesterday, but Mason told me not to because it would influence you. He said it would seem like I'm saying it to convince you to move to New York. But none of that matters because I'm moving here. I'm not forcing you to choose. I'm moving here. I'll go back up and get my stuff and find a place down here. And if you decide you want to be with me, that's up to you. But don't tell me I don't love you. That's not fair."

Rocky left Nikki standing in the hallway and went back to the couch. He was pissed and hurt. He put his head in his hands and waited for her to go back to her room. When the soft click of her bedroom door signaled she was gone, he leaned back on the couch and drew in a deep breath.

So much for thinking he knew what she would say.

18

———

Nicole pressed her back to the door and tried to pull in a breath. Everything she thought she knew was upside down, again. And it was all because of Rocky.

He wasn't supposed to say things like he loved her. He was supposed to pretend he cared about Sly and then disappear like everyone else in her life. Not that she wanted her son hurt, but that was what Nicole knew. It was what she expected. It was easy for her to understand a man, hell a person, that she couldn't count on. Having someone who kept insisting he was sticking around was more than she could handle.

Especially if he meant it.

She tried to tell herself he wasn't telling the truth. Maybe he thought he loved them or maybe he wanted to love them, but time and again, Rocky showed her that he was there. His friends were well aware of him leaving New York to move to be near them. Sure, they weren't happy about it, but they knew. He told the people who were the most important to him that he was leaving.

No, not the most important. Not if she believed what he

said and trusted that she and Sly were really the most important people to him.

Could she? Could she trust him? Could she let herself love him back? She thought she did once upon a time, but she told herself it was the romance of the weekend and the rush of emotions left behind. She convinced herself what they had wasn't really love, but what if she was wrong? Could she walk away from him and not let herself love and be loved?

Before she could second guess herself, again, Nicole pushed off the door and opened it. She drew a shaky breath and left her room. The lights were off in the rest of the apartment, but there was no doubt that he was watching her the moment she stepped into the living room.

Fear tickled the back of her throat, but she pushed past it and moved toward him. He didn't get up from where he sat on her ratty old couch. She hated the couch, but it was free. She hated that he saw the way she lived, but he never made her feel like that was all she deserved. She loved him for all those little things, the little things she judged herself for. He took it all in stride and continued to tell her how amazing she was. And she threw it all in his face.

Without a word, she straddled his lap. His hands immediately went to her hips and tightened on her. She paused, knowing she needed to say something.

Rocky stayed silent, letting her think without throwing her off his lap or demanding she tell him what she was doing. He just sat there, his thumbs making small circles on her hips and driving her crazy.

But that was only part of it. She was sex starved, but she'd survived seven years without sex. It wasn't sex that drew her to him, it was him. It was everything about him that made her ache to hold on tight to him and not let go.

And that was why she wanted to run as far and as fast as she could.

"I'm scared," she whispered in the dark.

"So am I," he said.

"This isn't easy for me."

He drew in a breath. "I got you. I'm not going anywhere."

His voice was strong and steady, and for once, she let herself believe him. She let herself go. She wanted what he was offering, what he promised her, and she was going to be selfish for once and take it.

"Love me," she whispered.

"Always."

He urged her forward with a gentle tug on her hips, letting her make the decision. She slid toward him until their bodies met. She ducked her head as he lifted his and their lips collided in a crash of desire. His hands slid up her back, drawing her tank top up and exposing her heated skin to the cool air of the apartment. A shiver rocked her, and she ground against his erection with a moan.

Rocky slowed their kiss and teased her with his tongue. He trailed his fingers down her back until they hit the waist of her shorts, then skimmed them up again, slowly up and down until she was squirming and desperate for his touch on more of her body.

Nicole leaned back and stripped her tank top off, exposing her chest to him. His body tensed beneath hers. Reverently, he cupped one breast and brought it to his mouth. He closed his eyes and hummed as he licked her nipple. She stared down at him as he tasted her skin. He sucked her nipple into his mouth and groaned.

"I love you, Nikki," he whispered as he moved to the other side and repeated the same torture.

The words hung on the tip of her tongue, but they were

rusty. The only person she'd said them to in seven years was Sly. It was easy to love her son, but it was painful to risk giving someone else that kind of power. To know he could hurt her just because she loved him.

So she kept her mouth shut and enjoyed what she could take from him.

Rocky kissed his way back to her lips and thrust his tongue into her mouth, shutting down her mind and opening her heart. She wanted to love him, and she did, but admitting it was a different thing. But if she couldn't say the words, she could show him.

She kissed him back and eased her body off his. She fell to her knees on the floor in front of him and urged his jeans off. He lifted his hips and let her remove his jeans and briefs, dropping them both to the floor. He leaned forward and stripped off his shirt, then laid back.

She didn't taste him seven years ago, and it was a big regret of hers. She wanted to, but she wasn't sure enough of herself to do it. Now, she still wasn't sure of herself, but she wanted to make him feel good.

She leaned forward and licked the tip of his cock. He sucked in a sharp breath and fisted his hands on the couch. She parted her lips and took him into her mouth. He groaned and thrust up, hitting her throat. Her eyes watered, but she wasn't giving up. If he could lose his mind that fast, she wanted more.

Rocky pulled her hair back from her face and held it behind her. She closed her eyes and braced herself on his knees and sucked him in again. She licked him on the way out and swirled her tongue around the tip, then sucked hard as she drew him back in again.

Over and over, she pumped him with her mouth. His

breathing grew erratic, coming in rapid pants. The whole time, he whispered how much he loved her.

Then, all of a sudden, he pushed her back and yanked her onto his lap. He forced his tongue into her surprised mouth and kissed her like a starved man. His hands were frantic, as if he was trying to touch her entire body at once.

When she finally pulled back from him, she asked, "Why did you make me stop?"

"Because I need to be inside you, Nikki. I need to feel you."

Heat pooled between her thighs at his words. She was wet and ready for him, her body pulsing already. She stood and stripped her shorts and panties off and made a move to straddle him again.

He reached for her, sliding his hand between her thighs. One finger entered her slowly while another teased her clit.

"Jesus, you're wet."

She nodded, unsure if that was good or bad.

"Fucking hell, sweetheart, I'm not going to last long with you like this. Did you like sucking me?"

She nodded again, a moan slipping from her lips as he stroked in and out of her.

"I love you, Nikki."

She finally met his gaze and almost said the words. They were right there, ready to break free. The look in his eyes said he knew, but that he wasn't going to push her into saying it.

"Do you want to come like this?"

She nodded and spread her legs. He added a second finger inside her and thrust deeper into her. Her thighs shook with the effort it took to stay on her feet, and her entire body threatened to revolt and collapse, but she focused on how good he felt.

"There we go, baby. Let go for me," he urged her. Rocky slid to the edge of the couch and wrapped his other hand around her waist, offering her his strength. She put her hands on his shoulders and bucked against his hand, letting the pleasure take over.

She fucked his hand hard, slamming herself down with every thrust inside. She gave him more of her weight, hoping he wouldn't collapse under her, and rode him through her orgasm. Every inch of her body vibrated with pleasure and burst with light and love for the man who made her feel like she was the most important thing in his world.

"You're so beautiful, Nikki. I love you. So damn much," he whispered in the dark.

She held onto him and gave in to the urge to collapse, letting him take all her weight. He easily adjusted her so she was on his lap again. She felt him hard against her thigh and tried to move to line him up with her entrance.

"I don't have a condom on, sweetheart," he said, not letting her move.

She hesitated for a minute, debating on not bothering. She trusted him, but she wasn't on the pill.

"I have one in my pocket. Don't move." He held her waist tight, as though he thought she was going to run if he let go of her. He leaned forward and grabbed his jeans. With one hand, he pulled out his wallet and removed a condom, tossing his wallet back to the ground. He used his teeth to open the foil packet and handed the condom to her.

Nicole held his gaze and saw the truth in his eyes. He was letting her decide if she wanted him. He'd made his choice, and he was giving her the chance to make hers.

She eased back and rolled the condom down his length.

They both groaned when he swelled in her hand. Rocky helped guide her onto him and he finally slid inside.

Nicole felt a rush of emotion with him in her. He stilled and kissed her softly, holding her face in front of his. He wouldn't let her hide like she wanted to.

Rocky locked his eyes on hers and said, "I love you, Nikki. I don't need to hear you say it back to me, but I will tell you until you believe me. This isn't a quick fuck to me, and this isn't a way to pass the time. This is me loving you. I need you to know that."

She nodded. All the emotions wrapped in her heart were there because of him. She opened her mouth to tell him she felt the same, but he leaned forward and captured her lips. Then he began to move.

He kissed her slowly while he shifted his hips beneath her. Shallow strokes built up her desire until she needed more.

Nicole pulled back from their kiss and lifted up on her knees. She lowered herself down onto him, meeting his stroke with her own. His hands went to her hips, guiding her gently. Their bodies synced almost instantly, both of them needing the same thing and taking it from the other.

Nicole put her hands on his shoulders and used him for leverage. She threw her head back and let go again, ignoring the burning pain in her thighs and the way her body jiggled and shook. Every word Rocky whispered made her feel like she had no flaws and was the most beautiful woman in the world.

"I need you, Nikki. I need you to come for me."

"Touch me."

He peeled his fingers off her hip and spread his hand over her thigh. He pressed against her clit with his thumb, and she lost it. She let go of all her fears and held on to him with both hands and her heart, trusting that he would take care of her.

Her orgasm grabbed a hold of her and refused to let go. She fought back the urge to scream as wave after wave crashed over her. She couldn't find her way back, her orgasms demanding she keep going.

"So beautiful," Rocky whispered. His thumb still stroked her, urging her on.

Nicole bounced and shook and whimpered. She lost her ability to support herself and sank onto Rocky. He wrapped both arms around her and held her sweaty body to his as he grunted and swelled inside her. She felt him come and held him tighter, unable to let go of him.

He held her close, his hands splayed wide on her back while their bodies cooled. Only when she sniffed did he move.

"Are you okay?" he asked, his voice worried.

She nodded against his shoulder and squeezed him.

"I'm right here, Nikki. I'm not going anywhere."

"Thank you," she whispered. It wasn't enough, but it was all she could manage at the moment. She only hoped he knew how much she meant by those two simple words.

ZEKE COULDN'T TAKE his eyes off the window the entire time. He wanted to kill that Navy son of a bitch for touching his woman, but he knew that wouldn't make Nicole come to him. No, he had to make sure she knew how much danger she was in, and that he was the only one who could make it better.

When she stepped into view, Zeke wrapped his hand around himself. He pretended he was the one she was topless for. That her full breasts were on display for him to taste and touch.

She was fucking perfect, and she was wasting that sweet fucking body on some asshole who couldn't be bothered to show up.

But Zeke was grateful he didn't because it brought Nicole into his life. She was his, and he was going to do whatever it took to make sure she knew it.

He groaned and came when she did, imagining the sounds she would make. Next time he was in there, he needed to put a listening device in the apartment so he could hear her come. Or better yet, make her come himself.

There was plenty of time for that. Plenty of time to show her what a real man could do for her. And he would protect her from his boss. They could run away together. Especially once Zeke got rid of the stupid kid.

Nicole finally stood, her entire body on display for him through the blinds. She closed the ones in her bedroom, but the living room blinds were open enough for him to see her. He took a few pictures using the lens he purchased specifically for watching Nicole. It was worth every penny.

She reached for the bastard and led him toward the hallway. Zeke took pictures until they disappeared. The man was going to pay for touching her. She didn't belong to him. She was Zeke's, and he was going to do whatever it took to show her.

No matter what.

19

———

ROCKY ROLLED OVER IN BED AND INHALED THE PILLOW NEXT to him. He groaned in his sleep and hardened. His hand reached out to find her, but he was met with cold sheets.

He lifted his head and looked around. Nikki was gone, the bedroom door was closed, and he was painfully hard. Just like the last time he spent the night in the same bed as her.

Damn, it was a good night, though. She never said she loved him, but he could see the truth in her eyes. He just had to prove to her that he wasn't going anywhere. And that started with not leaving her to deal with the day while he slept in her bed.

He walked naked to the bathroom, closing the outer door softly before he exposed himself to Sly. He stood facing the toilet and tried to think of anything but the way Nikki responded to him so he could take a piss. Nothing worked. He wanted her. No, he needed her.

Rocky stood there for a minute, not feeling much relief at all, then went back to Nikki's bedroom. His clothes were on the floor from where they tossed everything on their way in the night before. He used his one and only condom in the living room, so he got creative the rest of the night. Touching and tasting her until she came, then having her return the favors, would be some of his best memories for the rest of his life.

He just hoped he could repeat them a few thousand more times.

Rocky's phone buzzed in his pocket as he pulled on his jeans, reminding him that there was a world outside his family. He dug it out and saw a message from Mason asking if he was available to take him to the airport.

Instead of texting back, Rocky called him.

"What time do you need to leave?" Rocky asked when Mason answered.

"I need to be at the airport in a little over an hour. I wasn't sure what you wanted me to do with the SUV."

"I'll ride with you. Do you ever find out who's coming today?"

"Yep," Mason said. The grin in his voice was unmistakable.

"What does that mean?"

"Archer and Lily are already on their way. They should be landing around the time I'm getting to the airport, so you can pick them up when you drop me off."

"Oh, shit," Rocky muttered.

Mason chuckled. "Apparently, she berated all of them for not telling you not to move. She's coming down here to talk some sense into you."

"Dammit. I thought it was just a maybe that they were coming. Why didn't you tell me this before now?"

Mason snorted. "And risk pissing Lily off? Hell no."

Rocky groaned. "Fuck. Okay. I'll deal with it. Are you going to swing by and pick me up?"

"Yep. Heading out the door soon. I wanted to say bye to Sly and Nikki, if that's okay."

"Yeah, of course. I don't know why it wouldn't be."

"Are they up already?"

"Nikki is. I'm not sure about Sly."

"How do you not know?"

"Uh..." Rocky glanced around Nikki's room. He didn't have anything to be ashamed of or explain. He wasn't doing anything wrong by sleeping with her or telling her how he felt. Sure, Mason told him not to, but Mason had no say in how Rocky lived his life.

"You slept with her again?" Mason asked.

"Yeah."

"And stayed the night in her bed?"

"Yep."

"And by the way I'm having to drag it out of you, I'm guessing you also told her you love her. And that it didn't go as planned."

"Well, I spent the night in her room, so it wasn't that bad."

"Did she say she loves you?" Mason asked pointedly.

"Not exactly."

"That's either a yes or no question."

"Fine, then no. Are you happy?"

"No, I'm not. But my opinion isn't all that important. Hers is."

"It's fine. She's just scared. She told me so last night."

Mason drew a deep breath and blew it out slowly. "I hope you know what you're doing."

"Me, too."

A loud zipper echoed through the phone. "Okay, I'm all packed. I'm heading to you. I'll be there soon."

Rocky nodded. "Okay. Thanks."

Rocky hung up and looked around Nikki's room. He hadn't gotten a good look at it and wanted to explore, but he felt like a creep. He wanted to know everything there was to know about Nikki, but he wanted her to tell him what she wanted him to know. When she was ready.

He opened the door to her bedroom and listened to the sounds of the apartment. Sly's door was open, which meant he was likely awake. There was a soft sound that he thought might have been the TV. Noise in the kitchen forced him to walk that way, wondering what he would find when he got there.

"Hi, Daddy!" Sly shouted when Rocky stepped out of the hallway. Sly jumped off the couch and ran over to him.

Rocky ducked down and hugged Sly, resisting the urge to pick him up. His side was slightly sore from the activities overnight, and he didn't want to risk hurting Sly. "Morning, buddy. How's the day going so far?"

"Good. Mommy made me eggs for breakfast, and she said we can do anything I want today."

"Well, that sounds like a good start to the day. Is Mommy in the kitchen?"

Sly nodded and drifted back to the couch.

"I'm going to go say hi. Mason is on his way over. I need to take him to the airport, but two other friends of mine are coming in today."

"Another brother?" Sly asked.

Rocky nodded. "Yep, another brother. And his wife."

"An uncle and an aunt? So cool!"

Rocky chuckled and turned toward the kitchen. He leaned against the entrance and watched Nikki busy herself so she didn't have to look at him or acknowledge him.

When she finally glanced up, he pushed off the wall and

went to her, even though she was back to moving the second she saw him.

"Good morning," he whispered against her neck. He trapped her against the counter, one hand on either side of her hips.

"I need to clean up. And Sly can't see us like this."

"Why not?"

"Because he'll get his hopes up," she said simply, pushing away from Rocky.

"And you still don't think I'm going to stick around."

"I never said anything, Rocky. You have to make the decision that's right for you."

"You are the decision that's right for me, Nikki. You and Sly."

"We'll see," she said, somehow keeping her distance in the small space. "You got a lot of texts last night and this morning."

"What?" Rocky asked. He pulled his phone out of his pocket again and unlocked it. He had thirty-seven unread texts that he didn't notice when he hung up with Mason. He groaned. It was a group text with him and the women. Lily, Pilar, Ashleigh, Kelsea, and Kyra were ganging up on him and telling him he couldn't move.

"It sounds like you are pretty busy," Nikki said softly.

Rocky looked up at her and realized what was going on. "You read them and think I'm sleeping with five different women who all know about each other?" He chuckled.

Nikki's face turned stormy. "What you do with your time and who you spend it with is none of my business."

She tried to push past him, but he was ready for her. "It is your business because I love you, Nikki. These women are the wives and girlfriends of my teammates. I love them, but they're like sisters to me. And yes, they're upset that I'm moving, but Lily will be here soon and she'll understand."

Nikki's brows went up. "She's coming here? The one who told you not to move and asked what I had that was worth relocating for?"

"She didn't mean it like that," Rocky said.

Nikki drew in a breath and closed her eyes.

"Nikki, look at me," Rocky said softly.

A knock on the door drew her attention away from him. "I need to see who that is."

"It's Mason. He can wait a second."

"It might not be Mason. I need to see. Please."

The situation she was in the middle of rushed back to him. He spent the night because she was cornered in public. He was there because she was scared. And he forgot about it.

He stepped to the side and followed as she went to the door. She dried her hands on a dishtowel and looked through the peephole before she opened it.

"Hey, Mason," she said brightly. Too brightly.

"Morning. How are you guys today?"

"Great," Nikki said, keeping her fake smile in place. "Come in. I hear someone new is coming today."

Mason nodded and glanced at Rocky. "Yep. I'm on my way to the airport, but Archer and Lily will be here around the time I go. Rocky was going to pick them up when he drops me off."

Nikki's gaze cut to his. "That's good."

"Hey, buddy," Mason said, turning his focus to Sly with an exaggerated smile. "How are you?"

Nikki mumbled something about getting changed and left the room. Mason gave Rocky a look that screamed *I told you so.* Rocky just sighed and hoped he could salvage whatever he was starting to build with Nikki.

NICOLE WANTED to slap herself for getting her hopes up. Two nights with Rocky and she was planning a wedding and moving to New York.

Right up until his phone woke her up with all the texts. She would have been up before much longer anyway, but the incessant buzzing brought her out of whatever bliss remained from spending the night in his arms.

And then when she saw message after message from women... She wasn't sure it mattered that they were involved with his friends. He was getting texts from a bunch of women, and all of them were saying the same thing.

> You can't leave.
>
> You shouldn't leave.
>
> We don't want you to leave.
>
> I can't believe you would even consider leaving.

Maybe she wasn't being fair to him, but Nicole knew how people could influence each other. She grew up with it. Her father ruled things around their house, and her mother catered to him with everything she said and did. Nicole wasn't important unless her father decided she was, and most of the time, he decided she was not.

She could pretend Rocky's friends were just watching out for him, and she was happy for him that he had people like that, but Nicole knew the truth behind it. If his closest friends didn't want him to leave, they would make him regret it, and he would move back.

If he ever moved in the first place.

Which put Nicole right back to where she was before, wondering why she was getting involved with him. It was only going to lead to pain, and she'd had enough to last a lifetime. She didn't need more.

She drew a breath and closed her eyes. For one minute, she let herself live in the fantasy world she created where she and Rocky could exist in the bubble they were in. For one minute, they were happy and his friends weren't going to interfere.

Then she heard the front door close and knew he and Mason were gone and the next time she saw him would be with one of the women who spent all morning blowing up his phone.

She shook her head and bucked up. Her only option was to guard her heart and think with her head instead of her vagina.

Nicole dressed quickly, then packed a lunch for her and Sly. He wanted to go to a playground and she couldn't imagine anyone cornering them there. They would be safe, and the fresh air would be good for clearing her head.

The playground they liked to go to was quiet, especially for a Saturday. A few parents were there with young kids, most grouped together like they knew each other. Nicole sat on a bench by herself and opened the app on her phone to read a book.

It had been a while since she let herself indulge in a novel. Most of her reading had been information on kidney transplants and finding a kidney. Before that, it was understanding Sly's medical issues until she figured out what was going on. It had been years since she opened a real book.

The scene she opened to caught her attention quickly with the dirty words and hot sex, but she couldn't remember anything about the characters. She finished the scene and looked up to where Sly was, waving at him when he smiled. Nicole started the book over and kept an eye on Sly while he played.

Another boy who looked like he was a year or two younger followed Sly down a slide. He chased Sly up the cargo net and across the bridge. Sly giggled as they ran and ended up on the swings.

"Is he yours?" a woman said, sitting down near Nicole.

She nodded. "He is. Yours?"

"I haven't seen you here before. I'm Samantha."

"I'm Nicole. We haven't been here in a while. How old is your son?"

"Six. I homeschool him."

"Nice. I hear there's a good community for that."

"There is. You're not a part of it?"

Nicole shook her head. "He goes to school, but he's been off for a while. He just had a kidney transplant. I'm hoping he goes back next week."

"Oh, wow. I'm so sorry to hear that. That must be scary for you."

Nicole nodded and didn't elaborate.

The boys left the swings and ran around again. They went down slides and up ladders and laughed and finally ended up back on the swings. Nicole gave up on the book and tucked her phone back in her purse.

"Where do you guys live?"

"A few towns over," Nicole said, wondering why Samantha wanted to know.

"You should come visit us sometime. We live on the next street. We have a pool and big yard to play in."

"Why did you come here?"

Samantha shrugged. "Sometimes it's nice to get away from home a little bit."

Nicole forced a smile and stood. Something about the woman put her on edge. She'd met moms who were judgmental and odd before, but Samantha veered more toward the crazy end of the spectrum. They didn't know anything about each other and she was inviting them over?

"Are you leaving?" Samantha asked.

Nicole nodded. "We are. Sorry. We have to go meet my husband."

"Oh. I didn't realize you were married."

Nicole tilted her head. "I'm not sure why you would. We've only spoken to each other for a few minutes."

"Well, um, you're not wearing a ring. I just assumed."

"What difference does it make?"

"Oh, um, none. I, um, just thought we, um…"

"Sly, let's go."

Sly groaned and dragged his feet on the way over to her. His friend skipped behind him, then veered toward another group of parents.

Nicole glanced at Samantha. She'd barely noticed her 'son' with the other family. Nicole put her arm around Sly and forced a pleasant tone to her voice. "We need to go see your daddy. Sorry we can't stay longer."

"But I thought you said we could stay and have a picnic," Sly argued.

"No, we can't. Let's go."

Sly argued, but Nicole guided him firmly toward the parking lot. She let him in the car and got in her seat, searching the playground for the woman who called herself Samantha. She was gone, but her 'son' was still playing.

"Why did we have to go? I was having fun."

"I forgot about something we needed to do, honey. I'm sorry. We can maybe come back some other time."

"When?" Sly whined as she pulled out of the parking space.

"I don't know. We'll see," Nicole said, watching for cars and kids as she made her way to the street.

Sly grumbled in the back while Nicole drove away from the park. She didn't want Sly to worry about the woman and Nicole knew he would tell Rocky, so she had to come up with a reason they needed to leave.

The grocery store was out since they just went the day before. She was on paid leave, but she wasn't getting her full check, so spending more money was tough. But so was explaining the creepy feeling she got from a stranger at the playground.

Nicole pulled into the parking lot of the local ice cream shop and asked Sly if he wanted a treat. He forgot all about the playground and raced out of the car. He happily scanned the list of flavors and decided on peanut butter cup ice cream. Nicole asked for strawberry. They carried their dishes to a table closer to the parking lot and sat down.

"I didn't know we were going to get ice cream," Sly said as he licked drips from his hand. "You never let me have ice cream before lunch."

Nicole smiled and opened her mouth to tell him it was a special day when she spotted the same woman from the playground in the front seat of an SUV.

Nicole wanted to scream and run, but she knew that wouldn't do any good. Maybe it was a coincidence.

She finished her ice cream even as it turned to cement in her stomach. Sly ate his slowly, telling Nicole all about everything he wanted to do when Rocky moved to Tennessee.

"Unless we move to New York. I still think we should do that," Sly said.

"You do know you still have to go to school in New York, right?"

"I know. But we'll be with Rocky and all my uncles and aunts."

Nicole sucked in a breath. She dreamed of having a big family growing up. Both her parents were only children. She was an only child, and without any aunts or uncles, she had no cousins. She never wanted that for her own kids, but for six years, Sly hadn't had anyone except her.

Moving to New York and seeing Rocky's friends every day, the ones who didn't want him with her, was less than appealing, but Nicole made a vow to herself a long time ago to do anything she could to make her son's life better, even if it meant making her life worse.

Sly finally finished his ice cream. They went back to the car, ignoring the woman from the playground and the man in the dark shades behind the wheel. Nicole pulled out and headed toward home, watching her rearview mirror the entire time.

Sly chattered on as they drove. Nicole barely listened, choosing to focus on the road and the mirrors. She thought she saw the dark SUV a few times, but when she pulled into her parking lot, she didn't notice it.

Sly unbuckled and helped her get the cooler and blanket and her purse from the car. She was finally relaxing until someone walked up behind her without a sound.

20

——————

"Daddy!" Sly shouted, throwing himself at Rocky.

Rocky caught him and hugged him close while keeping his eye on Nikki. She tensed instantly and nearly threw the things in her hands at him. The fear in her eyes and the terror radiating from her said she wasn't just surprised to see him, she was scared out of her mind.

"What are you doing here?" she demanded.

"I wanted to show Archer and Lily where you live. Get an idea of the complex. We were going to drive around the area a little and grab some lunch. I thought you guys were out for the day."

"Then why are you here?" Nikki asked again.

"You said we were coming to see Daddy," Sly said simply, like it was no big deal.

Nikki's scowl slid off her face, and she averted her eyes. Something was going on.

"If you came here to see me, why are you upset?" Rocky asked.

"I didn't come here to see you," Nikki insisted.

"That's what you told that lady," Sly said.

"What lady?" Rocky demanded.

"No one. It was nothing."

"The lady at the park," Sly explained. "She was at the ice cream store, too."

Rocky stared at Nikki, but she did her best to ignore him. He saw right through it to the fear she was feeling. That was why she jumped when he walked up. She was being followed.

"Did you recognize her?"

"Do you think I'd have told someone I recognized anything?"

"I think it's easier to talk to someone you think you recognize than a stranger. Or someone who makes it seem like you're familiar."

"She told me her son was the one playing with Sly on the playground," Nikki said.

"And I take it he wasn't?" Rocky asked.

Nikki shook her head.

"Maybe we should all head inside," Archer said, joining the discussion.

Rocky looked at him and nodded.

"Who are you?" Nikki asked.

Archer extended his hand. "Archer Ford. I'm a good friend of Rocky's and here to make sure he's not exerting himself. This is my wife, Lily."

Nikki tensed again, but it was a different kind of tension. She shook Archer's hand and braced herself when Lily stepped in front and hugged her.

"It's so nice to finally meet you," Lily said with a smile. She stepped back and turned to Sly. "And you. I've heard a lot about you from Dex and Mason. It sounds like you're a really smart and strong kid."

"I'm strong like my daddy," Sly said proudly.

Lily grinned. "And smart like your mommy because your daddy isn't always so smart."

Nikki took a step back at Lily's dig. Rocky heard it the way she did but knew Lily was picking on him, not trashing Nikki. The look on her face said that wasn't what Nikki thought.

"I'm going inside," Nikki said with a forced smile. She turned on her heel and walked away from them.

Rocky flashed Lily a look that said *shut up*. Lily mouthed *sorry* and the four of them followed Nikki upstairs with Sly asking question after question of Archer.

Once they were inside, Nikki disappeared to her room for a minute. Rocky looked at the others and tried to pretend nothing weird was going on, but Lily wasn't one to let things go.

"I messed that up, didn't I?" she asked.

"You think?" Rocky said.

"I'm sorry. I didn't mean it that way."

Rocky sighed. "I know, but she doesn't know you. The only thing she knows is you don't want me to move here. She thinks you don't like her and you don't know her."

"Who don't you like?" Sly asked Lily.

"No one, Sly," Lily said with a smile.

Sly eyed her carefully, clearly not buying it. "Do you not like my mommy?"

"No, I do. I mean, I just met her, but I do like her," Lily said.

"She's the best mommy ever," Sly defended Nikki.

"I'm sure she is," Lily tried again. "I hope I get the chance to get to know her better."

Sly glared at Lily for another long moment, then turned to Archer. "Do you like my mommy?"

"Very much. Anyone who makes your daddy so happy is good in my book," Archer said.

Sly nodded, then went to the couch and turned on the TV.

Lily slapped Archer and glared at him. "Why are you making me look bad?"

Archer snorted. "You're doing that all on your own, woman."

Lily growled at him, and Archer laughed.

"I'm hungry," Sly said, still staring at the TV.

"I'll get lunch," Nikki said from right behind them.

Rocky spun around in time to see her go toward the kitchen. She was not happy about Lily and Archer being there. He had some major work to do to make things right between them again.

Rocky followed her into the kitchen. "I'm sorry we just showed up. I didn't think you would be here."

"It's fine," Nikki said immediately.

"It's not fine," Rocky argued. "Nothing between us is fine right now."

"There is nothing between us," Nikki said with finality.

Rocky stopped her movements around the kitchen and pinned her to the counter. He pressed his body to hers and waited until she stopped squirming and glared at him.

"What?"

"Don't start telling me how I feel again. You might not want me, but there is something between us. And it's not just sex and it's not just a son. I love you, Nikki. I told you I'm going to say it until you believe me."

"I can't do this," she said, her lower lip shaking. She caught it between her teeth and turned her face away from him.

Rocky pulled her into his arms and held her tight until

she sobbed silently against his chest. "What happened today?"

She shook her head and held him tighter.

He wanted to know, but if she needed to hold him, he wasn't going to argue. He held her tight until the trembling stopped and she tried to pull back.

"Lean on me, Nikki. That's part of why I'm here. I don't want you thinking you're alone because you aren't anymore. I have you. I have both of you, and if something is going on, I want to know."

She drew in a shaky breath and sank into him. He finally relaxed since she was. Until she started talking.

"A little boy started following Sly at the playground. They were playing together, which is totally normal. A woman sat down next to me and asked if Sly was mine. She said the boy was her son, and we started talking. It wasn't much, but after a few minutes, she was saying things that made me uncomfortable. Asking where I lived and inviting us over to her house. Not things you would do with a stranger. I told Sly we needed to go and said we were going to see my husband, and she said she didn't realize I was married."

"How the hell...?" Rocky muttered.

"That's why I asked her," Nikki said softly. "She knew who I was. She had to. Sly came over and we started to leave and the boy who was playing with him went to another parent, so he wasn't even her son. Since Sly was upset, we went for ice cream, and she showed up there in an SUV, but there was a man driving. When we finished, we came home."

"Did they follow you?"

Nikki shrugged. "I don't think so, but if she knows who I am, she probably knows where I live."

"I'm so sorry, sweetheart," Rocky breathed, pulling her in close again.

Nikki nodded against his chest and let him hold her. He hated how scared she was, and that he couldn't protect her from everything in the world. It could be a coincidence, but it wasn't likely that a random person would say those things if they weren't already involved in the situation.

"Oh, um, sorry," Lily said, walking into the kitchen. "I was wondering if you needed some help."

Nikki pulled back from Rocky and avoided looking at Lily. "I'm fine. Thanks. I was just going to grab the lunch I packed for Sly so he can eat."

"Well, we were going to go out and grab something. Do you want to join us?" Lily asked.

Nikki shook her head. "No, we're fine."

"Oh, um, okay. Maybe we can all go to dinner tonight?" Lily suggested.

"We'll see. Sly needs to stick to a schedule," Nikki said.

"I understand." Lily gave Rocky a look and stepped back before disappearing again.

"Come to lunch with us," Rocky implored.

"I am a single mom who isn't getting paid my full check right now. Taking him for ice cream almost emptied my bank account. I have been spending a lot of money lately, and I really need to stop."

"Let me pay," Rocky suggested.

"No." There was no negotiating with her tone.

He tried anyway. "Why not? I'm the one asking you to go. Why shouldn't I pay?"

"Because we're not together. We're not a family. He's your son, so if you want to take him out, I won't stop you." She paused and took a deep breath.

Rocky walked up behind her and nuzzled her neck.

She resisted him for a minute, then relaxed into him. "I want to spend time with both of you. And as far as I'm concerned, we are together, Nikki. I love you. You have cooked for me and taken care of things and given so many things to me, and to Mason. You bought us steak for crying out loud. The least I can do is buy you and Sly a sandwich or something."

She huffed a laugh and shook her head. "You're really good at convincing me to do what you want."

He chuckled and licked her jaw. "I'm hoping to convince you to do a lot more things that I want later."

She moaned softly. "I should be resisting you. I know this is a bad idea."

"What? Why is this a bad idea?"

She sighed and pulled away. "Because your friends are here to convince you not to move here."

"My friends are here to help me," Rocky said firmly.

Nikki snorted. "You don't know how women work. Lily isn't here to support you. She's here to check me out so she can undermine me and convince you that it's not worth moving here. She's not my friend, she's yours."

"Lily isn't like that," Rocky argued.

Nikki forced a smile. "Maybe not to you, but you're not an evil temptress trying to steal her friend away with a magical vagina or something."

Rocky wanted to laugh, but he could see in her eyes she meant it. She honestly thought Lily was there to make sure he didn't move.

Which meant she thought he wasn't man enough to make his own decisions.

"Lily doesn't get a say in where I live or who I love. She's a good friend, but the only one who chooses how I spend my time is me. I've chosen to spend it with you, and I love you, but you're making me pretty angry that you think I'm just going to blow you off because someone else says so."

NICOLE COULDN'T REMEMBER SEEING Rocky angry before. Smiling, laughing, and playing around, absolutely, but angry? Nope, it wasn't there.

But holy shit was it hot.

She felt guilty for the thought as soon as she had it, but it was too late. She could tell the moment he noticed the desire on her face. His anger morphed into something darker, something much more dangerous for her.

He stepped into her space and pressed her against the counter. His erection grew hard against her belly. Her eyes widened and her chest expanded with the breath she took.

And then his lips were on hers, demanding she open to him. His hands threaded into her hair and pulled to angle her mouth exactly where he wanted her.

Nicole was useless to fight him. She'd never been attracted to men who got jealous or angry, but it seemed Rocky broke every rule she'd ever set for herself, and then some. There wasn't a thing about him she could resist, and when he ground his cock into her stomach, she knew he'd be spending the night in her bed again.

With lots of condoms.

Rocky broke their kiss with Nicole's mouth still open and begging for him. He stepped back, leaving her to sag against the counter before she fell. The look in his eyes was blazing with desire and anger and love, and it made her knees even weaker than his kiss did.

"Don't doubt me, Nikki. Don't you dare fucking doubt me. You can get mad at me and yell, you can tell me off, but don't doubt me. You've been doing it too much lately, and I'm not okay with it."

Nicole stared at the man she loved and tried to wrestle her emotions back under control. A part of her wanted to tell his friends to take Sly to lunch so she could have Rocky instead. She stared at him as he watched her and knew her emotions were all over her face.

"You have to trust me, Nikki," he said softly. "I love you, and dammit, do I want you, but I need to know you trust me. If you don't, then you're right. This is a bad idea."

She drew in a breath and closed her eyes. She wanted to tell him everything that was racing through her mind, but she didn't know where to start.

"Nikki?"

"I trust you, Rocky. And I'm sorry I've been doubting you so much. I'm just not used to counting on other people. At all."

"I'm not other people, sweetheart."

She breathed a laugh and smiled up at him. "No, you're definitely not."

He inhaled deep and pulled her into his arms again. "God, I love you."

She closed her eyes and said the words in her head. She wanted to open her mouth and say them out loud, but the voice in the back of her head said *not yet*, so she waited.

"I'm hungry," Sly said from the other room.

Nicole pulled back from Rocky. He cupped her jaw and brought her lips to his for a gentle kiss that was just as hot as the demanding one. She trembled against him and told herself it didn't matter if she said the words, she loved him and didn't want to let him go.

He took her hand and led her into the living room.

"We're all going to get some lunch," he announced to everyone.

Sly jumped and said, "Yes!"

Nicole grabbed her purse and followed the others out of the apartment and down to the parking lot. She said she would drive, but Rocky insisted they all ride together. He got Sly's booster out of her car and buckled him into the center of the backseat, then slid in on one side. Archer got behind the wheel, and Lily asked where Nicole wanted to sit.

"I'll sit with Sly. Thanks." She was trying.

Lily nodded and got in the front. Archer immediately reached for her hand and held it the entire time he drove to the restaurant.

"Did you grow up in this area?" Lily asked when they were seated at a table.

"No. We've been here almost seven years," Nicole said.

"Where did you live before?"

"Texas."

"I've never been there. Which do you like better?"

Nicole forced a smile. "Here."

Lily shut up at the tone of Nicole's voice, and she immediately felt bad for snapping at the other woman.

"I didn't have a great relationship with my parents, and when I found out I was pregnant... they're dead now, to me. So being here is much better," Nicole explained, hoping Lily picked up on all the things she wasn't saying.

Lily nodded. "Parents aren't always easy. I'm sorry for your loss."

Nicole smiled. Olive branch extended, she went back to studying the menu.

Rocky squeezed her hand under the table and whispered, "Thank you."

Nicole looked up at him and smiled. She was going to try.

LUNCH WAS BETTER than Nicole thought it would be. Archer was funny and kind to Sly. He obviously worshipped his wife and bowed to her on just about everything. But Lily was just as devoted to Archer by Nicole's observation.

They were the kind of couple she always wanted to be a part of. Two people who loved each other and trusted each other and would do anything for each other.

On the ride back to Nicole's apartment, the conversation turned to sleeping arrangements.

"We haven't been to the hotel yet," Lily said. "There's two rooms?"

"Yeah. We figured it would be easier to get a suite like that instead of two separate rooms," Rocky explained.

"Definitely," Archer agreed. "Are you staying at the hotel?"

Rocky turned his gaze to Nicole. Her cheeks burned. She wanted to invite him to stay with her, but with everyone in the car waiting for her to speak, she felt ridiculous.

"Can we have a sleepover like you did with Mommy last night?" Sly asked.

Nicole closed her eyes and wished for... something that would take away her embarrassment.

"That sounds great," Rocky said. "What do you want to do?"

"We can stay up all night and watch movies," Sly said. "And if I get tired, you can sleep in my room with me."

Nicole tried not to be disappointed that her son was cock-blocking her. It wasn't fair to think of it that way, but she was hoping to get some time with Rocky alone overnight.

"Sounds like fun. But I'm not sure your bed is big enough for me and you," Rocky said.

"Then maybe we can sleep in Mommy's room and she can sleep in my room. Her bed is big enough for both of us since it was big enough for you and her."

Nicole was wondering when that miracle was going to happen that would take her away. She stared out the front window but ended up catching Archer's gaze and wry grin in the mirror. Her cheeks blazed all over again.

"We'll figure something out," Rocky said with a laugh.

Archer parked the SUV and the five of them headed back up to the apartment. Sly immediately commandeered the two men into playing a game with him, which left Nicole alone with Lily.

Time to face the music.

21

———————

NICOLE WANTED TO RETREAT TO THE KITCHEN, BUT SHE TOOK a seat at the table and watched the men try to sit on the floor with Sly. Rocky grinned at Archer and the two of them shared some kind of silent communication that Nicole wondered about.

"I'm sorry I've been kind of bitchy to you," Lily said, taking the seat next to Nicole at the table. "I love Rocky and will hate to have him leave."

"I didn't ask him to move here," Nicole said, facing Lily. The other woman was pretty, but not what Nicole expected. She figured Lily would be a thin, petite, perfect woman married to a former SEAL. She never thought she'd find a woman she could almost imagine being friends with.

"I know," Lily said. "Rocky is the kind of guy who will do anything for the people he cares about. He's very kind and I'm just having trouble imagining him not being in my life."

"You've known him long?"

Lily shook her head. "A few years. I met Archer before the rest of them. His brother and I went to college together.

Archer moved to Niagara Falls to be with me and the rest of them decided to stay."

Nicole's eyebrow went up in question.

Lily laughed. "Okay, yeah, I know how much of a hypocrite I sound like."

Nicole didn't comment.

"I am sorry I've made you uncomfortable. I don't mean to. Sometimes these men just lose their minds. I've sort of taken the role as annoying little sister to them and call them on their shit."

"Like falling for a magical..."

Lily twisted her lips and grimaced. "Yeah. Sorry about that. I've just never heard of Rocky acting like he is now. He's never gotten seriously involved with anyone. He's had a few hookups, but nothing that involved more than a few nights. Moving to a whole new state really threw me off."

"Again, I didn't ask him to do that."

"I know," Lily said with a nod. "And I'm not being fair to you by assuming you did something to trick him or trap him. I wanted to come down here so I could meet you."

"And drag him home?"

Lily had the decency to shrug. "It crossed my mind. I would never keep him away from his son. And now that I've seen how he is with you..."

"What do you mean?"

Lily smiled. "He clearly adores both of you. And that's a good thing. So, I hope we can get to know each other. This group of men... I never thought I'd know people like them. I never imagined having them in my life. They're amazing and they're my family. My mom wasn't the best, and I always assumed I would be alone forever. But Archer..." She looked across the room and smiled. She spun her wedding band around her finger, then met Nicole's gaze again. "I don't do well with goodbyes. I don't know if I'll be able to say goodbye to him. We will be down here to visit a lot, and that means I want us to be friends."

Nicole studied the other woman and wondered if they could be friends. Under any other circumstances, she thought there was a chance, but Lily blamed Nicole for breaking up her family. A family Nicole didn't know existed a few weeks ago, and one she secretly wished she could be a part of.

"You're a phlebotomist, right?" Lily asked.

Nicole nodded. "I am. I was in school when I got pregnant. I was planning to go to nursing school, but being a single mom is a lot harder than it looks."

Lily laughed. "I can't even imagine. You're stronger than I would have been."

Nicole looked at Sly and shook her head. "Not even a little. He's given me my strength. I made a vow to myself when I moved here that I would do everything in my power to give him the best life possible."

"And you've done that. You're a great mom from what I can see."

"Except for keeping him from his father and letting him get sick and getting caught up with people who have no problem hurting me or killing him to pay my debts."

"Rocky said you didn't know his name, so that one is not on you. I work in a hospital, so I know for a fact him getting sick is not on you. And the last one is just another example of you being a great mom. You were doing whatever it took to make sure your son didn't die. There's nothing wrong with that."

Nicole stared at the scratch on her hand-me-down table and tried to absorb Lily's words. She felt guilty for years for all the things she did wrong. Rocky could say he forgave her for keeping Sly from him, but until Lily said it wasn't her fault, Nicole wasn't sure she believed him.

"Does he hate me?" Nicole asked softly.

"Rocky?" Lily asked with brows up.

Nicole nodded.

"I'm pretty sure he's in love with you. Why do you think he hates you?"

Nicole shrugged. "For Sly."

Lily huffed a laugh and shook her head. "I've never seen him this happy. He wasn't exactly miserable before, but he was sort of neutral. Like he was existing instead of really living his life. He's a different person. It's only been a few hours since we got here, but I can tell he's where he's supposed to be with you and Sly."

Nicole drew a breath and looked at Rocky. He was laughing at something Sly did. He looked relaxed and happy. He rubbed Sly's head and hugged him to his side. Nicole's heart felt like the Grinch and grew in that moment. Grew to let in all the people she'd been trying to hold at a distance. Lily, Archer, Mason, Dex, and especially Rocky. She already knew she loved him, but knowing he wasn't just saying things to get her to let her guard down gave her the courage to love the people he loved.

"So, you work in a hospital?"

Lily nodded. "I'm in IT, but yeah. I get to know I'm doing good while not actually having to deal with blood and guts. I'm a bit squeamish."

Nicole smiled. "Do you know if they're hiring?"

ROCKY KEPT GLANCING at Nikki and Lily, wondering what they were talking about. Nikki was smiling more than anything, so he assumed it was going well, but he couldn't hear them.

"It's fine," Archer said quietly.

Rocky looked at him and shrugged. "I hope."

"She's worried."

"I know, but it's not her business."

Archer chuckled. "Have you met her?"

Rocky grinned. He loved Lily and would do anything for her, but if she messed things up for him with Nikki, he'd be pissed.

They went back to the game Sly made up and kept playing, trying to keep up with the changing rules as Sly made them up to try to keep things fair. Fair for himself, Rocky realized as Sly took more points from him.

"What was that?" Rocky asked with a laugh.

"You can't do that," Sly said.

"Why not?"

Sly kept playing and ignored his question.

Rocky looked up at Archer and they both laughed.

"He needs to play cards with us sometime. He'd beat everyone," Archer said.

Rocky nodded, then realized what Archer said. Sly wasn't going to be at their get-togethers because Sly wasn't moving to Niagara Falls. Rocky was moving to be near him.

"Excuse me," Rocky said, scrambling to his feet and heading toward the bathroom. He closed and locked the door, then closed the one that led to Nikki's room and locked that, too. He took a deep breath and closed his eyes as the pain sank in deep and took a hold of him.

He hadn't let himself think about walking away from his brothers. In the back of his mind, he knew it wasn't going to be easy, but living in the bubble he'd been in for the last few weeks with Nikki and Sly made it easy for him to ignore what was coming.

Archer's offhand comment brought the truth in front of Rocky and forced him to acknowledge that Sly wasn't going to be meshing in his life. For years, Rocky lived and worked and played with the men who were his family, and he was saying goodbye to all of it.

It was the right choice, but that didn't mean it was going to be easy. And to make it worse, he had to keep his thoughts from Nikki or she'd pull back again like she did every time things between them seemed like they might be hard.

Rocky knew from watching his brothers fall in love that nothing about relationships was easy. Finding the right person, falling for them, loving them, marrying them... none of it was easy. But his mother told him loving someone didn't mean deciding once and then living with it. Loving someone meant waking up every day and knowing the person you chose to love was the person you were made to love every day for the rest of your life. She was still grateful for the years she had with Rocky's father, even though she didn't get enough of them.

Rocky wasn't willing to walk away from Sly or Nikki. He hated walking away from his brothers, but he knew every single one of them would do the same thing if they were in his position.

Rocky took a deep breath and pulled himself together the best he could, then went back to the living room. He took his seat without meeting the gazes of any of the people in the room and asked whose turn it was.

Archer reached over and put his hand on Rocky's knee. He squeezed it and let go. He never looked at Rocky or said anything, but it told Rocky that Archer understood. He wasn't alone.

They finished their game, and Sly won, of course. Archer asked him how he always won.

Sly shrugged. "I'm really good."

Rocky chuckled.

"It helps that you're the only one who knows how to play."

Sly shrugged again. "You'll learn."

Archer rubbed his head. "I will, buddy."

Rocky, Archer, and Sly kept playing games that Sly made up. Lily and Nikki disappeared into the kitchen. Rocky wondered what they were talking about and doing but stopped wondering when the smells from the kitchen made their way out to them.

"Are you baking?" Archer asked without looking up.

"Always," Lily replied. "Nikki was kind enough to let me use her kitchen. We need to buy her groceries tomorrow because I used up a lot of stuff."

"Make a list," Archer replied.

"Already have one started."

Archer just chuckled. "Are you making dinner in there, too, or just dessert?"

"Just dessert. We'll grab stuff to make dinner when we go to the store tomorrow, too."

"The hotel has a kitchen," Rocky said.

"Yeah, but it's always more fun to cook for more than just two people. Besides, I need the practice," Lily said.

Rocky tilted his head. "You cook for more than two people all the time. What kind of practice do you need?"

"I'll be cooking for three soon," Lily said.

"Three? Why would you..." Rocky looked at Archer. "Is she...? Are you...?"

Archer grinned and nodded.

"Holy shit, dude! That's awesome! Congratulations!" Rocky pulled Archer in for a man hug and jumped up to hug Lily. She laughed and let him spin her around. "You're having a baby."

She nodded. "I am. It's really early, though. I'll only be thirteen weeks tomorrow so we haven't told many people yet."

"That's understandable," Rocky said, although he really had no clue.

"Dunn and Ash are the only ones who know," Archer said. "I wanted to make sure he is prepared for me to take some time off when the baby comes."

Rocky nodded. The things he would miss were stacking up. "Wow. A baby. We need to go out and celebrate."

Archer and Lily were on board once the cupcakes were out of the oven. "She's been baking more lately and trying out new recipes. If she's already this bad in the first trimester, I know the last one is going to be torture. And she's looking at houses so we have more space. She's got all these plans."

Rocky nodded and put his hand on Sly's shoulder. He missed so much. He didn't know what Nikki was like when she was pregnant, or how it was to find a new place to live with a baby. He never got to hear a heartbeat or let her squeeze his hand when she was in labor.

He didn't realize he missed all those things, and knowing he had made him want them. All of them.

He looked at Nikki, standing in the kitchen with Lily, and imagined her pregnant. Another baby of theirs ready to welcome into the world. More love to share.

Damn, when the hell did he turn into a sap? He shook

his head at himself. Love makes you do crazy things, his father used to say. Yep, it definitely did.

NICOLE CAUGHT the looks Rocky was giving her during dinner and wondered what was going through his head. He sat between Sly and Archer, but he looked like he couldn't decide where he wanted to be.

When Lily told Nicole she was pregnant, she knew asking about a job was the right thing. Moving to New York was the right thing. It made no sense that someone else being pregnant meant she had to move, but she had nothing in Tennessee besides Sly's doctors. She adored Dr. Andrews, but there were great doctors in New York. Lily already had a list of names for her and promised to make a few calls about jobs first thing Monday morning.

But until she knew something more definite, Nicole didn't want to tell Rocky about her decision to move to New York.

Lily was kind and funny, and with every passing moment, Nicole liked her more and more.

"What do you think we should name the baby, Sly?" Lily asked at one point.

Sly tapped his French fry on his lower lip and stared at the ceiling thoughtfully. "Hmm, what about Billie if it's a girl and Sylvester if it's a boy."

Lily grinned. "We can't have two Sylvesters! That would be so confusing."

"Fine. What about my middle name? Edward."

Rocky turned quickly to look at him. "Your middle name is Edward? His middle name is Edward?" he asked Nicole.

"Um, yes. Why?" she asked hesitantly.

Rocky pressed his lips together. "Edward was my father's name. Did I tell you that?"

Nicole shook her head. "No, I don't think so. I always liked the name. And it worked with Sylvester."

Rocky swallowed thickly and nodded. "It does." He reached for her hand behind Sly's seat and squeezed it.

"Edward is a great name," Lily said. "I think that should be on the top of the list. And Billie is pretty cool for a girl. You're good at this."

Sly nodded and ate another fry.

Rocky insisted on paying for everyone's dinner. Nicole wanted to argue, but she really didn't have the money to do so and simply thanked Rocky. He held her hand on their walk to the car on the way out of the restaurant.

"I can't believe his middle name is Edward. That's pretty cool."

Nicole nodded. "I'm glad he ended up named after you and your father. It sounds like he was a great dad."

"He was," Rocky said thickly. "The best."

"You take after him," Nicole said with a hip check.

Rocky chuckled. "I hope to be half the man he was."

Nicole smiled. "You can stay at the hotel tonight, if you want."

"You don't want me invading your bed again?" Rocky teased.

Nicole shook her head. "It's not that. I know you miss your friends, and this is big news. I just want you to know I won't be upset if you want to stay with them."

Rocky shrugged. "It's tough to know I'm saying goodbye soon."

She nodded. "I know. So spend the night there. Enjoy some time with them. Lily looks like she's falling asleep on her feet. It'll give you and Archer a chance to talk. You can give him some advice on being a great dad."

Rocky chuckled. "I'm not sure I know how yet. Are you sure you'll be okay?"

Nicole nodded. "We'll be fine."

Archer drove them back to the apartment complex. Rocky walked up with Nicole and Sly and said goodnight to Sly. While he was getting changed for bed, he gave Nicole a kiss that was guaranteed to keep her up for hours wishing he was in her bed.

She waved and locked the door behind him, then went to Sly's room. He was already under his covers with droopy eyes. Nicole opened his favorite book and left after only three pages when he was sound asleep.

She walked back through the apartment and double checked that the door was locked and the blinds were closed on the windows. She ate one of Lily's cupcakes and groaned with pleasure at the sinfully sweet taste. She debated eating a second one but decided against it, knowing if one wasn't enough, two might not be either.

Nicole went into the bathroom and got ready for bed. Teeth brushed and pajamas on, she pulled back the covers on her bed and froze.

Rose petals covered her sheets like a bloodstain, a thick blanket that was impossible to miss. On top was a note.

TIME'S UP.

22

Rocky and Archer were sitting in the common area of the hotel room when his phone rang. He didn't expect to hear from Nikki again and was surprised to see her name on his screen.

"Hey, babe. Miss me already?" he joked with her.

"Rocky?" she said.

Immediately, he was on his feet. She sounded small and scared, two words he hadn't yet thought of when it came to Nikki. "What happened? Are you okay? Sly? What's wrong?"

"Someone was in my apartment," she said. "Left... bed... scared." Her sentence was broken up by soft sobs.

"I'm on my way," Rocky said. "Stay on the phone with me."

He turned to Archer, whose face was hard as steel. "What happened?"

"She said someone was in her apartment. They left something in her bed," Rocky whispered, turning the phone away from his face to talk to Archer. "I can't leave them."

"Do you want me to come?"

Rocky shook his head. "No. Let Lily sleep. We might be

back here before long. I don't want her staying there. Either of them."

Archer nodded and followed Rocky to the door. "Call me."

Rocky waved as he ran down the hallway and out to the parking lot. Nikki's soft sobs and intermittent gasps echoed through the phone while he raced to her apartment. He was sure he would get pulled over, but no one pulled up behind him.

He was out of the SUV and running up to Nikki's apartment while she still cried on the phone. "I'm here, baby. I'm outside your door right now. I'm going to knock so you know it's me." He knocked on the door. "Let me in, sweetheart."

He heard the click of the lock through the phone and through the door. Nikki practically fell into his arms when she opened the door. He kicked it closed behind them and locked it, then carried her to the couch and sat down with her.

Rocky's heart pounded as he tried to calm her down. He never should have left her. He should have been there for her all night. He knew she was in danger, but he was selfish and wanted to spend time with his friends before he walked away from them. By doing so, he left the woman he loved and his son exposed.

It could have been minutes or hours by the time Nikki calmed down enough to tell him what happened. As soon as she did, he called Archer and relayed it to him.

"Those sons of bitches were in her home," Rocky spat.

"This is not your fault," Archer said.

"It sure as fuck feels like it is."

"My wife was kidnapped. Taken. Someone used me to snatch her right from under my goddamn nose. Was that my fault?"

"No," Rocky said vehemently.

"Then this isn't yours. People are fuckers and they deserve all the bad in the world to rain down on them. Nikki isn't one of those people. She deserves good, and so does Sly. And so do you. Now, pull your head out of your ass and check on your woman. Are you coming back here?"

Rocky sighed heavily. "She doesn't want to move Sly."

"Understandable," Archer said. "We'll come by first thing in the morning and get you guys."

"I took the SUV," Rocky said.

"Shit, that's right. Okay, well, we'll figure it out. But I'm calling Dunn. We can't wait for more intel. We need to stop this now, and we need backup," Archer said.

"I know. Thanks."

Archer hung up with promises to keep him posted. Rocky hated that he hadn't taken care of this for Nikki. He was too wrapped up in how he felt about her to notice how much danger she was in. He trusted his team was on it and would keep him informed about what was going on, but they were missing something. Something that meant Nikki was in more danger than they realized.

"Do you want to go to bed?" he asked Nikki softly.

She shrugged against his side.

"It's been a long day. Let's go lie down. If you don't sleep, that's okay, but you can try."

"What about Sly?"

"I won't let anything happen to either of you," Rocky assured her.

"What does that mean?"

"It means no one is going to hurt either of you." He crushed her against his side and pressed his lips to the top of her head. He waited seven years to find her again and only found her on a chance. He wasn't going to lose them.

"Maybe we should just stay here," Nikki said.

Rocky nodded against her head and settled back against the couch. Nikki stretched her feet up on the other end and snuggled tight against him.

Rocky rubbed her back and prayed she would get some sleep. He knew he wouldn't, but he could handle it. Years of training taught him how to survive with little to no sleep, especially when he was in danger.

After a while, Nikki's breathing steadied, and she went limp against his side. He slowed his own breathing to match hers and listened to the sounds of the apartment complex, praying backup would arrive before he needed to protect his family.

ZEKE WANTED to break down the door and rip that asshole to shreds. He could do it, too. He was the muscle, and he wasn't afraid to get his hands dirty.

He thought for sure he could get Nicole when the asshole walked out earlier. Zeke waited for all the lights to go out, but the dickwad was back before Nicole went to sleep. And it looked like he was there to stay.

"Fucking hell," Zeke muttered to himself.

He only needed to get Nicole alone to take her. She would learn to love him. And he could protect her. The other guy could have the kid for all Zeke cared, but he was going to have Nicole. She'd have his kid and forget all about the other one.

Zeke settled in for another long night of watching her when his phone rang. He didn't want to answer it, but he knew if he ignored his boss, he'd be on the list next. And then he couldn't protect Nicole.

"Yeah?"

"Where the fuck have you been?"

"Working."

"Doing what?"

"Keeping an eye on things."

The boss sighed heavily. "You're supposed to be taking care of things. Instead, I have to bring in a second person to handle the fucking mess you made."

"Second person?" Zeke asked, his hair standing on edge.

"Yes, a second person. Since you're incapable of doing your fucking job, someone else will have to do it for you. You have twenty-four hours to bring her to me, or someone else will do it for you."

"Fuck," Zeke whispered.

"I suggest you decide whose side you're on," Jon said in a voice that left zero interpretation.

"You know what side I'm on."

"I used to. Now, I'm not so sure. You've been spending a lot of time watching that woman and not so much getting anything from her. My wife said she didn't look like anyone had laid a hand on her, even though I told you she needed a reminder that she owed me."

"Your wife?" Zeke blurted.

He laughed. "She saw you, too, Zeke. It's funny how easy it is to watch a person when all their focus is on someone else. Maybe I'll let you watch."

"She's not yours," Zeke growled.

"And she's not yours either. I'm guessing that's the problem. But that'll change tomorrow. For me, at least."

"What about your wife?"

He snorted a laugh. "She lives a very comfortable life."

"She has no problem with you cheating on her."

"It's not cheating. It's training."

Zeke's stomach turned over. He'd been guard for training sessions in the past. Some of the women didn't survive. Zeke could not let that happen to Nicole. She was his. Which meant he was out of time. He had a day, less than, if he was going to get her away from his boss.

And Zeke would protect what was his.

NICOLE WOKE UP SLOWLY, the bleary light of day tickling her brain and telling her to wake up. She felt like there was something she was supposed to do, but the warm body she was wrapped around begged her to forget about the outside world and lose herself in him.

Him?

Her eyes flew open. Rocky. Living room. Rose petals.

The fear rushed back in like a bucket of ice water over her head. Her stomach dropped to the floor and left her feeling like she was going to be sick.

"It's okay, baby. I got you," Rocky whispered softly.

"I wish I'd never met him."

"I know you do, sweetheart. But we'll take care of it."

"I'm sorry."

"You have nothing to be sorry for," he said firmly. "Don't think about that at all."

She nodded, wishing she felt the same.

"What do you want to do? I need to go get Archer and Lily at some point so they have the SUV. I'm assuming we can use your car?"

She nodded and pushed herself up to sit next to him. She missed the heat of him against her side, but she needed to stand on her own. She refused to be the kind of woman who couldn't take care of herself, even if she felt like she was. The men Zeke worked with were deadly. They could make her disappear in a heartbeat if they wanted to. Just the thought sent a chill through her.

"I'm not going to let anything happen to you," Rocky said.

Nicole knew he meant it, but that independent part of her said she didn't need him to protect her. "We'll be fine. You should take the SUV back to Archer."

"There's no rush, Nikki. There's nothing they need it for right now."

Nicole stood and shook her head. "It's fine. I'm sorry I interrupted your night. You should spend time with your friends."

"Nikki," Rocky groaned. He stood and trapped her in his embrace. "Don't pull back from me right now, sweetheart. We will take care of this. I should have already taken care of it. These men... I won't let them hurt you."

"I can take care of myself," she said.

Rocky nodded. "I know. I've never doubted that. You've been taking care of yourself and Sly for years. You're strong, Nikki. But I'm not going to let you take care of yourself. I'm going to be by your side."

Nicole drew a breath and nodded. She was tired of doing it all herself. He wasn't telling her she couldn't, he was telling her she didn't have to. And that was more important to her.

"What time will Archer and Lily be up?"

"I'm sure they're already up. They usually get up fairly early."

"Take the SUV back now before Sly gets up."

"I don't like leaving you here alone," Rocky said.

Nicole drew a breath and forced a smile. "I don't like it either, but you can't be with me every hour of the day. Sly goes to see Dr. Andrews today, and I'll be back to work soon. You can't sit in my office with me."

"No, but I can sit outside."

Nicole chuckled. "You need a job. And we can't live like this forever. We need to resolve this."

"We will. But that doesn't mean I should walk away from you right now."

"I'll be fine," Nicole said. "Go quickly and be back soon. Sly goes to see Dr. Andrews at nine."

Rocky checked the time on his phone. "Okay, but keep the door locked and don't let anyone in."

Nicole shivered. "Didn't stop them yesterday."

Rocky kissed her hard on the lips. "I won't be long."

Nicole nodded and drew in a breath. She closed the door behind him and locked it. His footsteps hurried to the stairs, echoing off the metal as he raced down to the parking lot.

Nicole pushed away from the door and tried to tell herself everything was fine. She would make breakfast and Rocky would be back before she knew it. She had nothing to worry about.

She opened the fridge and looked inside to see what she had for breakfast when there was a knock on the door. She laughed to herself and shook her head. She knew he wouldn't be able to leave. Truth be told, she was happy he'd come back. Listening to him rush off made her more anxious with each step he took away from her.

She unlocked the door and swung it open with a smile. "Couldn't stay away?"

"No, I couldn't," Zeke said, pushing his way inside.

Nicole opened her mouth to scream, but he clamped a large hand over it and pressed her against the door.

"Scream and your kid is dead. I don't think you'd like that, would you?"

Tears ran down her face as she shook her head. His breath was hot and stale against her cheek. His weight crushed her to the door. Everything inside her screamed to fight, but Sly... She couldn't risk him hurting Sly. He was still asleep and likely would be for another thirty minutes. She just had to find a way to get rid of Zeke by then.

"Now, you're going to pack your shit and leave a note for Daddy Dearest. Tell him you don't love him and you don't want him or the rugrat and that you're leaving them."

"No," burst free from Nicole, the sound ripped from her chest.

He yanked hard on her hair, tilting her head to the side. Pain echoed inside her head and speared through her neck. "I told you to be quiet. Or should I go take care of the kid now?"

Nicole shook her head. She could barely see Zeke with the tears flooding her vision. She couldn't lose Sly. Even if she had to do what Zeke said, she couldn't risk him hurting her son.

"Good girl," Zeke soothed. "That's my good girl." He slid his hand around her waist and pushed her shirt up. His erection grew against her back. "I can't wait to have you. But we don't have time for that right now. We need to go before your boyfriend gets back or my boss finds us."

He moved away from her, letting her spin to face him. "What do you mean?" Nicole demanded.

"He wants you for himself. He's going to train you, Nicole. I won't let that happen to you. You're mine, not his. We're leaving town. He'll never find us."

"I'm not yours."

He slapped her hard, the pain radiating through her

cheek before she even realized he hit her. "Don't you dare talk back to me."

Nicole held her hand to her cheek and tried to figure out how she could get out of the situation. Sly was the most important thing, but she didn't want to think about Sly growing up without her. Rocky was a good dad, and he would take care of him, but it broke her heart to think she might never see either of them again.

"Move it," Zeke said, pulling a gun from his waistband. "Now."

Nicole sucked in a breath and went still at the gun. She didn't know much about them, but she knew enough to be scared. Especially when one was pointed at her face.

She walked quietly down the hall to her room. She ignored the bed and headed for her closet, wishing she had a phone in there and could text Rocky. Her phone was on the coffee table, and there was no way to get it without Zeke noticing.

Zeke closed the door to her room and looked around. "I always wondered what the inside looked like."

"What?"

"Of your room. I can't see enough through the blinds to really get a feel for the room. Not that I cared when I got to see your tits on display. I can't wait to taste them and fuck them."

Nicole gasped.

"And to watch you when you come. The only time I got to see that was when you were on the couch with that fucking... He's not going to touch you ever again. You're mine, Nicole. Do you hear me?"

Nicole trembled. "You... watched me?"

Zeke stared at her breasts and licked his lips. "Every chance I got. I've been sitting outside for months. You like to walk around your room naked, and the blinds are just right for me to be able to see in. It was like you wanted me to watch you."

"No, I didn't," Nicole spat.

He crossed the room and grabbed her arms, slamming her against the wall. He pressed his entire body to hers and sealed his lips over hers. She clamped her mouth shut, but he squeezed her arms tighter until she gasped and he plunged his tongue inside.

He tasted like stale cigarettes and morning breath. She could smell his BO and feel his erection against her stomach. All she could think about was being subjected to that every day for the rest of her life. Until he tired of her and killed her.

Vomit raced up her throat and pushed out. He threw her to the ground, spitting as she gagged and choked on the floor.

"Fucking bitch!" Zeke spit on her back.

Nicole almost felt guilty for throwing up in his mouth, but he didn't exactly give her a choice. Karma was a bitch. She only hoped Karma had a few more tricks in store for Zeke before the day was over.

And if she was lucky, a few for Nicole, too.

23

————

THE WHOLE TIME ROCKY WAS WALKING AWAY FROM NIKKI, something felt off. He didn't want to leave her side, and it wasn't just not wanting to be without her. They were after her. They'd threatened her. They'd made it clear they were coming for her.

He knew she could take care of herself, but he didn't want her to have to. He never should have left.

Rocky told his phone to call Archer as he drove through the next light.

"Morning. How was the night?" Archer asked.

"Uneventful."

"That's not what I expected," Archer said.

"Everything was quiet. I didn't hear anything. Something feels off."

"These are not people who wait around for what they want. Dunn was in touch with some contacts at Homeland before we left, and they got back to him yesterday. This group... they're bad news. We're talking drugs and people and weapons. Anything they can move, they move. And they have no loyalties to anyone. The guy who runs the operation settled here years ago because it's quiet. No one else that big operated in the area, so he thought it was a good place. And with the mountains so close, they can disappear, or make others disappear without a trace."

"Fuck," Rocky breathed. "It's worse than we thought. I figured this was a small town group who needed the money."

"Not at all. This is a massive operation who won't take no for an answer because they don't show kindness. If they make a deal, you better hold up your end. Dunn and the rest of the team are on their way down here. They should be on the ground in just over an hour. They're going to work with the local unit to bring this operation down."

"Shit," Rocky breathed. He turned on his signal and made a fast U-turn. "I need to go back."

"Go back? Where? What do you mean?"

"I was on my way to pick you up so you guys would have wheels, but something doesn't feel right."

"I was going to call a ride and come to you. Nikki and Sly can't be alone. These guys could have planted something in her place. They might have known you were there and exactly when you left," Archer said, his voice showcasing the same tension that was racing through Rocky.

"I never should have left her alone."

"Don't beat yourself up. It might be totally fine. I'll get a ride. I'll be there as soon as I can be. Be careful," Archer said.

"Thanks," Rocky said as he hung up. He drove way too fast on the way back, but he didn't care. No one stopped him.

He pulled into Nikki's complex and told himself he was being ridiculous. She was safe. Nothing would happen to her.

Even as he ran up her stairs, he knew it was all lies. He wasn't in a war zone anymore, but he saw the ugly side of humanity on a daily basis. He knew how evil people were.

He paused at Nikki's door. He didn't tell her he was coming right back, so she could be doing anything. He didn't want to risk waking Sly, but he knew Nikki locked the door.

He knocked softly and sent her a text at the same time to let her know it was him at the door. He waited a few seconds, listening without hearing a sound in the apartment.

The hairs on his arms stood on end. Something was definitely wrong. He was used to being calm and in control when they were on a mission, but this wasn't a mission. This was his family, the people he loved more than anything in the world. His future wife and his son were inside, and he had no idea if they were safe or not.

Rocky tried to take a deep breath and faced the parking lot. The same black car he noticed days ago was parked at the back of the lot. Backed in where no one could see a plate. It was out of the way enough that you wouldn't notice it unless you were looking for it. But Rocky was looking for it.

It was possible he was wrong, but Rocky learned what a lot of SEALs learned over time. To trust his instincts. Every cell inside him was screaming that there was something else going on. That the car wasn't there because the person who drove it lived there, or was involved with someone who did. No, he knew that car was there for one reason.

Nikki.

Rocky reached for the doorknob with a steady hand. If someone was inside the apartment, Nikki and Sly were both in danger. His only option was to sneak up on him.

The knob turned under his hand, a soft click the only indication that he could enter without being invited in. He heard the lock engage when he left, so he knew it wasn't good. Nikki wouldn't have unlocked the door for any reason. Not until Rocky returned. She was scared, and she was not stupid. Which only left one explanation.

Rocky looked around for something he could use as a weapon. He never thought he'd need a gun when he was going to donate a kidney and found himself ill-equipped and unprepared. He would normally be able to count on his team to show up fully armed, but if they were arriving in an hour, they wouldn't make it fast enough. Archer might, but Rocky wasn't sure if he could wait for him.

A noise from the bedroom drew his attention. Nope, definitely not waiting for backup. He wanted to run in and help her, but it was very possible he would do more harm than good if he walked in without a plan. First, he needed a weapon.

Rocky moved quietly into the kitchen. He grabbed a knife from the drawer, praying the creak of the drawer didn't alert whoever was in the bedroom with Nikki. He left it open, not willing to risk more noise.

Both bedroom doors were closed. With any luck, Sly would sleep a little longer. Rocky had no idea what his normal routine was, but he sent up a prayer to whoever was listening that his son didn't get hurt in the crossfire of whatever was about to happen.

He sent up another prayer that Nikki didn't get hurt, either.

Rocky crept down the hall soundlessly. At the door, he paused, wishing he had some gear to see who was where in the room. Nikki cried out, a little to the left, and Rocky had to grit his teeth to stop from charging in and ruining the element of surprise.

He reached for the doorknob and was about to grab it when the door swung open. Rocky drew back, surprised at being caught in the hallway. The other man, Zeke he assumed, wasn't nearly as surprised.

Rocky swung the knife, but Zeke sidestepped the attack quickly. He caught Rocky on the back of the neck with the butt of the gun, sending him to his knees.

"This is who you fucked? He can't even hold a knife. Give it to me," Zeke growled.

He towered above Rocky, a big man before Rocky was on his knees. The smell coming off him said he hadn't showered in a while. He was huge with muscles that told the story of what he did for a living. And it wasn't helping old ladies across the street.

Rocky's head spun, and his eyes blurred. His only chance at getting out of this alive was to get the knife back. He tried to reach for it, but it was too far away. Movement caught his attention across the room. "Nikki."

"Nicole is no longer interested in you," Zeke said. "She's mine." He turned to her. "Go ahead, tell him."

"I'm sorry, Rocky," she said. Tears ran down her face. A red mark marred her cheek with a bruise forming around the edges. Her hair was tangled in a knot on the side of her head from where he'd obviously been dragging her around.

Rage welled up inside Rocky, but the pain from the blow to the back of his head made him too dizzy to stand. Or maybe that was the combination of Zeke's odor and vomit that overwhelmed him and made him think he was going to throw up, too. "Nikki."

Nikki moved toward him and kicked the knife in his direction. She tried to scramble out of the way, but Zeke grabbed her by the hair. She yelped and reached for her scalp.

"Fucking whore. Why the hell did you do that? Now I'm going to have to make you pay for it and watch him die. Is that what you want?"

"No, please," Nikki cried.

Rocky fumbled for the knife and finally managed to pick it up again. He stood on wobbly legs and held it out. "Let her go."

Zeke turned back to Rocky and chuckled. He waved his gun around and said, "Do you see this? I can end you before you even think about slicing into me."

"Trust me, I'm already thinking about it," Rocky growled.

"Yeah? What about her?" He turned the gun toward Nikki and pressed it to her temple.

Fear flashed in her red eyes. More tears poured down her cheeks. She whimpered. "Please."

"Okay. All right. Fine. I'm putting it down. Just let her go." Rocky dropped the knife at his feet and put his hands in the air.

Zeke tugged on Nikki's hair. "Give me the fucking knife." He threw her onto the floor at Rocky's feet.

Rocky crouched down and helped her to stand. He brushed the hair back from her face and asked if she was okay. She shook her head.

The gun cocked behind her, and Nikki's eyes went wide. "Take care of Sly for me. Tell him I love him. I always will."

"Tell him yourself, Nikki."

She shook her head. "He'll kill Sly if I don't go with him."

"He's going to kill you."

She shook her head again, determination and strength in her eyes. "No, he won't."

Rocky met her gaze and understood. Zeke wasn't taking her to his boss. He was taking her for himself.

"Nikki, no."

Nikki stepped back with the knife in her hand and handed it to Zeke. Rocky saw the pain in her eyes. She was sacrificing herself to save him and her son. Giving herself up. She knew what she was doing, and she knew how she would spend the rest of her life, but she was doing it for them.

He wasn't having that.

"Back up. Let us out of the room," Zeke said firmly. He kept the gun trained on Nikki.

Rocky had enough training to know attacking someone head-on in a situation like that was rarely successful. He tried to surprise Zeke, but that didn't work, either. Instead, he was going to have to outsmart him. Piss him off. Make him attack Rocky and give Nikki a chance to get away.

Rocky moved out of the way and down the hall. He stepped into the kitchen to let them into the living room. Only when he knew he had the advantage did he open his mouth.

"Good luck trying to get her to come for you. She only likes my cock inside her," Rocky said with a smirk.

"That's just because she hasn't had mine."

Rocky snorted. "Yeah, because a pencil dick like yours can't satisfy a woman, especially when you force it on her."

"Fuck you, asshole."

"Nah. You're not really my type. But Nikki is. I can still feel those sexy lips of hers wrapped around my dick. She sucked me hard. And she moaned when she did it. Turned her on, didn't it, babe?"

Nikki stared at him like he'd lost his damn mind.

"Guess you're wrong about that one," Zeke said with a laugh.

"No, he's not," Nikki finally said. Her voice was rusty and broken. "I almost came just from that. But he's the only one who knows how to make me come."

"Yep," Rocky said with a pop. "She can't get enough of me. You're going to have a challenge. She makes herself come by thinking about me, and when I'm inside her, she loses her mind. As bad as you smell, she'll probably throw up all over you if you even try to kiss her. A shower could help, but maybe you can tell her to just fantasize that it's me and she might be willing. Maybe give you one O."

"She doesn't need to fantasize about you when she's with me, you fucker. She's mine. All mine!" Zeke lunged at Rocky and swung. Rocky avoided the knife and delivered a blow to Zeke's throat. He dropped the gun at his feet and grabbed his neck.

Rocky moved forward to grab the gun while he was distracted. Rocky kept his eye on Zeke right up until he looked down for the gun. His fingers brushed the edge of the metal...

"No!" Nikki shouted.

IT ALL HAPPENED SO FAST, but Nicole saw it in slow motion. When Rocky started talking, she didn't know what he was doing, but it distracted Zeke enough that they didn't run out, so she figured he was stalling.

Then Zeke attacked him.

Nicole watched as Rocky fell to the ground at Zeke's feet. The knife stood straight up out of his back. Red stained his shirt quickly, the fabric held close to his skin by the knife.

Nicole fell to her knees. Every last shred of hope she had that she would make it out of there alive disintegrated. She didn't know what to do. If she pulled out the knife, he could bleed to death. If she left it in, she had nothing to defend herself.

Either way, the man she loved was lying motionless on her living room floor. And she never had the chance to tell him she loved him.

"See if he can make you come when he's dead," Zeke growled, reminding her she wasn't alone.

He grabbed Nicole by the hair again, dragging her to her feet. Nicole yelped and tried to pull free, but he was too strong. He was almost to the door when she heard Sly's voice.

"Mommy?"

"No, no," Nicole cried. "Go back to bed, Sly."

"Mommy? What's going on? What happened to Daddy? Who is that?"

"I'm a friend of your mom's," Zeke said with a smile. He released Nikki's hair and smoothed it down roughly. "I was going to take her to the doctor because she wasn't feeling well. You stay here with your daddy, okay?"

"But he's hurt. What happened to him?" Sly asked. His voice wobbled with his chin. He moved closer to Rocky and his big brown eyes widened, then flipped from Rocky to Nicole and up to Zeke.

Nicole dropped to her knees in front of Sly and took his hands. He stood next to Rocky, protecting the father he loved after a short period of time. She prayed she would always be able to remember them, and that they would always have each other. If nothing else worked out, she hoped her son wouldn't lose both of his parents. "I love you, Sly. I'll always love you. Don't ever forget that. Do you hear me?"

"I love you, too, Mommy."

"Good. Then turn around and cover your ears. Now."

She picked up the gun from under Rocky's side and turned. She didn't care where she shot, as long as it was Zeke. She pulled the trigger over and over until the gun clicked, telling her she was out of bullets.

She forced herself to watch him. His eyes widened with shock. His shirt turned red in three spots. He looked down like he couldn't believe she shot him, then lifted his gaze to hers.

"I loved you," he said. His knees hit the floor and his whole body shook. He grabbed at his chest where one of the gunshots was pumping blood onto his shirt faster than the other two. "I loved you," he said again. Then he fell face first onto the carpet.

"Mommy! Mommy!" Sly screamed.

The door burst open as Nicole reached for Sly. She shielded him with her body and screamed.

She only stopped when Archer asked, "What the hell happened?"

24

———

Warmth and comfort were the first things Rocky felt when he woke up. Safe. Like nothing bad was going to happen.

Then he moved, and pain laced through his back. "Oh, fuck," he groaned, stilling immediately.

"Don't move," a voice said softly. "You're bandaged up pretty well, but it's going to hurt for a while."

"What happened?" he asked, forcing his eyes to open. He didn't recognize the woman in front of him. Her scrubs said she was a health care professional, which meant he was in the hospital.

"You don't remember?" she asked, her eyes narrowing as she checked the monitors he was connected to.

Rocky shook his head, then stopped. "Nikki. What happened to Nikki? Did he take her? I need to go get her." Rocky tried to push up. He kicked the blankets off his feet and winced. He had to swallow back the bile rising in his throat.

The woman pressed on his shoulders and urged him to

lie back. "You need to stay in this bed. You need rest. And you need to let me do my job."

"I need to know what happened to my family," Rocky insisted. He glared at the stubborn woman even though it held zero malice. Even if she stepped back and told him he could go, he wouldn't make it to the door before collapsing or throwing up and they both knew it.

"I will find out about your family. All I know is about you. Please try to rest."

Rocky nodded, knowing he had no choice, and laid back on the bed. She walked out of the room, and his eyelids drooped again.

The next time he woke up, no one was in the room with him. He reached back for a call button and hit it.

"Can I help you?" someone asked, walking into his room.

She was different from the woman who was there when he woke up the first time. "My family. Where's my family?"

"Your brother went to get coffee. He'll be right back."

"My brother?" Rocky asked.

The woman gave him a sharp look. "You do have a brother, don't you? Because he told me he was your brother."

"I do," Rocky said. "I just didn't know he was here."

"Mm hm," she said with a look that said she knew he was lying. "I'll tell him you're awake."

She walked out, leaving Rocky alone again. The pain in his back wasn't as bad as before, but he was definitely in a lot of pain. And on some heavy drugs to keep his head funny.

He had no idea how long he'd been out or what happened to Nikki and Sly. Or Zeke. Or Archer. It was dark outside his window, which could mean it was nighttime or it could mean it was a cloudy day. He had no clue what was going on.

"Don't fucking scare us like that again," Mason said as he walked in. "What the hell?"

"Where's Nikki?" Rocky demanded.

Mason grimaced and took his time sitting down.

"I might be injured but I will kick your ass somehow if you don't tell me where she is."

"She's in jail," Mason admitted.

"What? Why?"

"Because she killed a man."

"Who?"

"That Zeke guy. You don't remember?"

Rocky shook his head and tried to pull something from his memory, but the last thing in there was Zeke... "Did he stab me?"

Mason narrowed his eyes. "You really don't remember?"

Rocky shook his head again. The hospital gown was scratchy and tight all of a sudden, like it was trying to choke him. He pulled at the collar. "He was going to take her. It was self-defense. He was going to kill Sly if she didn't go with him. You have to tell the police."

"She already did," Mason said.

"Then why the fuck is she in jail?"

"Because they have to do their jobs," Mason said softly.

Rocky drew a breath. He knew what Mason had been through, and even though they never talked about it, Rocky knew Mason killed his wife in what he thought was self-defense. Since he wasn't actually in danger, he was convicted and sentenced. The same thing could happen to Nikki. She killed an unarmed man with his own gun. A gun that likely wasn't registered at all, let alone registered to her.

"Where's Sly? What happened to my son?"

"He's with Dex. Archer got there right after Nikki shot Zeke. They called the police and told them everything. Nikki told Sly to stay with Archer, but the rest of us got there around the time they were taking Nikki. He knew Dex and I the best, so he stayed with Dex while I'm here, since I'm your brother and the nurses would let me in."

Rocky snorted. "The nurses know you're full of shit."

Mason shrugged. "It doesn't matter. Until everything is sorted out, I'm all you got."

"How long has it been?"

Mason checked his phone. "About fourteen hours."

"Nikki's not getting out tonight."

Mason shook his head. "No, she's not. She has a hearing first thing in the morning. Dunn was in touch with the FBI and Homeland yesterday, and they moved on Zeke's boss today. They got everyone, and Dunn gave all the credit to Nikki. Someone is supposed to be at her hearing tomorrow to vouch for her."

"I can vouch for her. I need to be there," Rocky said.

"You need to rest up. You were stabbed in the kidney, and when you only have one, it's not good when it's damaged," Mason told him.

Rocky sobered quickly and stopped fighting to get out of bed. "What?"

"These guys knew what they were doing. Zeke knew all about the surgery. He went after you where he could do the most damage."

"Fuck. What does that mean for me?"

"It means you have to take it easy and recover. Dex will bring Sly over tomorrow. I'm sitting here with you tonight. And Dunn will get Nikki out. Until then, get some sleep, take all the meds they'll pump into your body, and let us do our jobs."

Rocky nodded. He laid back against the bed and tried to force his mind to relax. "Thank you for being here. I don't know what I'm going to do without you guys."

"We'll make it work," Mason said, sounding as happy about Rocky leaving as he was. "The most important thing is your family. The rest will come."

Rocky nodded. It was just too bad his families didn't live in the same city.

NICOLE STARED up at the ceiling and tried not to throw up. When she first walked in, she did. The smells of people and alcohol and waste all mixed together, and she couldn't hold it in. The fear had gotten to her, but the fear only lasted so long. Then the reality slammed her in the face and invaded her senses and she lost it. Literally.

Since she was arrested but not officially booked, she was in a holding cell alone. For that, she was grateful, but spending a night away from Sly wasn't easy. He'd never even gone to a sleepover. She'd never spent more than a workday away from him. And she was locked in a jail cell because she tried to protect him.

After she created the mess they were in.

Tears leaked from the corners of her eyes and slid back into her hair. She'd screwed up everything. She could tell herself she was being a good mom and doing whatever it took, but the reality was, she messed up. For that, she'd never forgive herself, and she was sure Rocky would feel the same.

Rocky. She closed her eyes and said her millionth prayer that he survived. Seeing the knife sticking out of his back...

she'd never get that out of her mind. She was to blame for him getting hurt.

Archer told her it would all be okay, but how? How could it all be okay? She was a felon, and she got the man she loved stabbed. And she never even told him she loved him. Even if he survived, she'd never get the chance because he wouldn't forgive her for it.

"Burke, time to go," the guard said, standing in front of her cell. She waited for Nicole to hold out her wrists and snapped the cuffs on her.

Nicole did her best not to cause trouble, hoping that helped her case. She followed the guard to the door and waited to be let out.

They walked a few hallways and then buzzed through a door that led directly to a courtroom. Nicole followed the others who were there, all ready to sit before a judge and have their fate decided.

Nicole had a lawyer assigned to her by the county since she couldn't afford her own. Rocky's boss, Dunn, said they'd take care of everything, but she wasn't counting on it. They had to make sure Rocky was okay, not worry about the woman who put his life in jeopardy.

When Nicole's name was called, the guard helped her stand and led her to the defendant's table.

The judge addressed her directly. "Do you have representation, Ms. Burke?"

"Yes, your honor. Someone was assigned to me."

"Are they here?"

"We're here, we're here," someone said from the back of the courtroom. "Sorry, I'm late, your honor. Ms. Burke is being represented by DHS."

"Excuse me?" the judge asked. "What does the Department of Homeland Security have to do with this case? Aren't you usually responsible for putting people away?"

"Yes, your honor, but Ms. Burke was critical in taking down a criminal organization that we had been following for years. We couldn't have done it without her assistance, and we believe she was justified in her actions," the woman said. She made her way to the front and stood next to Nicole.

Nicole looked at the perfectly dressed woman in a navy suit and four-inch heels. Her sleek, black hair was brushed behind her shoulders in a style that didn't dare defy the woman it grew from. She didn't bother to look at Nicole, just stared at the judge.

"Is this true, Ms. Burke?"

Nicole shrugged and mumbled something incoherent.

"You have to answer her," the lawyer said. "She needs to hear you say a word."

"Yes," Nicole said, wondering how in the world all this happened. She had no idea what she'd done, but if it meant she could walk out of jail and never go back, she would do it.

"Am I to assume this means Ms. Burke pleads not guilty?" the judge asked.

"You have to say it," the lawyer whispered.

"Yes, your honor. Not guilty," Nicole said. Her entire body shook.

The judge nodded and turned to the men at the other table. "Do you have anything to add to this?"

They shook their heads. "No, your honor. We agree with Ms. Monroe."

"Okay. Case dismissed," the judge said. She hit her gavel and called out, "Next."

Nicole wasn't sure what she was supposed to do. The guard walked over and unlocked her cuffs and handed her a slip of paper. The lawyer took it and said, "I'll collect your belongings. Wait for me outside. We still need to talk."

Nicole nodded, afraid to do anything other than what the woman said. She turned and walked through the courtroom, feeling extremely out of place. She made it to the hallway and looked around, wondering where she was supposed to go.

"Nikki," she heard to her left.

She nearly cried when she saw Archer to the side.

"Sorry we were late. We didn't get word until an hour ago that you were on the docket for this time. We tried to get here in time to make it into the courtroom," Archer said.

Nicole shook her head. "I'm surprised you made it at all. And the lawyer? Who is she?"

"Dunn had all this in the works before he got here. You were supposed to be called as a key witness to everything. They had your name before, so when he told them you were arrested, they jumped into action."

"Who are they? What is going on?"

"We took down Zeke's entire organization yesterday. Everything you shared with Rocky, he sent to us. It took us a while to figure out who they were, but once we did, we went to the local network. They were watching them and your intel helped to put a few pieces together. The whole network crumbled because of you. What Ms. Monroe said in there, every word of it is true. None of this would have been possible without your help."

Nicole's head spun with all the information Archer told her. She wasn't upset with Rocky, but she didn't know he was telling them about everything. She wasn't directly involved, yet they gave her credit for it all and helped her.

The enormity of the situation and exactly what she was involved in sank in, and Nicole stumbled. She reached for the closest bench and fell onto it, unable to keep herself upright.

"This is a good thing," Archer said. "A very good thing. You helped get a bunch of criminals off the street. I know it's a lot to digest, but you did great work."

"Yes, she did. Nice to see you again, Mr. Ford. How is our patient?" Ms. Monroe asked.

"Rocky's better today. They were able to fix him back up and he'll be back to annoying the shit out of everyone before too long."

"Glad to hear it. I need to head back to the office. I'm assuming you can take Ms. Burke home?"

Archer nodded. "That's why I'm here."

"Good." She handed over Nicole's bag of possessions. "It was nice to meet you, Ms. Burke. Thank you for what you did."

Nicole nodded numbly and shook Ms. Monroe's hand. The other woman smiled and waved and disappeared into the crowd.

"Are you ready to go?" Archer asked.

"Rocky's okay?" Nicole asked softly.

Archer nodded. "Yes. He's been asking for you. Lily insisted I bring you to the hotel first, and then we'll all head over to the hospital."

Nicole nodded, going along with whatever she was supposed to do. She felt broken and bruised, like she'd been beaten up and was still in a daze. She let Archer guide her out of the courthouse and to the SUV he had. The ride to the hotel was quiet as she stared out the window. He drove and let her have the peace.

Archer led her to the hotel room and unlocked the door. There were voices inside, but they all stopped when Nicole and Archer walked in.

"Mommy!" Sly shouted, racing over to her. He collided with her and nearly knocked her over. Archer stabilized her and squeezed her shoulder before leaving them to have a moment.

Nicole's eyes filled again as she hugged Sly to her side. She wasn't sure she'd see him again and being able to hold him overwhelmed her.

"Are you okay, Mommy?"

Nicole nodded. "I'm much better now."

"Good. You have to meet all my uncles. Most of them left already, but Uncle Dunn is still here. So's Uncle Dex and Uncle Mason, but Uncle Mason is at the hospital with Daddy. Can we go see him now?"

Lily walked over and put her hand on Sly's head. "I think Mommy might need a shower and something to eat. How about we fix her something while she takes a shower and then we can all go to the hospital?"

"Yeah, let's do that. Is that okay, Mommy?"

Nicole nodded and found she couldn't choke out any words. These people, these amazing strangers, took care of her son and made the entire ordeal almost fun for him. She was sure he was scared, but he was acting like nothing was out of the ordinary when he raced back to the living room of the suite and jumped on the couch next to Archer.

"Are you okay?" Lily asked.

Nicole shook her head, not really sure what to say.

Lily nodded to one of the bedrooms and closed the door behind them. "It's not easy. I've been there. It'll take you a little while to get past it, but you will. And, if you're still interested, I have a job for you. Whenever you're ready to move."

Nicole started crying. Lily wrapped her in a hug and held her.

"Is this a good cry or a bad cry?"

Nicole shook her head. "I don't know why you're all so nice to me."

Lily laughed. "Because we take care of our own, and you're one of us, Nikki."

"I'm not sure Rocky wants me to be. Not after all this."

Lily chuckled. "The only reason he isn't here right now is because we left Mason at the hospital with him. The guys told Mason if Rocky leaves that he's to blame. He's not going to let anything happen."

"Mason?"

Lily nodded. "Rocky can't take Mason on a good day, let alone after he's been stabbed. He's not leaving the hospital until the doctors tell him he can."

"You think Rocky still wants to be with me?"

"Absolutely. You have nothing to worry about."

"I hope not," Nicole said, wishing she had Lily's confidence.

25

———

ROCKY WATCHED THE NURSE LEAVE HIS ROOM AND WONDERED if he was ever going to get out of there. He hadn't heard anything about Nikki's hearing, and he was crawling out of his skin waiting for news.

"Nothing?" he asked Mason for the hundredth time.

Mason checked his phone again and shook his head. "I will let you know."

Rocky groaned. He hated being stuck in a bed. When he was in the hospital for his donation surgery, he could move around and went to visit Sly every day. This time, there was nowhere for him to go, and they wouldn't even let him use the bathroom on his own. He was losing his mind.

A knock on the door brought his attention to it. He pushed himself up higher on the bed and stared at the curtain until someone walked around it.

He tried not to be disappointed when it was Lily.

"Where's Nikki? Is she out yet?" Rocky asked.

"Well, good morning to you, too," Lily said.

"I love you, Lil, but I need to know Nikki is okay. I need to see her or talk to her or something," Rocky grumbled.

"Okay, fine," Lily said, a cheeky smile on her face.

She turned back to the curtain, and Rocky wondered what was going on. Then he heard the soft footsteps and held his breath.

Nikki appeared in front of him like he'd dreamed her up. She was in jeans and a loose top. Her hair was free around her shoulders, and her face was bruised from where Zeke hit her the day before. Rocky's heart broke for her.

"Nikki," he breathed.

She bit her lip and stayed put, rooted to the ground. "I'm sorry for everything that happened. For you getting hurt."

"Jesus, baby, I don't care about that. I care about you. Are you okay?"

She nodded and squeezed her hands together.

"If you don't get your ass over here, I'm getting out of this bed and dragging you over here. And then Mason will kick my ass." He reached out to her.

Nikki finally moved, slowly, and took his hand. He yanked her down, and she fell onto him. He pressed his nose to her hair and breathed her scent in deeply.

"None of this is your fault, Nikki. God, I love you. I was so worried about you."

"You're the one who's in the hospital," she said.

"Yeah, and you're the one who was in jail. Did Dunn take care of everything?"

Nikki nodded.

"Good. You're safe now. We can move on with our lives."

Nikki pulled back and stood. "I... um... I don't want you to move here."

Rocky's heart fell. Everything inside him burst with pain. She couldn't mean it. "Nikki, don't..."

"I don't want you to move here because Lily already got

me a job at her hospital. If you're okay with all of us living in Niagara Falls."

"What? She did what? When did this happen?" Rocky asked. He couldn't keep from smiling like a fool.

"When we talked the other day, I told her there was no reason for me to stay here and asked if she knew of any openings. She made some calls this morning. She's a miracle worker. And I just thought... I don't know. You have this whole life up there, and we don't really have anything here. I always wished Sly had family and people to count on besides me, and you love what you do and the people you work with, and I can't ask you to leave all that. It wouldn't be fair. And—"

"Nikki," he interrupted.

"Yeah?"

"You don't have to convince me, sweetheart. If you're sure about this, I'm sure. You're my home. You and Sly. I love you."

"I love you, too," she said softly.

"What? You do?" Rocky asked.

Nikki chuckled. "You know I do. I have forever."

Rocky pulled her in close again. "Yeah, but damn, is it good to hear you say it."

"ARE YOU READY?" Rocky asked Nikki.

She watched him in the mirror as he walked over to her. She waited until he slid his hands around her waist and set his chin on her shoulder to nod. "I am."

"I think we should stay home."

"Why?"

Rocky looked down the mirror at her body. "Because I'm

not going to be able to keep my hands off you all night. We should just stay here so I can have you over and over again."

"I'm ready!" Sly announced, walking into the bedroom.

Nikki met Rocky's gaze in the mirror and grinned. "Sorry."

He kissed her cheek with a loud smack and whispered, "You'll be mine tonight."

"I'm always yours," she said.

He pressed his growing erection to her back and groaned. "I love you."

"I love you."

"Can we go?" Sly asked, oblivious to the moment he was interrupting.

Nikki laughed and said, "Yep, we're ready, too. Daddy was just telling me about jumping out of airplanes when he was a SEAL."

"You did?" Sly asked with his eyes wide.

Rocky nodded. "I did. Hundreds of times."

"Wow. I want to do that. What was it like?"

Nikki smiled as the two of them walked out of the room. She sucked in a breath and still couldn't believe this was her life. Rocky spent a week in the hospital to recover, hating every second of it. Lily helped Nikki pack up her apartment, and Dex and Mason drove the moving truck back to Niagara Falls and unloaded all of Nikki and Sly's things into Rocky's house. Dex moved in with English so Rocky, Nikki, and Sly could have a home to themselves.

Nikki never thought she'd have a home like she did with Rocky. It wasn't just that the place was nice, but she felt like she was finally where she was supposed to be and who she was supposed to be. And she felt safe there. Like nothing else bad was going to happen. And with a legit badass in bed next to her every night and more watching over them all the time, she couldn't imagine anything bad happening.

Sly fell hard for all his new uncles. He even liked his new school and was making friends. And Nikki had a group of friends that welcomed her in without question and made her feel like she'd always been one of them.

Her boys were already in the car when she made it there. Rocky asked if she was ready and backed out of the driveway when she nodded. She was more than ready.

Slade's house had become her second home in the month since they moved to Niagara Falls. Nikki and Kyra had grown close, and Kyra adored Sly, so they spent a lot of time together when the guys were away. Sly loved Howler and begged Nikki daily to get a dog. She hadn't given in yet, but she was getting closer.

Everyone else was already at Slade's when they arrived, and the women immediately pulled her into the extra bedroom.

"How are you?" Ashleigh asked.

"I'm good," Nikki said with a deep breath. "Definitely ready for this."

"Good. Does Sly know?" Lily asked.

Nikki shook her head. "I don't think he'd be able to contain himself. He did complain about wearing something nicer than sweatpants. He wants to roll around on the floor with Howler."

Kyra laughed. "He still can. Just not until after the ceremony."

Nikki nodded. "I told him to try to keep his clothes clean for ten minutes. Hopefully that's long enough for us to get started."

"It will be. Everyone is ready. The only thing left to do is wait," Pilar said.

Nikki took a breath and nodded. She smoothed a hand down her lavender dress and hoped her son said yes to her marrying his father.

ROCKY WAS sure Sly was going to be okay with the wedding, but Nikki insisted on him asking Sly before they went through with it all. She didn't want Sly to know ahead of time because she was sure he'd be excited, but now that the day was here, Rocky wondered if there was another reason she hesitated to tell Sly.

Dex and Rocky led Sly to the couch and sat him down. They both sat on the coffee table across from him and waited until he and Howler were listening.

"Sly, you know I love you, and I love your mom," Rocky began.

Sly nodded. "I know."

"Well, I wanted to ask you if it's okay if we all become a family."

Sly tilted his head to the side. "I thought we already were."

Rocky grinned. "I think we are, too, but, if you're okay with it, I want to marry your mom today. And we're going to add me to your birth certificate so there's no question that I'm your father."

"You are my father, right?"

Rocky nodded. "I am. But your mom and I want to make everything official, and we want you to have a say."

Sly shrugged. "Okay."

"I can marry your mom?"

Sly looked closely at Rocky. "Are you going to make her cry?"

"I hope not."

"Okay, then you can marry her."

Rocky pressed his lips together as Dex choked on his laugh. "Thanks, buddy."

Sly went back to playing with Howler and forgot all about their conversation. Dex nodded for Rocky to talk in the dining room.

"They're good for you."

Rocky nodded. "They're the best things that have ever happened to me."

"I never thought I'd see the day you married someone. For years, you were hung up on Nikki. I'm glad you finally found her again."

Rocky chuckled. "Someone knew what they were doing."

Dex slapped Rocky on the back and nodded. "Yeah, your dad definitely did."

Dex walked away to let Nikki know the wedding was a go, and Rocky faced the rest of his brothers.

"You ready?" Archer asked.

Rocky nodded. "Absolutely."

"Good, because if you fuck this up, I'm going to fuck you up," Mason said.

"No need. I'll get to him first," Slade said.

"We are all going to fuck him up," Dunn said. "Nikki is perfect for him, but he's not going to mess it up. He waited too long for her to be his."

Rocky nodded and exchanged a look with his boss. Dunn knee exactly what Rocky was feeling because he'd been there. Losing the woman he loved and finding her again wasn't easy. But it happened. And Rocky wasn't going to lose her again.

"Ready," Dex announced when he came back into the living room.

Slade started the music, and the rest of them took their places. The living room wasn't that big, but it would do. Rocky didn't need fancy, he just needed Nikki.

He stared at the hallway as the rest of the women filed out. Each of them went to their partners and shared a private moment. Rocky just stared, waiting, knowing she was coming.

Then she stepped into view, and he lost his breath. It didn't matter that he'd already seen her that day or that he spent almost every day and every night with her for almost two months, she still stole his breath whenever she walked into a room.

Her lavender dress hugged her curves and accentuated her breasts. He was definitely a breast man, but he loved every inch of her. She'd added a tiara in her hair and tied it up so her neck was exposed. She winked at him and knew she was thinking about the way he feasted on her bare skin whenever he had the chance.

He couldn't wait for her to reach his side and met her halfway through the living room. He grabbed her hand and resisted the urge to kiss her right there. He wanted her to have a perfect wedding, and that meant waiting.

"Are we ready?" Kelsea asked when they made it to the sliding glass door.

Rocky looked at Nikki, and they both nodded.

"Good. I think this crowd is, too."

Kelsea kept the ceremony short, which worked for Rocky. When Kelsea asked them to say their vows, he turned to Nikki and smiled.

"Nikki... I've wondered what happened to you for years. I missed you every day. And when you sat down next to me,

I thought someone answered my prayers. Then you told me we had a son, and I knew my life would never be the same. You are my world, my everything. I can't imagine a day without you, and I don't want to. I will work every single day to be worthy of the love you give me, and I will never stop trying to make you happy. I love you."

Nikki blinked tears from her eyes and smiled up at him. Rocky wiped her tears away and leaned down to kiss her. Kelsea cleared her throat, and Rocky froze. He growled. "The next time I kiss you, you're going to be my wife."

Nikki laughed. "I like the sound of that."

"Nikki, do you want to say your vows before Rocky says screw it and carries you out of here?"

Nikki laughed again and nodded. "Rocky... I honestly never thought I'd see you again the night I walked out. I thought I was doing the right thing, but nothing has felt right since I left your side. Until you were next to me again. I wanted to be strong enough to stand on my own, but you taught me strength doesn't come from being alone. Strength comes from the people you love. And with your love, I have enough strength to do anything."

Rocky pulled her in close and breathed in her scent. Then he turned to Kelsea. "Hurry up. I'm almost out of patience."

The rest of them laughed, and Kelsea shook her head. "May I have the rings?"

Rocky barely noticed the rest of the ceremony. He repeated Kelsea's words and waited not so patiently for her to tell him he could kiss his wife. And he did not hold back when she finally said the words.

Rocky stepped closer to Nikki and slid his hand low on her back. He pressed her body tight to his. Everything was right in his world with Nikki in his arms. His wife. The love of his life.

She smiled as he leaned in to kiss her. "I love you, husband."

"I like the sound of that." He sealed his lips to hers and cupped the back of her neck. He tilted his head to the side and licked his way into her mouth.

She opened for him and sighed happily against him. She held on to him like she didn't want to let go anymore than he did. He kissed her like he had all the time in the world, because he did. She was his now. Forever. And she was never going to leave him.

Their friends cheered and whistled until Rocky finally let his new wife up for air. He didn't let her go far, keeping their lips close enough that they brushed when he spoke.

"God, I love you. Thank you for marrying me."

She laughed. "Thank you for waiting for me to get here."

Rocky kissed her again, quickly, and said, "I'd have waited forever if I needed to. But I'm happy it didn't take that long."

"I love you," she said.

"I love you. Now, let's get this party started."

Nikki nodded. "I like the sound of that."

They finally turned to everyone else and held up their hands. More cheers echoed through the house, which set Howler off. Sly sat on the floor next to him and howled, too, making everyone laugh again.

Life was definitely better with the people you loved.

"THANK YOU FOR FINDING HIM," Dex said to Nikki.

"What do you mean?"

Dex looked at Rocky. "He changed after you two met. I didn't think he'd ever get over you, no matter how much he insisted he was. But he's happy now. He deserves it."

"I love him. Walking away wasn't easy, but I really thought it was what he wanted."

Dex nodded. "I know. He's kind of stubborn like that. I'm just glad you two found each other again."

"Me, too."

Nikki got her food and joined the women at the table to eat. Sly was entertaining the men in the middle of the living room, and the women were talking and laughing.

"Favorite position?" Lily asked.

"On top, definitely," Ashleigh said. "We started doing it that way when I was too pregnant to lie on my back. Changed my life."

"I'm a shower fan," Kyra said.

"Ooh, I like that, too," Pilar said. "But we need a bigger shower to really enjoy it. I'm a fan of against the wall. When he shows off how strong he is. I lose my mind when he just picks me up."

"I agree," Kelsea said. "I never thought I'd be with a man who could, but Jaymes... yeah, that's nice."

"What about you, Nikki?" Lily asked.

"Ah, we haven't experimented much. With a six year old in the house, we're limited. But I would say anything where I can look at him," Nikki said.

"Yes," Lily agreed. "Archer's a fan of reverse cowgirl, and while it feels good, I don't like not seeing his face. I want to watch him lose his mind."

"Seeing him lose it always pushes me over the edge. Or when he holds back to wait for me," Kyra said.

"Right?" Ashleigh agreed. "So sexy."

Rocky walked over, and the conversation halted. "What are you ladies talking about?"

"Sex," Nikki told him.

Rocky drew back and tilted his head in question. "Um, okay. Maybe I should stay here and get some tips."

"Not unless you want to know what all your friends are like in bed," Lily said with a snarky grin.

Rocky froze. "Yeah, I definitely belong over there. You can show me what you learn later." He kissed Nikki soundly on the lips, thrusting his tongue into her mouth for a quick swipe and pulling back before she had a chance to catch her breath.

He walked away without a backward glance. Nikki just grinned at his back. "Damn, I love that man."

"And he's your husband now," Lily said.

Nikki's grin grew. "He's all mine."

The other women laughed. "We can drink to that."

MASON COULDN'T HELP but remember his own wedding. It was in a church and bigger than Rocky and Nikki's, but no less fun. Megan was the love of his life. He thought they'd be together forever.

She always looked at him the way Nikki looked at Rocky. Like he was the most important person in his world. But after his last tour, the way she looked at him changed. She was wary. Maybe even afraid of him. Like she knew he would hurt her.

If he could go back and not marry her, Mason would. He would save her from the pain he caused. Pain he hoped none of the people in the room around him would ever know.

"The women are talking about sex," Rocky said as he joined the men at the table. "It's not safe over there."

"I know about sex," Sly announced.

Rocky drew back. "You do?"

Sly nodded. "Yep. Mommy told me about it."

"Really?" Rocky didn't look convinced.

"It's what people do when they love each other. Like kissing, but with their pants off."

Mason snorted before he could stop himself. The kid was funny as hell. And smart.

He looked straight at Mason and asked, "Is that wrong?"

"Nope. That's a good description," Mason said.

Leave it to the kid to make relationships sound easy. All you had to do was love someone, take off your pants, and kiss them. Hell, with Megan, it almost was that easy. Loving her was the only thing Mason was good at.

That was how he knew he'd never get involved with another woman. It would never be that easy again. And even if it was, the nightmares he had every so often would scare off any woman who ended up in his bed.

"That's what Mommy and Daddy are going to do to make me a new brother or sister," Sly added.

Mason rolled his lips in and tried hard not to react, but damn. How could he not? "They are?"

"Yep. I want a brother first, but Mommy said we'll see."

"A little brother to play with would be fun," Archer said, drawing Sly's attention and giving Mason a second to compose himself.

He hadn't been around many kids. He didn't know if all of them were like Sly, but he was fairly sure Sly was a special one.

"A sister is cool, too," Slade added. "I have a younger sister."

"Daddy has two younger sisters," Sly told them. "My aunts. I haven't met them yet. But I like having so many uncles."

Mason grinned at the kid. He called the group of them his uncles and the women his aunts. He didn't care that they weren't related, he just enjoyed being a part of something.

Mason understood that feeling. It was why he joined the Navy in the first place, and why he started working with F-BOMB. Both came at a time when he needed something else to believe in.

But Mason also knew all of it could be snatched away at any moment. He never got too comfortable. He thought he had everything once, but it vanished as quickly as any other dream. He vowed to never let his guard down like that again. To never let someone in. To never let himself be so vulnerable to destroying it all. Because if there was one thing Mason knew, it was that he didn't deserve another shot at happiness.

THANK **you** for reading Nikki and Rocky's story! They were so sweet, but I adored Nikki — that strong mom type who is just as fierce of a protector as the sexy man she loved. And of course, Sly was a lot of fun to bring to life, and who doesn't love a kid who brings his parents together.

Mason's story is up next. When he runs into someone from his past, he lets his guard down. Waking up the next morning with his friend's sister in his bed was definitely not a part of the plan, but he finds it impossible to resist her. Read Forbidden today!

.   .   .

ARE YOU READY FOR MORE? Newsletter subscribers get *exclusive* bonuses like short stories, bonus scenes, and a first look at everything new. Sign up for my newsletter today so you never miss a thing!

ZOEY FELL for Sebastian when she was barely old enough to understand love, but she walked away before giving it a real chance. Now, she's back in MacKellar Cove with her two kids and a shattered confidence she might never repair. Zoey and Sebastian fight their attraction, but when two people are meant to be together, nothing will stop love from conquering all. Start His Curvy Ex today!

ABOUT THE AUTHOR

USA TODAY Bestselling Author Mary E Thompson spent most of her childhood wishing she had a few less curves. She hid in the pages of books because her favorite characters never cared what size her clothes were. Now, neither does Mary, and she writes stories that celebrate women like her. Real women who have curves, chase dreams, and find love, because we should all be happy, no matter our dress size.

Mary spends her non-writing time with her husband and two kids, watching too much TV, cheering for her hometown football team (Go Bills!), and hiding chocolate from her family.

Visit https://MaryEThompson.com/ to sign up for Mary's newsletter, **Romancing the Curves.** Subscribers get free ebooks and other fun stuff, like exclusive, members only content and giveaways, plus are the first to know about new releases and sales!

www.ingramcontent.com/pod-product-compliance
Lightning Source LLC
Chambersburg PA
CBHW051549030726
47592CB00001B/206